HARD, FAST AND MADLY: PART 1

THE DARK AND DAMAGED HEARTS SERIES, BOOK 7

WHITLEY COX

ISBN: 978-1-989081-12-9

For the Small Human and the Tiny Human,
You are the beats of my heart, my reason for living.
Thank you, for picking me to be your mama.
The moon and back isn't far enough for how much I love you.

PROLOGUE
JAKE

Shit! Where the hell are my headphones? I could have sworn I packed them in my carry-on. Where the hell are they?

"This is the final boarding call for Flight 173 to Victoria," the nasally woman called out over the loudspeaker.

Fuck! Shit! Fuck!

"Here!" I panted, thrusting my boarding pass into her tiny hand. "Sorry I'm so late."

"Everyone is waiting for you, sir," she reprimanded as she looked over my boarding pass and passport before scanning it. I rolled my eyes and nodded. *No shit.* "Have a good flight, Mr. Leeman."

I gave her a nod of thanks as I chucked the empty container of NyQuil capsules into the trash can next to the reception desk. I'd tossed them back twenty minutes ago but in the panic of not being able to find my headphones, stuffed the box into my pocket. If I didn't have my headphones, I definitely needed to be knocked out for the flight over The Rockies, and Gravol just wasn't going to cut it. The box said take four every two to six hours. Seemed excessive, but whatever. Probably better to be overdosed than underdosed. I certainly didn't want to remember this flight, no matter how short it was going to be.

I hate flying. And flying over The Rockies is even more nerve-wracking.

As I booked it down the jet bridge, my internal conversation was interrupted by heavy breathing coming up behind me. I craned my neck around, stunned for a second about how woozy and fuzzy my brain suddenly felt, only to see a spray of flaming red curls and a box of candy fall to the ground.

Bending down to grab them, I took in the cute little black flats and no-nonsense beige trousers only to be hammered in the chin with a very hard head springing up.

"Ouch!"

"Oh my God! I'm so sorry! Are you okay?" I saw stars and was beginning to think that there might be blood when the curls parted to reveal a beautiful flushed face and the biggest yellowy-green eyes I'd ever seen. She was tall, almost as tall as me, and her face was covered in an adorable smattering of freckles that just added to her beauty.

I blinked for a couple of seconds, letting the black spots fade from my vision. "Uh, yeah." I rubbed my chin. "How's your head?"

"Fine, thanks."

"Sir, Miss, could you please board the plane?" the tiny little brunette with way too much eye makeup squawked.

"Oh, sorry," we both said in unison. I let her go ahead of me and then I was literally like a moth to a flame, following her flowing mane of fire down through the aisle.

"I'm right here," she whispered, stopping at row seventeen and scrunching in so I could move past. Her taut little ass stuck out into the aisle and was being ogled by the creepy mustached man in the row across.

I looked down at my boarding pass again and grinned. "Looks like I am too."

She quickly stowed her carry-on in the overhead and tucked her e-reader and cardigan under her arm as she shuffled to her window seat, buckling up and then looking out the window while desperately pretending that the rest of the plane no longer existed.

I absolutely hate flying. Too bad Justin's jet was being used.

I took my seat, then heard the main door seal shut.

Looks like the middle seat is empty. It's just me and Flames all the way to Victoria, and she is doing everything she possibly can to avoid looking at me.

The jet lurched, and I felt my burrito from lunch do a somersault as it churned in my stomach and threatened to make an appearance.

Fuck, I hate flying.

White-knuckling the armrests, I made it through the demonstration of what to do if we crashed. I knew this was for our safety and necessary, but it almost made the whole experience worse. Just reminded you of what *could* happen.

Why did I decide to fly? Why didn't I just rent a truck and drive? Because you hardly have any shit and it wasn't worth the time, dumbass.

I caught Flames watching me out of the corner of her eye while pretending to read her book.

Holy Jesus, is she fucking blind? The font on her e-reader is enormous. There's like twelve words on each page.

I leaned back as the plane left the runway and began to read over her shoulder.

Patience studied Drake with hooded eyes. Her hand trembled as she reached out and gripped his quivering member, curiously stroking him and marveling at how soft his skin was. Meanwhile, Drake wasted no time in relieving Patience of her shift, ripping the thin straps at her shoulders and sending the loose piece of fabric fluttering to the ground. Her nipples grew hard and crimson as the cool autumn breeze washed over her creamy flesh.

"Have you ever had a man put his mouth on you before, Patience?" Drake asked, his raspy drawl sending a shiver down her spine while the twitching hairs of his mustache had her aching to know what it felt like to have those whiskers rub against her body. Were they soft? Did they scratch, or did they tickle?

"N-no," she panted, suddenly breathless, yet having not moved an inch. "Th-the vicar will be back soon with his Lordship, s-so we must make haste."

Gently Drake took Patience's hand and relieved her of her efforts, kissing *the inside of her wrist and each finger before dropping to his knees and planting more sensuous kisses down her abdomen.*

"Oh Patience," he drawled, "I'm going to savor you. Ain't no way a man can make haste with such sweetness." And his fingers softly parted the downy curls on her mound, his mouth came forward and his tongue darted out with inquisitive little licks.

Holy shit! This chick is reading porn!

I tried to keep reading, but my seatmate caught me, shooting me a look of mild irritation mixed with embarrassment.

Don't be embarrassed, honey, you read this stuff and I watch it. If only women knew that men LOVE it when we find out that they like porn.

The jet pitched and rocked, and I grabbed the armrests again, my breath ragged like Patience's, while my heart felt like it was going to punch a hole in my chest.

The cover of the magazine in the front pocket seemed to be floating off the page. Was that the NyQuil kicking in or was I just sleepy?

I needed a distraction.

"Um, hi," I said casually, "I'm Jake."

"Hello," she murmured, not bothering to look up.

"What's your name?"

Her eyes darted across her e-reader as she hesitated. Still not bothering to look up at me, she finally whispered, "Uh, Sandra, Sandra Macey."

"Nice to meet you, Sandra."

Turning her body away from me, she brought her e-reader up again and began to read. "Yeah, you too."

What's this chick's problem? I've done nothing wrong. Just trying to engage her in some harmless conversation. Pass the time. Make a friend.

I stopped myself from laughing. She'd turned away from me so I would stop reading over her shoulder, only now the e-reader was directly in my line of sight.

Hot damn, she was cute. I had to get to know her.

"Are you married?" Her head snapped around and she gaped at me, an incredulous look on her face, as if I'd just asked her if red was her natural color.

"No!"

"Okaaaay." Why was she acting so skittish? "Dating anyone?" Figured there was no harm in trying to make a friend ... or maybe more. I was leaving all my friends behind in Edmonton. Barely knew a soul in Victoria and needed to start somewhere.

"No!"

The plane tilted again, and the whole cabin shook. The seatbelt light flashed on overhead.

And that's when the NyQuil decided to kick in. Then the plane, my world, the seat and the eyeballs in my head all started to spin and go blurry.

Fuuuuuuck.

"Good evening, folks, this is your captain speaking. We're experiencing some mild turbulence as we make our way over The Rockies, so please remain in your seats until the seatbelt sign turns off."

Motherfucker.

Great, we were going over rigid mountains that were most likely covered in snow, so even if we did survive the terrifying plummet and managed to evade getting impaled by the shards of land sticking out into the air, we'd fucking freeze to death. Or get eaten by a bear or a pack of wolves.

Fan-fucking-tastic!

"You ... uh ... you wanna make out?" Jesus Christ, my mouth was now apparently working independently from my brain when scared shitless. God, what must she think of me?

That you're a fucking nut-job creeper. Shut up now.

But it wasn't me doing the talking anymore, it was the cough medication. Oh fuck, what had I done?

I fought the urge to put my hand over my mouth to shut myself up. I couldn't get over my gall. With death practically imminent, all I could focus on was getting laid? Good luck getting out of this one. I could practically hear a door slam in my head as my brain left the situation entirely, floating away on a NyQuil-fueled cloud never to be seen or heard from again. The conversation was being entirely run by my penis.

My penis on drugs. This wasn't going to end well. This wasn't going to end well at all.

"Excuse me?" She looked at me like I'd just sprouted another head.

"Fuck. Sorry. I hate flying and I think I took too much cold medicine. My brain isn't working."

"Clearly," she said snippily, giving me the death stare.

I shrugged. Meanwhile, inside I was anything but relaxed and mentally berating myself for my stupidity. "I apologize. I'm not normally this big of a dick."

Her posture softened just a touch, but her glare didn't. "It's fine."

I let out a breath. "I mean you are crazy hot. And if you agreed that'd be cool. But I get it."

Shut the fuck up, you moron! You're creeping her out.

"You're not serious?" she said slowly, trying to gauge whether I was a threat or just completely delusional.

I shook my head. "Only if you are."

Take your socks off and shove them in your mouth. Just. Stop. Talking.

"You're insane," she said with a low hiss.

Jesus Christ, I'd apologized. What was this chick's problem? I brought my voice down to mirror hers. "I'm not the one reading porn on my e-reader with hundred-size font. Are you blind?" I snapped back, my nerves taking hold of my charm and pummeling it into a pulp.

She glared at me. "It's NOT *porn*." She snorted. "And not that it's any of your business, but I packed my glasses in my checked baggage."

"Looked like porn to me."

"You're a jerk."

"Hey!" I said, holding my hands up in surrender. "I think it's hot. You're not getting any complaints from me."

She reared back in her seat and glared at me, her perfectly straight white teeth bared as if ready to strike. "Leave me alone!"

"Suit yourself, sweetheart."

What the fuck is wrong with me? I'm never this big of an asshole. And certainly not to someone so fragile-looking as Sandra.

"Just leave me alone." Her shoulders slumped, and she swallowed, the last word coming out as a whisper. "Please."

Suddenly, as if flying through cotton candy, the plane leveled out and everything was smooth again. The seatbelt light flicked off, and a sigh of relief echoed throughout the cabin. I pried my cramping knuckles off the armrest and bent and flexed my achy fingers.

"I'm sorry," I muttered, too ashamed to look at her. "I don't like flying, and it kind of turns me into an asshole."

She shot me a side-eye but didn't move. "It's fine."

Only then did I see on her e-reader the author of the book she was reading, *Sandra Macey.*

Well, fuck me! She gave me a fake name.

1

FREYA

Leaning over Stacey's enormous belly, I gave her an awkward but affectionate hug. Her straight strawberry-blonde bob tickled my nose. "You call me if you need anything, okay?" I murmured against her ear, hating that I had to leave her, leave them, like this.

She nodded as we came apart, unshed tears welling up in her light brown eyes. Three-year-old Connor lifted his arms, beckoning to be picked up. I watched her hoist him up onto her hip with a grunt, his leg draped nonchalantly over his little brother or sister.

"It'll be okay," I reassured her, knowing full well that they were just words and we'd both just entered a giant storm. All she could do was continue to nod. "I've got to go. My cab is here." I lunged forward and gave her one more quick hug and a peck on the side of her head, along with one on Connor's cheek. His big baby blues blinked at me with open curiosity. Then with a smile and wave, I was out the door.

"The airport, please," I said to the cab driver as I met him on the curb. He loaded my suitcase in the trunk and I climbed into the back.

What a weird week, was all I could think as we drove in silence the thirty minutes to the airport. I know I should have been chattier with the taxi driver, and normally I am, but my mind was racing after the whirlwind week I'd just had meeting Stacey and Connor.

Never in a million years would I have thought that Stacey and I would have become friends, especially given the way we were thrust into each other's lives. Yet, there I was, leaving her home after a week getting to know her and her son, having arrived as a stranger, almost an enemy or a rival, and leaving as something I could only describe as akin to family. And in some weird convoluted way, we kind of were.

"We're here, Miss," the driver announced. I'd been so caught up in my thoughts that the last half hour just flew by. I paid him, grabbed my suitcase and rolled through the doors and up to the front desk.

I was just about to head through security when it hit me like a baseball to the face that I'd forgot to grab my father his favorite maple candy from the gift shop. He wouldn't know if I'd forgotten to buy them, but I would, and it'd been a tradition for nearly thirty years. I couldn't break it now. Finally, after about four different gift shops, I spotted a tiny box of the sweet little treasures and nearly had a stroke when I turned it over and saw the price. *Airports are such a rip-off.* But I bought them anyway, and that's when I heard the announcement.

"This is the final boarding call for Flight 173 to Victoria."

How the heck did I not hear the first, second and third boarding calls? Was I really that far off in la-la-land? I hurriedly paid for my overpriced candy and then started running.

"Hi!" I grinned, a tad out of breath but not too bad, silently saying a small thank-you to myself for getting to the gym as often as I do. I hadn't even broken a sweat. "So sorry I'm late. I didn't even hear your previous calls. I was across the airport at the gift shop. Thank you so much for waiting. I apologize again."

"It's fine." The woman smiled politely, though the irritation in her tone was clearly detectable. I decided to kill her with kindness instead of stoop to her level.

"I'll be sure to write a glowing review of the airline when I get home. And make special mention of," I leaned forward to read her name tag, "you, Maria, and how helpful you've been. I really do appreciate you being so understanding."

Her face transformed, and this time the smile reached her eyes. "Not at all. Have a wonderful flight, Miss Lapierre."

"Thank you."

I continued to speed-walk down the jet bridge, loathing the idea of being that one person holding up the flight for the other hundred or so passengers. I mentally prepared myself for a slew of glares and plastered on a big, apologetic smile.

Oh, thank goodness, I'm not the only Last-Minute Lucy.

I saw the back of a very tall man as he lazily made his way toward the plane doors. He must have heard me, because he spun around, and that's when everything in my arms decided to plummet to the ground, making a godawful racket and delaying our flight even further. Hastily, I bent down to pick up my purse and candy, berating myself and my clumsiness, only my fellow tardy passenger must have attempted to do the same, and the back of my head bashed him in the chin.

"Ouch!"

"Oh my God! I'm so sorry! Are you okay?" I stammered, my own head a little sore. Dad always said I had the hardest Irish head he's ever seen. I brushed my untameable mop out of my face only to look up into the face of a very handsome young man. I'd say twenty-five, maybe. With eyes the same color as the ocean on the postcards people send you from tropical havens like Barbados and Aruba. Messy brown hair brushing just over his ears and high-cut rosy cheeks, burning bright when I asked him if he's okay. Combined with an intoxicating scent of fresh linen and just a hint of—was that cinnamon?—and the guy was practically perfect.

He blinked for a couple of seconds. "Uh, yeah." Then rubbed his chin, his stubble making a raspy sound against his hand. "How's your head?" I watched as his eyes raked my body from head to toe, a small smile playing at the corner of his mouth.

"Fine," I replied and then immediately looked down at my feet. "Thanks." Something about him was flustering me. I hoped we weren't sitting together. Who smells like cinnamon? Was that his natural smell, or was it in his body wash? I shook my head to dislodge the cinnamon-scented cobwebs and blinked a couple of times. Meanwhile Handsome Harry or whatever his name was continued to stare at me.

"Sir, Miss, could you please board the plane?" the flight attendant interrupted.

She's very pretty. I wish I was able to do my eye makeup like that. And she's so little. Men love short and tiny women.

"Oh, sorry," we both say. He let me go ahead of him, but the entire time I led us down the aisle I could feel his eyes on me, past all the annoyed glares from the other passengers who were forced to wait for us.

"I'm right here," I whispered, stopping at row seventeen and scrunching in so he could hopefully move past.

He looked down at his boarding pass again and grinned. "Looks like I am too!"

_____

2

We landed without issue, and when the light came on for everyone to grab their bags, thankfully my seat companion avoided making eye contact with me and immediately headed toward the door.

Good riddance!

It was still light out, so after getting in my car I decided to stop off and grab some grocery store sushi and then head over and see my dad at the assisted living home, taking him his candy and filling him in on my trip.

"Hi, Dad," I said, finding him just finishing up what looked to be fruit salad and ice cream. I kissed the top of his curly, gray head. I'd have to take him to get a haircut soon. Things were getting a little unruly.

"Hello," he murmured, not looking up from his dish but instead chasing a grape around his bowl with a spoon, the Parkinson's interfering with his success.

I put the box of maple candy next to his elbow. "I brought you something."

His bright brown hawk eyes shifted to the box, and his face lit up. He abandoned his grape and instead tore into the box with childish enthusiasm. I watched as his gnarled and liver-spotted hands trembled, but even with arthritis and now with the Alzheimer's and Parkinson's, he was determined and swift, opening up the box to reveal the candy inside with the speed of a kid on Christmas.

"You went on a trip?" he asked, twisting open a wrapper and popping one in his mouth, eyes closing as he savored the sweet treat. "Where did you go?" he tucked the candy into his cheek to continue talking. "I just got back from Anchorage, was a visiting professor for a semester. Former professor of mine went on sabbatical, asked me to fill in for him. Incredibly cold but breathtaking in beauty."

"You haven't been to Anchorage in years, Dad," I said softly. "Remember, I told you I was going to Edmonton to meet Stacey?"

He nodded absentmindedly. "Must have forgot, must have forgot." A dining room attendant came over and took his bowl away. "She smells like smoke!" he muttered.

I rolled my eyes. "You say that every time."

"Well, she does. Filthy swine!"

"Dad! You can't say those things."

He glared at me, bushy eyebrows furrowing. "I'll say whatever I want to, young lady. And that woman smells like smoke. Don't ever let me catch you smoking." A deep growl in this throat made his neck skin jiggle.

I smiled at him, laughing through my nose. "I know, Dad, you'll be so disappointed in me, and disappointment is much worse than anger, because it means I've lost your trust, and trust is one of the hardest things to rebuild once it's been broken. Trust is the foundation of all relationships, and when it cracks or crumbles, it compromises the integrity of the whole structure. If you can't trust me to behave, then how can you trust me at all?" I recited his lecture verbatim as I'd memorized it many years ago, after the first time I'd misbehaved when I was five or so.

It was the same thing every time. He'd sit me down on his lap in his giant tweed recliner, with a big stack of books perched on the desk next to it, and then he'd hold my hand and look at me with such sadness that tears would well up in my eyes and I'd beg him to trust me and I'd promise to never misbehave again.

I wasn't sure if that kind of manipulation and guilt is now recommended by today's parenting experts, but I've got to say that it worked. I was rarely disobedient as a child; I toed the line and did as I was told. Maybe because it was just the two of us and I knew how hard things were for my dad, so being bad would have just made it harder, but I strived to please him. To excel and succeed and make him proud, make him trust me. And he did. We were best friends until the day I moved away, and even then, we spoke on the phone nearly every night, talking about our day and watching *Jeopardy* and *Wheel of Fortune* together over the phone.

He went to reach for another candy, but I gently grabbed his hand. "Let's pace ourselves. Maybe just one more for tonight and then you can have some more tomorrow. Looks like you already had some sweets. Was that ice cream?"

Giving me a petulant scowl, he batted my hand away and snatched the box. "Yeah, vanilla. I keep asking for mint chocolate chip, but they don't have any."

I smiled. "I'll bring you some mint chocolate chip tomorrow."

"Have you seen your mother?" His big hands fumbled with the wrapper, so he brought it to his mouth and opened it with his teeth.

I shook my head with a big sigh. "No, Dad, I haven't. Mum's been gone for some time now, remember. She died when I was six."

"You should really go see your mother," he said, ignoring me and reaching for another candy.

"Want to go watch *Jeopardy*?" I asked cheerfully, hating when he would ask about my mother, forgetting that she's been gone for twenty-four years. Oftentimes, it would end with him getting upset and crying or denying that she was dead and throwing a fit.

His eyes came alive and he nodded. "Yeah, *Jeopardy*. And then *Wheel of Fortune*."

I let out a small sigh of relief that he was able to move on to a new topic so quickly this time. I helped him from his chair and tossed the box of candy in my purse before looping his arm through mine and shuffling the two of us off to his private room.

Like most nights, my dad fell asleep halfway through *Wheel of Fortune,* while I mindlessly ate my dinner and muttered the answers to the puzzle far sooner than the contestants were able to solve them. After the show was over, I made sure that he had a full glass of water on his nightstand, hung up his robe and put his slippers next to his bed, pulled the blanket up over his arms and kissed his forehead before I turned off the light and quietly slipped out.

Once I got home, I hung my purse on the hook behind my coat closet, tucked my shoes into their rightful place and rolled my suitcase into my bedroom, heaving it onto the bed and unzipping it.

I hated unpacking.

As I threw all my clothes in the laundry hamper and mindlessly put away all my toiletries, my thoughts started to wander back to the weird and awkward flight. Who the heck was that Jake guy? Was he from Victoria? Was I going to have to worry about running into him? Was he on some kind of medication besides the cold medication he said he'd taken? He didn't seem like a threat, though. He just seemed like a cocky weirdo. Terrified of flying and willing to do anything to take his mind off his fear. The man had been so rude. However, he'd also called me hot. I was so confused as I stripped off all my clothes and climbed into the shower. I'd never been called "hot" before. Did he mean it? Or would he have made out with a dust pan, had it been available and willing?

I welcomed the warm water as it beat against my skin, a tad too hot, just the way I liked it. A much-needed cleanse after the crazy week I'd just endured, not to mention the weird flight. My life had never been eventful. Sure, my mom had passed away when I was six but after that, life with my dad had been pretty even-keel. He traveled a lot, leaving me with family and friends, but I'd always felt safe, cared for and tended to.

And then in the first year of my master's, I'd met Ted, a respectable and nice, albeit plain man. He, too, had cared for me and never given me any reason to worry. Our life together was predictable and pleasant, if a tad boring, and the days and weeks he'd be away from work, I'd find myself itching for entertainment and a purpose. But he always assured me that my place was in the home, to make sure that the china cabinet was dusted and dinner was on the table, so that's what I did. It didn't seem to matter to him that I had a master's degree in education and was a certified teacher. Ted said I didn't need to work.

He didn't want me working.

But I wanted to.

I hadn't gone to school all those years for nothing. So, going against my husband, I signed up for the on-call teachers list. I taught a bit when we moved to Victoria, substituted every now and then, but nothing was steady, and Ted was adamant that I stay home when he was in town. So for seven years my life was easy, predictable and bland. And then in a matter of three months, my entire world blew up.

I was just getting out of the shower when I heard my phone ringing from the bedroom and haphazardly tossed a towel around my body before I raced out to grab it.

"Hello?" I panted, not bothering to look to see who it was on the call display.

"Hey, Freya! How was your trip?" It was Emma, my new friend, well really my only friend since Ted and I had moved to town.

"It was good. How're you and the girls?" I could hear the coo and babble of one or both of Emma's twin girls in the background. "Who do I hear right now?"

"You hear Claire. I'm nursing her. Grace is with her dad upstairs, getting ready for bed."

"I'll tell them apart one day." I sighed.

"What are your plans for dinner tomorrow night?"

"Nothing that I can think of. I'll probably go see my dad at some point. Why?"

"You want some baby snuggles?"

"Always." I smiled as my biological clock punched me in the ovaries at the sound of Claire guzzling and humming.

"Then be here at five. I'll be sure to send you away with a care package for your dad."

"Deal!"

"Okay, gotta go." She made an irritated groan. "I think she just shit herself ... again!"

I laughed. "Okay, bye."

After I got off the phone with Emma, I tossed on my favorite ratty old Backstreet Boys T-shirt and a pair of pajama shorts, popped some popcorn, poured on way too much butter, decanted a bottle of very cheap "red wine" as the label indicated, and flicked on Netflix. I was halfway through the second season of my newest obsession, a zombie romance thriller where the female main character was a hybrid zombie and the male main character was still full human and they went back and forth between being in love and needing/wanting to kill/eat each other.

It was nearly three o'clock in the morning when I finished season three, and I finally decided to call it a night and head to bed. My head hit the pillow, and all that flashed through my mind was that idiot Jake from the plane and his handsome and cocky smile and those Caribbean-blue eyes that seemed to look right through a person and see their very soul. I tried to push him out of my head as hard as I could, but in the end, I wound up falling asleep to the images of me saying yes when he asked me to make out with him, and visions of the two of us locking lips and heavily petting while still belted into our airplane seats. Why'd I have to go and notice how the yellows in his checkered shirt brought out the flecks of gold in his eyes, like the Caribbean at sunrise? Why?

3

The following day I found myself in a perpetual state of unrest. I hadn't been able to sleep very well the night before, despite my late bedtime and how drained I'd felt from my trip to Edmonton. I'd tossed and turned until nearly seven o'clock in the morning when I finally decided to call it and get up for the day. I made myself a double shot of espresso in my super fancy coffee maker before I headed out on my morning run.

Ted and I had moved to Victoria around nine months ago, so I was still learning the city, choosing to drive out to a different neighborhood each time I went for a run, to explore and decide—if I ever had the chance—where I'd like to raise a family. I'd park my car in a safe and open area, like a church parking lot or next to a busy playground, and then wind and wend my way through side streets and foot paths, up and down hills until I either made my way back to my car by sheer fluke or found myself completely and utterly lost and had to whip out my phone and ask Siri for help.

But today I didn't really feel the pull to venture off into suburbia. The vision of families walking down the sidewalk pushing a stroller with a dog on a leash made me want to toss up the oatmeal I'd had for breakfast. Because now, more than ever, I felt as if that dream, that life, a husband, a house, kids and a dog were so far out of my grasp, it was darn near impossible.

Instead I decided to head down to the water and run along Dallas Road, immerse myself in the throngs of people while not having to interact with a soul. I tossed on a pair of navy capri tights and a turquoise tank top before slathering on some sunscreen. Then, wrestling my untameable mane of fire into a white hat, I pulled it down low over my eyes, put my earbuds in and headed out the door.

Ted had opted to live right downtown. He said he liked having everything within walking distance and that it eliminated the need for two cars, and after moving from a small town in rural B.C. to the quaint but bustling Victoria, I had to agree that being downtown was pretty great. Once you learned how to tune out the din of the endless street noise, sirens and crazy people bellowing nonsense at all hours of the night, it was a wonderful place to live. Lots of culture, fantastic restaurants and tons of kitschy little shops to spend an entire Sunday perusing with a latte in hand. When Ted would go away for work, I'd often take an entire Sunday to just wander up and down the one-way streets, buying myself a smoothie or a coffee when I felt like it or some sushi or a box of noodles, while aimlessly drifting in and out of antique stores, shops in Chinatown, and one-of-a-kind clothing stores. I'd never been in a city like Victoria before, and after nine months, I quickly realized that there was nowhere else I'd rather be. This place had it all.

It was just a five-minute jog to Dallas Road, the sun was hot and high, and I was quickly cursing myself for not packing a towel as the sweat dripping into my eyes was starting to sting. But I loved it nonetheless. It was a picturesque place for a run, with the ocean on one side, sparkling with millions of diamonds, cargo ships blotting the view of the Olympic Peninsula and a beautiful beach for exploration and fun. And then a park on the other side, complete with a petting zoo, zany ducks with a death wish who'd dart in front of your car, and noisy peacocks who flashed their plumage like a creepy naked man in a trench coat, and always when you least expected it.

I stopped for a second to catch my breath, wiping my face with the hem of my shirt and bending down to tie my shoe. Only when I was popping back up, blue shorts and orange sneakers came into view, and before I knew it, I was bulldozed over and sent flying into a bush by a freight train made of muscle.

"Agh! Ouch!" I cried, as branches scratched up my face and arms and I struggled to right myself, my legs kicking up in the air.

"Oh my God, I'm so sorry, are you okay?" came a deep masculine rumble from behind, followed by the faintest smell of cinnamon. Strong arms gripped my waist and hauled me out of the shrubbery. I turned to face my clumsy assailant, but the sun was in my eyes, and he just looked like a shadow with the sun haloing his big head. "Hello," he said, humor and surprise in his voice. "We meet again."

Tilting my head up, I shielded the glare with my hand and came face-to-face with my flight-hating, make-out propositioning jerk of a plane companion. "YOU!" I exclaimed. "What are *you* doing here?"

His eyebrow quirked up. Clearly, he was over the sickness from the plane and was back to being completely insufferable. "I live here."

"Oh!" was all I could think of to say. "W-well ... next time, watch where you're going!" And without any further need for chit-chat, I took my scratched and bruised body and headed off in the opposite direction toward the breakwater.

"I wasn't the one who decided to bend down in the middle of the path!" he called back with a chuckle. "Maybe move over next time, *Sandy*." But I refused to look back. The man was an absolute jerk, more brawn than brain. A Neanderthal with nice biceps and a cute face. Sexy pond scum. I wasn't about to waste any more time staring into his eyes, no matter how fathomless and hypnotic they might be.

My run was not nearly as restorative or therapeutic as I had hoped or intended it to be. I kept my eye out for Jake or whatever his name was, but thankfully he was long gone, and hopefully for good. By the time I got home, I was a hot mess and decided to jump in the shower, only not even the thrumming of the warm water could soothe my temper. This *child*, because that's what he was, a *child* in men's clothing, was occupying my every thought, and he had no right to. He was nothing, nobody and he never would be, so why couldn't I stop thinking about him?

I made myself a lunch of spinach salad with cranberries, pecans, goat cheese and Cajun chicken. Then, I googled a sweet and spicy vinaigrette that wound up being one of the best things I'd ever tasted, so much so that I licked the bowl when I was done. I lived alone. No one was around to judge me.

I then proceeded to spend the rest of the afternoon sitting out on my veranda with my e-reader and a pitcher of pink lemonade while the sounds of the city and all its wonders, ripe and fresh on a beautiful spring afternoon, lulled me into an impromptu nap. It was nearly five-thirty when the sound of a police car roaring past and my phone ringing inside the house roused me from my slumber and I woke up with my face glued to a flyer for Bed Bath & Beyond by an attractive puddle of drool.

"H-hello?" I asked, my voice hoarse. I knuckled sleep out of my eyes.

"Hey! Where are you? Everything okay?"

It was Emma. "Oh no!" I sprang up from where I sat, my brain still half asleep. "I'm so sorry. I fell asleep. I'm on my way." And without even waiting for her to respond, I hung up and grabbed my purse, not bothering to check my face in the mirror or brush my teeth, and was out the door.

"I'm so, so sorry," I sighed, trudging in through Emma's and James's front door about fifteen minutes later, only to have a beautiful, little pudgy-faced baby thrust into my arms at the same time a black and white fluff-ball bounced and hopped around my feet. "Hi, Dave," I cooed, crouching down to rub the dog's head.

"It's okay." Emma smiled. "Is everything okay? Dave, off!"

I kissed the little one in my arms and smelled her head, not knowing which one of the twins I had but not caring. They were both tiny bundles of perfection. "Yeah, I'm okay. I just had a rough flight home last night, and I can't shake it."

"Was there a lot of turbulence?" she asked. I followed her into the house and to the kitchen. I loved James's and Emma's house. It was enormous, for one thing, but also homey and welcoming with rich earthy tones of greens and browns and wheat colors, lots of wood, high-beamed ceilings, an open-concept kitchen and sunken living room. It was a perfect representation of them as a couple, with both masculine and feminine touches here and there but, most of all, a sense of cohesion and compromise. It was *their* home. The scent of barbecue hit me like a gust of wind, and my mouth started to water. Both of them were incredible cooks, so I made sure never to turn down an invitation for dinner.

"No ..." I groaned. "There was this really annoying—" but we were interrupted by the sound of two male voices coming in through the French doors from the patio, one of them James's as he cooed at a garbling little baby.

"Hello ... *Sandra.*"

I nearly dropped the baby I had when I saw him follow James into the kitchen.

What the heck was he doing HERE?

"Sandra?" James and Emma said at the same time, giving each other quizzical looks. James, who was carrying a big tray of meat, set it down on the counter, his muscular arms bunching and flexing.

"Is this not the bestselling historical erotic romance author *Sandra Macey,* who wrote such classics as *Patience's Virtue, Faith's Pride,* and *Destiny's Surrender* and the most recent one that is getting a lot of buzz, *Charity's Wish?*" Jake asked, bouncing one of the twins on his hip.

I ground my molars together and glared at him. "What are you doing here?"

"You two know each other?" Emma's hazel eyes shifted back and forth between us as we continued to stare at each other.

"Unfortunately," I murmured. "We met on the flight."

"So, what's your real name?" He laughed, wandering around to where he apparently had an open beer and juggling the baby into one arm so he could take a drink.

James was chuckling as he took a sip of his own beer before helping his wife carry all the food to the dining room table. "Why'd you give him a fake name?"

"Because he was rude and inappropriate on the plane, and I didn't feel like giving him my real name." I held my chin up and looked Jake square in the eyes, driving home the fact that he wasn't going to intimi-date me or make me feel like a fool.

"Ah, let's be honest here ... " His grin was cocky and far too sexy for anybody's good. "Seriously, what is your name?"

I rolled my eyes. "Freya."

He stiffened and looked at me, his blue eyes flashing something I'd never seen before. But he quickly sobered and gave me a curt nod. "*Freya.*" He rolled my name around on his tongue like he was tasting it for the first time and it was the most decadent of chocolates.

I felt an odd stirring in my belly, and my palms were all of a sudden sweaty. What the heck was wrong with me?

"You're right," he said, causing me to stop and gape at him. "I was rude and inappropriate."

"I ..."

"I hate flying. More like am terrified of it. We were on a flight to England when I was a kid, and the plane hit some crazy turbulence in a big hurricane over the Atlantic. The oxygen masks came down. We all thought we were going to die. So I get a little neurotic when I'm forced onto a plane. And there always seems to be turbulence over The Rockies."

My eyes went wide. "Oh my goodness."

"Holy shit," James said behind me.

Jake nodded. "I mean it's no excuse for how I behaved, but that wasn't me. I usually put my headphones in, either get drunk or take a bunch of cold medication or Gravol and then sleep. But I'd forgotten my headphones in my checked bag and took too much NyQuil. Turns out I read the box wrong. It said take *two* every four to six hours, and I read it as take *four* every two to six hours."

"Better not be fucking up at work like that," James said. "Your ass will be grass if you make an error like that with my buildings."

Jake's cheeks puffed up and he blew out a big long breath. "I won't. I promise. I'm good at my job."

"Better be," James said with a grunt.

"Anyway, Jake went on, apparently, too much cold medication combined with—"

"—The fear of shitting your pants," James added helpfully.

"Yes, that," Jake said, glowering at James. "Is a recipe for me being a complete *inappropriate* ass. I'm really, very sorry."

"Thank you," I said softly, stunned at how candid and vulnerable he was being. This was not the same man I'd met on the plane.

"So what exactly did you do?" James asked.

Looking convincingly sheepish, Jake bowed his head and toed at the wood floor. He was probably feeling a lot like me at the moment and hoping not to relive the awkward flight. James seemed to be getting a kick out of Jake's predicament. "I asked her if she wanted to make out. Then I accused her of reading porn."

"You what?" Emma squawked, batting him on the shoulder with the back of her hand before tying her long flaxen locks up into a messy bun. She came over to grab the baby from me, taking her over to a waiting high chair. "Come here, Gracie Bean. Let's go have some supper."

Jake lifted his head. "Yeah, not my finest moment."

James rolled his eyes as he took the other twin, who I now knew was Claire, from Jake and started putting her in the other high chair. "Dude, seriously? Give me my kid! Come here, Claire Bear, in ya go."

I had to admit it, since meeting James several months ago, I'd developed a tiny bit of a crush on the man. He was positively perfect. Gorgeous but in a vaguely menacing way, with dark, almost black, hair that constantly looked as if he'd just rolled out of bed, deep and piercing blue eyes that saw everything, even your very soul, and an enigmatic smile that, although rare, practically lit up a room. For his mid-forties, the man was built, not more-muscles-than-brains built, but he had tone and definition and cords along his arms that flexed and bulged when he strapped his daughter into her high chair as carefully as if she were made of porcelain.

But I think what drew me to him the most was how he absolutely worshipped Emma. I'd never seen a man look at another woman the way James looked at his wife. Complete and utter obsession. And the more I thought about it as I got to know them, the more I thought I had a crush on his behavior more than the man himself. I yearned for someone to be that obsessed with me, to feel their love as if it were actually tangible, it was so strong. Ted had never looked at me like that, never made me feel like I was more important than air. Whereas James made his choice very clear every day. He would choose Emma over his last breath any day of the week.

"I can't believe you asked her to make out," Emma said, clucking her tongue as she began placing pieces of minced-up food on the girls' highchair trays.

"I know, I know," Jake said, taking a seat. "But I apologized on the plane, and I'm apologizing now. That's got to count for something?" He looked at me pleadingly.

"I do appreciate your apologies," I said.

At this point in my life, after the disaster Ted had left me with, there were only two men I had any respect for, two men I trusted: my father and James. All other men, in my opinion, were untrustworthy scoundrels, and I was better off without them.

I fixed him with a curious but wary stare. "What are you doing here anyway?"

Emma and James took their own seats. Emma gave me a sympathetic look. "Jake is Justin's brother. I've mentioned Justin and Kendra to you before, right?"

I nodded. "Yeah, I met them at the girls' baby shower."

"Right, right. Anyway, Jake just moved here to work for James. His lead structural engineer just moved away, so Jake agreed to come on and help out. He's living in our garage apartment until he finds a house. And he's helping James rebuild the back fence that was knocked down when a big tree fell on it in that huge windstorm we had in March."

Jake gave me a "please don't hate me" look as he speared a baked potato off the platter and onto his plate. "I'm really not a creeper," he said.

"You just play one on television?" James asked with a chuckle. "Or when you're hopped up on cold medication and afraid you're going to shit your pants."

"Yeah, that," Jake agreed, shamefaced.

"Maaaybe," Emma sang, spooning some kind of indecipherable

sludge into Grace's pouty little mouth, "you guys could bow and shake hands. Call a truce. Start over. I mean Jake's going to be here for a while, and you're here all the time, Freya, so you *will* run into each other again."

Jake's lip tilted up into a cute little half smile. His big man hands dominated his silverware and began cutting into his steak. "What do you say? I promise to never bother you again. And I'll *definitely* never ask you to make out again."

"Or take too much cold medication ever again," Emma added.

Jake nodded. "Or that."

"Or shit your pants," James said with a devious grin.

"You're not helping," Emma chastised.

"Fine," I said, taking a bite of salmon. James and Emma were amazing dinner hosts—surf and turf with all the sides. "We can start over."

"Good!" Emma smiled. "This was not at all how I thought this evening was going to go, but I guess you two are just preparing us for when we have to referee such childish arguments between the twins." She rounded on Jake. "But seriously, dude, asking a random woman to make out with you. Even I would have responded unkindly. That's just creepy."

He managed to look wounded but took a sip of his beer and nodded like a child who had just been reprimanded.

James just shook his head and smiled. "Ah, I dunno. When we first met I would have done absolutely anything to get you to kiss me. Had it been on a plane, I probably would have come up with some lame-ass line as well." His eyes softened as he gazed at his wife across the table.

Emma blushed. "Well, if that had been the case, we probably wouldn't be sitting here right now with twin babies," she retorted.

"That's what you think." He winked.

4

After dinner Emma and I took the girls upstairs to get them ready for their baths and bedtime. The men were busy with the dishes, and I was happy to finally have her alone.

"So how was Edmonton?" she asked, peeling Grace's diaper off and popping her into the tub with her sister.

"Really good." I nodded. "Surprisingly good. Stacey and I have a lot in common, besides the obvious. Connor, her little boy, is delightful, and she's really nervous about having another baby without anyone around to help her. I think a few days before her due date I'm going to fly back and help her. She doesn't have anyone. Maybe stick around for a bit. You don't mind, do you?"

"Why would I mind?" she asked, making goofy faces at her babies while they blinked and smiled at her.

"Because you're kind of my boss."

She snorted and shook her head. "I'm not the boss there anymore, remember? And I'm pretty sure the *boss*," she looked at me and narrowed her eyes, "can do whatever she wants. Right, Boss Lady?"

I rolled my eyes. I still didn't feel like the boss, even though that had been my title for several months now. Emma had managed to give it her all until nearly seven months into her pregnancy, which is when her back started to give her problems and the doctor put her on bedrest. She was the director of studies at an English as a second language school for adults and had hired me almost on the spot when we first met. I'd started working pretty much the next day, moving into her role when she went on early maternity leave, as my master's in education made the most qualified instructor, despite the fact that I'd never taught abroad. It also helped that no one else *wanted* the job.

It wasn't glamorous, just tedious and time-consuming. But my obsession with order and organization proved to be useful, and I found the job to be easy and therapeutic. I was finally working and using my education, which made me all the happier. But to me, Emma still felt like the boss.

"There are plenty of teachers," she went on. "Just give one of the part-timers more hours or hire another part-timer. There are always people who have taught abroad looking to teach here." When Ted and I moved to Victoria, I had a hard time getting any work as a substitute teacher in the public school system, and despite the fact that Ted said I didn't need to work, I wanted to. I wanted to do something with my days, contribute to our household and contribute to society.

"Yeah, but I don't want to be *that* boss. The one with all the drama who never shows up and just takes sick day after sick day simply because she can't be bothered to get out of bed."

She gave me a poignant look. "You have a very good reason to take those sick days. And you're not *that* boss. Just relax." She squirted a delicious-smelling baby body wash on to a couple of cloths. "Everyone at the school knows what happened, and they're all very understanding. Just lean on Allan. He keeps texting me asking if you need anything. He's afraid to call you. He doesn't want to upset you."

I let out a big sigh and took the soapy washcloth she gave me and started washing Claire's perfect little chubby body. At least I was pretty sure it was Claire.

"I know you think I'm your only friend," she continued, "but I'm not. Other people want to be your friend too. You just need to let them in."

"I know."

"Like Jake, for example. He doesn't have any friends either. Why not be friends with him?"

I gave her an incredulous look as I gently poured water over Claire's belly to rinse away the soap. She blinked up at me, her bright blue eyes —the same as her daddy's—wide with wonder as her limbs kicked and punched the water like the tentacles of a spastic octopus.

"What? I thought you two were starting over?" she asked, grabbing two towels off a warming rack in the corner and handing me one. We lifted the girls out of the tub and folded them up in the warm terry cloth.

"Starting over and becoming besties are two very different things," I retorted. "Just because I'm not trying to blow his head off with my mind power anymore does not mean I want to go rollerblading down the sidewalk while holding hands."

"Well, I think you guys'd make a cute couple," she sang as she stood up and headed off to the nursery. I followed her and laid Claire down on the change table, watching Emma for guidance on how to diaper and dress a squirming six-month-old.

I gave her a sarcastic look. "Uh, robbing the cradle isn't my style."

"He's not that much younger, and James and I are twelve years apart and it works for us. And weren't your parents like ten or fifteen years apart too?"

I nodded and let out an exasperated sigh as I massaged a sweet and powdery scented lotion into Claire's warm little body.

"Just think about it."

Leaving Emma upstairs to feed the girls and put them to bed, I wandered downstairs, where I found James and Jake sitting out on the patio, each nursing a bottle of beer.

"Bear and Bean down for the count?" James asked, tipping the bottle up.

"I think Emma is just feeding them now," I said, making sure to walk around to James's side of the table and avoiding eye contact with Jake, even though his eyes never left me.

"Boobs are awesome!" James sighed. "Fun to play with, and they feed your kids. Sometimes I wish I had them."

Jake and I both gave him a weird look, our eyes locking for just a second as smirks tugged at the corners of our mouths. James was such a raw and commanding alpha male, a true man's man, so a wish for boobs was about as bizarre coming out of his mouth as me wishing for a penis or a hairy chest.

"Yeah, man, they're great." Jake snorted, shaking his head. "I'm as big a fan as any, but I can't say I'd like a pair myself. I feel like they'd be a hassle when you run. Or a distraction. I'd spend my entire day playing with them." He looked to me for confirmation, but I averted my eyes.

James looked up at me with a curious expression. "You okay? How was your trip to Edmonton? Did you find out what you needed to?" He was remaining cryptic, and I appreciated it. The last thing I needed was Jake finding out why I'd gone to Edmonton. I'd never hear the end of it.

I let out a big sigh and let my shoulders slump forward. "Yes and no. It was great meeting Stacey and her little guy, but we both still have so many questions. There are still a bunch of papers I need to go through but keep avoiding. I'm hoping maybe they have answers. One of these days I'll work up the courage to do it."

He nodded methodically. Jake's eyes darted back and forth between us with overwhelming curiosity, willing one of us to stop and explain. But I think James was enjoying keeping him in the dark just as much as I was.

"All in due time. No sense rushing it if you're not ready."

"That's kind of how I'm viewing it. And I'm just not ready. I mean the news about Stacey and her kids was a big enough surprise, and I've had enough surprises for the year. For a lifetime, really."

He nodded again. "There's more beer in the fridge if you'd like." He stood up. "I can grab you one. Jake?" Jake nodded. I shook my head. I'd never been much of a beer person.

And then Jake and I found ourselves alone on the patio, the setting sun falling across his face and playing up his high, rosy cheekbones and causing his eyes to shine lambent as though the sea was on fire.

"Now that we're alone for a moment, I'd really like to express my apology one more time," he started. "I know I said I'd leave you alone, but ... " he shrugged, "maybe we could be friends? I don't have any in town, and from what James has said, neither do you." He paused. "But *just* friends. I promise." I looked up at him from where I'd been staring at my shoes, and his breath caught. "Your eyes look like when the sky is stormy but there's just a peek of sun poking out of the clouds and it's shining right down on a big towering red cedar. They're practically on fire," he said with awe in his tone.

Now he was a poet?

"Are you Irish by any chance?"

My smile came on before I could stop it. "That obvious, is it? Pretty much your quintessential Irish poster child: pale skin, curly red hair and green eyes. Stick a potato in my mouth and a shamrock on my shirt, and I'm your St. Patrick's Day mascot."

He chuckled. "That's not a bad thing."

"No." I shook my head. "I've learned to live with it. My mom was from Ireland."

"Cool." He twisted his lips. "So, friends?" He surprised me again and stood up out of his chair with an extended a hand.

I took his hand. The spark that flowed between us made us both jump and lock eyes.

"What's going on out here?" James chuckled. "Calling a truce or setting up a time and place to duel?"

"Truce!" Jake smiled, looking to me for agreement. I nodded. The hand that he'd just released felt all tingly and warm.

"Yeah, a truce."

"Good, good," James cheered, handing Jake another beer. "You sticking around, Freya?" He took his seat again and propped his feet up on a vacant one. "Because if you are, you're allowed to sit down."

I rolled my eyes and let the corner of my mouth quirk up in a grin as I pulled out a chair across from Jake, his eyes following my every move with conspicuous fascination. I swallowed the lump in my throat only to realize that my pulse was racing. "I, um ... I'm going to go grab myself some water. Be right back." And without bothering to look at either of them, I dashed inside and poured myself a tall glass from the faucet.

"Everything okay?" Emma whispered, adjusting her tank top so that her already enormous breasts weren't spilling out of the top (as much).

"Yeah, fine. Just needed some water."

"Things better with you and Jake?"

I nodded and chugged. "I think so. We've called a truce. Shook hands and everything."

She got a mischievous glint in her eye, and I fought the urge to back away. "Could it be *more* than a truce?"

I made a dismissive face. "Cool your jets, matchmaker lady. I don't want to jam a fork in his hand ... anymore. That's enough for one day, wouldn't you say?"

"Fine, fine! You spoilsport." Her lips turned down into mock pout as she made her way around me into the kitchen to pour herself some wine. "You want any?"

"Sure. May as well."

"Don't sound so enthused," she chided, giving me the side-eye. "No pressure or anything."

"Sorry."

Passing me a glass half full of what looked to be a rich red, she gave me a sympathetic smile. "It's okay. You've got a lot going on. I can only imagine how this can all be weighing on you."

"Yeah, but your life is crazy too. Twin babies! I don't want to sit here and whine on your shoulder all the time."

She rested a hand on my shoulder. "It's what *friends* do. It's okay. Besides, if you don't bitch and complain, then I will."

"Oh?" She wandered into the living room, shooting a look out to the patio, where Jake and James seemed to be immersed in a deep conversation about cars and engines. Letting out a big sigh, she flopped down into their brown leather couch. I curled up in the matching chair. "Okay, spill."

She took a sip of her wine and glanced at the baby monitor. "It's nothing, really. Things are just hard, having kids and all. James and I used to be so in sync and all over each other. Now ... now we're both just so tired. I honestly can't even remember the last time we had sex. I gave him a blow job last weekend but wound up passing out while he was returning the favor."

I looked down at my wineglass and traced the rim with my index finger. I'd never talked about sex with anyone before, not even Ted. It just wasn't something we did. Our sex life when he was home was ... pretty straightforward, once a week, with a little bit of foreplay to set things up and then missionary position for roughly seven to twelve minutes, and then we'd both roll over and go to sleep. I usually orgasmed, but not always, but from what Ted said, it was all very typical and a fact of life that some women never orgasmed, so I should consider myself lucky.

But we never talked about sex, not ever.

"Am I weirding you out?" she asked, reading my body language perfectly. One thing about Emma was that she was a very empathic and astute woman, quickly homing in on other people's feelings and behaviors and responding in kind.

"N-no," I stammered, a slow warmth creeping up my neck and into my cheeks. "I—I'm okay."

"You're not comfortable talking about sex?" There was no judgment in her tone, just curiosity, so I forced myself to look her in the eye and gave her a small shrug.

"It's not that I'm not comfortable. Well, maybe I'm not. I dunno. It's just that I never have. Not with anyone."

"Not even your husband?" she asked with a surprised squawk.

I shook my head. "No."

"Oh, but that's half the fun, half the foreplay, setting the scene, talking about what you're going to do to each other and then chatting about it after." Her face took on a whimsical look of longing. "About what you liked and didn't like, what turns you on, what kind of things you'd like to try, hidden desires and secret fantasies."

"And what kind of things would you like to try, my love?" James interrupted, his voice a low and primal tenor that set the hairs on the back of my neck on end. Jake was in his wake, an amused grin spreading across his face. Dave jumped up on the couch and put his paws on Emma's lap. She reached out and started stroking his head without taking her eyes off her husband.

She gave him an appraising look. "Anything and everything, dear, you know me."

"I do," he murmured, his gaze focused solely and completely on his wife. Jake and I could have been lamps or throw pillows for the amount of attention he paid to us.

"I'm going to go to my place now. Freya, I think we should probably go," Jake said with a wink. "Leave the parents."

"I ... uh ... yeah," I muttered, standing up and draining my wine.

"No ... no, you guys don't have to go," Emma pleaded half-heartedly. She licked her lips and continued to stare at her husband, who slowly prowled toward her.

"Let's go, Freya," Jake encouraged again. A warm hand came under my arm and urged me to follow. "I'll walk you out."

"Okay." I nodded, continuing to watch the exchange between my two friends and feeling a small stirring in my belly. My own heartbeat picked up. He looked like he was ready to devour her.

"Good night, guys," Jake called out as he shut the front door with a chuckle. "Well, I guess their dry spell is over."

"James talked to you about their sex life?" I squeaked before I knew what I was saying and realizing that Jake was walking me to my car like a gentleman.

"No." He smiled, opening my door for me. "We heard you guys talking."

"Oh."

"So what happened?"

"To who?" I climbed into my brand-new Volvo XC90 and buckled myself in. Smiling inwardly at how *safe* my new car was. Built like a tank.

"Your husband. You guys get divorced?"

I put the key in the ignition and started it up, loving the sound of the engine and the way the vehicle purred and hummed beneath my hands and feet, a man-made beast under my control.

"No, he ... he died."

His eyes flashed with surprise, and then he looked down at his big, sandaled feet, holding on to the door so that I couldn't drive away. "I'm sorry. Now I feel like an even bigger ass for asking you to make out with me."

"It's okay." I swallowed. I looked at the clock on the dash. "But I should probably go, though."

"Yeah ... yeah, right, sorry." He made a disappointed scowl but then released my door and closed it for me, the smell of cinnamon and man drifting into my car with a small gust of air. "I guess I'll see you around."

"Yeah, see you," I whispered.

And I did see him again, only much sooner than I had anticipated, because Jake the flight fraidy-cat was the male lead in a very unexpected, very dirty dream I had that night, one that had me waking up with my pulse racing and my thighs damp. And all that I could think when I sat up at three in the morning and took a drink of water and mopped up the bead of sweat along my chest was: Who was this guy? And boy, was I in trouble.

5

The following evening, I went to the gym. Despite the beautiful day and the fact that I should've been out running, I really wanted to lift some weights. I'm one of those girls that most women hate. I have a hard time gaining weight, no matter how much I eat. I'm a bony stick, rail-thin with a mediocre chest and no hips or muscle tone.

I'd spent the last several months really trying to add some definition to my arms and legs so it didn't just look like strands of spaghetti were falling out of the arm and leg holes of my clothes, and so far, I was pleased with the results.

I put my headphones in and was busy doing some bench presses with a couple of free weights when a shadow behind my head and a muffled "hello" made me lose track of how many reps I'd done. I tilted my head up only to find an upside-down smiling Jake looking at me.

Sitting up, I pulled out my earbuds. "Oh, hey."

"We meet again." He grinned. "But this time as friends. Right, *Freya?*" There he went again, rolling my name around on his tongue like it was bloody foreplay.

"Right."

"How're you?"

I nodded. "I'm okay." I tipped my water bottle into my mouth and took a sip. "Had a good day back at work. You?"

He shrugged. "Can't complain. Haven't started my job yet. Spent most of the afternoon test-driving some trucks with James."

"Yeah? You buy anything?"

He nodded, and then a big, satisfied smile took over his face, showing off perfectly straight, white teeth. "A motorcycle."

"Really?" I grabbed my towel and mopped up my face. "That doesn't sound very safe."

He shook his head, still grinning. "It's perfectly safe. I've had a bike license since I moved to Edmonton and away from my parents."

"What do your parents have anything to do with it?" I asked, lying back down and motioning for him to move back so I could start another set.

He backed away and gave me a lifted eyebrow. "They're overbearing nutjobs. They still don't know I can ride a bike. You wanna come for a ride sometime?"

I gave him a dubious look. "Uh, never in my life would I be caught dead on one of those death machines."

"You sound like my mother," he joked. Just then my phone started to vibrate on my hip. Jake noticed and swiftly took my weights from me so I could answer it.

"Sorry," I murmured, seeing that it was Stacey and quickly pressing the little green button on the screen. "Hello?"

"Freya?" she panted, out of breath and in a state of panic.

"What's wrong?"

Jake looked at me with curiosity. I must have appeared scared out of my skin.

"The baby, it's c-oh." She growled. "Oh God, it's coming."

"But ... but it's early, too early. It's not due for another three weeks."

"It's coming now!"

"Okay ... I'm on my way. I'm not sure when the next flight to Edmonton is, but I'll be on it, okay? Hang in there. Is there anyone that can stay with Connor while you go to the hospital?"

"Noooooo," she wailed.

"Okay ... okay, if your contractions get too close together, call an ambulance, okay? Otherwise, I'll be there as soon as I can."

"They're still about twelve or so minutes apart. I have some time."

"All right, good. I'll call you when I'm booked on a flight." I hung up. "I—I have to go!" I crammed all my stuff into my gym bag, only to look up and find Jake on his phone.

"Perfect, thanks, bro ... An hour? Great. Okay, bye." He hung up and looked at me. "How soon can you be home, showered and packed?"

"Why?"

"I've acquired my brother's private jet to take us to Edmonton. It can be at the airport within the hour." My mouth hung open, but nothing came out, so Jake just continued to talk. "If you're not comfortable riding on my bike, would you mind picking me up on your way?"

"Um, thank you."

He shrugged. "No worries. Now let's go."

I blinked rapidly but composed myself and then followed him out of the gym to the parking lot. "I can't believe your brother has a jet," I finally managed to say. "How come you weren't on it the other day?"

"Someone else was borrowing it."

"Oh." The realm of private jets was so out of my field of knowledge or expertise that I had no idea what else to say.

"All right." He stopped in front of a brand-new shiny motorcycle and pulled a helmet out of his gym bag. "This is me. I'll see you in about half an hour?"

I nodded. "Sure. See you in a bit." And then without looking back, I zombie-walked to my car and drove home.

True to his word, we were in the air within an hour or so, cozily tucked into the plush, cream-colored leather seats of Justin's beautiful private jet, while Jake sat on the edge of his seat rocking back and forth with his eyes bulging out of his head.

"You okay?"

"I hate flying," he muttered. "Hate it!"

"Do you have your headphones? I don't mind if you listen to them if it'll help you."

He shook his head. "Left them at home, I was in such a rush to pack. I'll buy some for the flight back."

"You didn't have to come with me, you know? I mean, I appreciate that you organized this for me, but," I shook my head in confusion, "you hate flying."

He shrugged but then made a face as if that shrug was about ready to send him over the edge. "You're going to need someone to look after your friend's little boy while you're at the hospital with her. Besides, it's what friends do. And now I can go to my storage locker and bring back some more stuff, not that I have much. Mostly clothes."

I rolled the words around on my tongue. "What friends do ... "

"We're friends, right?"

I nodded slowly. "Riiiight."

He swallowed. "And as much as I'm hating this right now, I promise not to ask you to make out with me. But I do need a distraction. I'm losing my shit."

"Oh, uh, okay. Do you know if there's a deck of cards in here? We could play a game."

He swallowed again, his face having taken on a greenish hue. "Over ... over in that cupboard there are board games and stuff."

I unbuckled my belt and got up to go and check it out, coming back with a crib board and a deck of cards. "So you've been on this plane a fair bit then? Even though you hate to fly?"

Taking a sip of his water, he nodded. "Justin and Kendra have been kind enough to take my sister and I on a few trips. It was either give in to my fear and not see the world or suck it up and have some amazing adventures."

"Where all have you been?"

He shuffled the deck, our conversation proving to be a successful distraction to his fear and nausea. "A few years ago they took us to Utila, a small island off Honduras where we did a bunch of diving, then they took us to Turkey for a month one summer as well as Portugal and to James's island in Belize."

"Wow." I set the pegs in the board. "You've been all over the place."

Nodding absentmindedly, he continued to shuffle. "I love traveling. But what I'd really like to do is fly somewhere and then take a train or bus around to different countries. You see more of the land that way." He scrunched up his nose. "What is this game anyway?"

"You don't know how to play cribbage?" I squeaked, surprised that this worldly young man didn't know how to play such a popular card game.

He shook his head. "Where'd you learn?"

"My dad taught me when I was seven. It was our Friday night ritual. We always ordered pizza, which was a huge treat, and played cribbage."

"Can you teach me? Is it easy to learn?"

"Do you know how to count?"

He nodded with a sarcastic smile.

I just grinned back at him. "Then I think you'll be fine."

"**B**eginner's luck!" I scoffed, rolling my eyes and scooping up the cards to shuffle them. Jake took out the pegs and put them back at the beginning.

"Winning four in a row is beginner's luck?" He chuckled. "I'd say that it's the student surpassing the master."

I shot him an irritated glare. "What'd you say you did for work again?"

His smile nearly made me swallow my tongue. "I'm an engineer."

"So, numbers and math and problem-solving is your thing then?"

"My life," he affirmed.

"Well, maybe I should go grab the Scrabble board then, because words and letters are *my* life."

He chuckled again and raised a sexy eyebrow at me. "Yeah? I'm up for that."

"Hey there, folks," the captain boomed over the loudspeaker, "just wanted to let you know that we're about thirty minutes out of

Edmonton and are going to be starting our descent in about five or ten minutes."

Jakes face went ghostly white.

"Looks like Scrabble will have to wait." I winced as he stood to put the game away. "You going to be okay?" Just then the plane lurched to the left, causing him to fly across the aisle from where he had stood up to go and put the board away, and then fall right into my lap.

"Sorry," he mumbled, righting himself. Our eyes locked, and before I knew what I was doing, I reached for his hand and guided him to sit down next to me, lacing our fingers together and giving them a reassuring squeeze.

He looked at me like a lost puppy, smiling hesitantly.

"Just close your eyes, and I'll tell you when you can open them, okay?" I said slowly, as if trying to coax a kitten out from under the bed. "We'll be safely on the ground in no time."

Swallowing, he nodded and then closed his eyes, leaning his head back against the headrest and gripping my hand as if it were a life preserver.

I took this time to look around the inside of the jet. It was lavish and luxurious, with dark wood accents and paneling. I'd noticed before that there was a big bedroom at the rear of the plane as well as a bathroom and I wondered, just for a second, what it'd be like to make love at thirty thousand feet. Had Jake ever done it?

"Hey," I whispered a short while later, tapping his shoulder with my free hand and squeezing the hand that was laced with mine again. "We've landed. It's okay."

Over the last thirty or so minutes, Jake hadn't moved. There had been a bit more turbulence and even then, the only change had been his breathing and his pulse, which I felt beating against my own. He'd also squeezed my hand tighter, darn near cutting off the circulation at one point, but I didn't complain. We all had unexplainable fears, and I wasn't about to ridicule him for his.

He popped open the eye closest to me. "All good?"

"All good." I smiled. "We're back on good old terra firma."

He let out a big long exhale and stretched his neck from side to side, the move making long cords stand out, and for some reason I felt a stirring in my belly and my mouth was suddenly sandpaper dry.

He looked at me. "Thank you. You didn't have to do that."

When I realized I'd been staring at him with my mouth hanging open, I quickly closed it and gave him a curt nod, which promptly earned me an enormous, knowing grin.

"So." He yawned, stretching his whole body like a lithe puma, making my knees turn to jelly. "Do you just take a cab to her house?"

I nodded. "Uh, yeah." I shook the cobwebs out of my brain. "But I need to call work and get Allan to fill in for me."

"Okay. You call work. I'll grab our bags. Let's go."

6

"They're about four minutes apart now," Stacey huffed as we made our way into her small two-bedroom apartment forty-five minutes later. "And lasting about thirty or forty seconds each."

"I don't know what any of that means," I said, dropping my bag on her couch. "When are you supposed to go to the hospital?"

"When they're four minutes apart, lasting for one minute each for at least one hour," Jake interjected, plopping his own bag down and crouching down to say "hi" to Connor, who was busy watching some animated sing-along show with a bowl of Cheerios in front of him. "Hi, buddy. I'm Jake. Whatcha watching?"

"How do you know these things?" I asked, giving him a skeptical look.

He shrugged. "You pick things up. Plus, I was visiting when my sister-in-law went into labor with my nephew."

"So ... so we should go to the hospital now, then, if they're four minutes apart?" I asked, searching Stacey's face for answers.

He nodded. "Yeah, you guys go. Keep me posted. But Connor and I will be just fine." He turned to Stacey. "The little guy have any allergies or anything?"

Her eyes darted back and forth between me and Jake. I wasn't sure if she'd ever left her kid with anyone before, let alone a man she'd just met. And I couldn't blame her if she didn't exactly *trust* men. Neither did I. But at this point, we didn't really have a choice.

Jake was all we had.

I saw as that realization dawned on her, she shook her head. "No, no allergies. But I'm allergic to strawberries, so the doctor said to just watch him when we feed them to him. No reaction ... so far." And then another contraction ripped through her body, forcing her to bend over the arm of the couch, breathing deeply while she went as still as a statue.

"I told the cab to wait outside, so he's there if you need him," Jake said, ruffling Connor's strawberry-blond hair.

"Okay, thanks. Stacey, you ready to go?"

She nodded, her brown eyes wide with terror, darting around the room frantically, looking for something, "M-my bag's right there." I reached for her bag and mine, slung them both over my shoulder and headed out, giving Jake a beyond appreciative look over my shoulder as I left.

———

Time seemed to stand still while Stacey and I were in the hospital. When we arrived at the entrance to labor and delivery, her contractions had already increased to three minutes apart and lasted a minute or longer each. I wasn't sure what that meant, but if movies and television shows were any indication, I felt like I should have packed ripped sheets and boiled water with us in the cab. Thankfully though, she managed to keep her legs crossed until we reached the hospital. The sun was nearly set, and a soft brush of magenta clouded the indigo sky while the city lights prevented me from being able to see too many stars. Already it had me missing Victoria. For a city, you could still see a lot of stars at night.

I wasn't sure how long we'd been in the delivery room. Minutes turned to hours. Even though I thought for sure when we arrived that the baby would be out by midnight, it was encroaching on morning and light was peeking out from behind the drawn blinds as I pressed hard on Stacey's back while she wailed and cried in agony.

"I can't do this," she whimpered, coming off another contraction. They'd managed to slow back down to five minutes apart, but they seemed to be getting more intense and lasting longer.

"Yes, you can," I soothed, dabbing a cold wet cloth on the back of her neck and pushing her braid over her shoulder so I could dab between her bare shoulder blades. "You're so strong. You can do this." I wasn't sure what else to say. I'd never been to a birth before, barely knew any people who were pregnant. I'd met Emma when she was pregnant, but she had her husband with her. One day I saw her and she was as big as a house, and the next day, she had two little babies in her arms. I knew the fundamentals of childbirth, but the intricacies of it all were scaring the daylights out of me.

She looked over her shoulder at me and made a face that was so mixed with emotions it made my heart physically ache. "I hate him!" she cried, fear and anger and hurt all comingled. "I HATE HIM!"

"I know, honey, me too. Me too."

"He did this! He did this to me! To *us!* I HATE HIM!"

"Then prove that we don't need him. We can do this together. You and me, Connor and this baby. We'll do it together. You don't have to be alone."

She let out a low and guttural moan as another long and painful contraction took over, making her toes curl and her back arch. All I kept doing was what the nurse had showed me, a hip squeeze, wet washcloth on the forehead, and let her grip my hand until her nails dug deep wells into my palms.

"Okay," came the much too perky voice of a very young, very handsome doctor with bright blue eyes and golden hair. He looked like he should be off catching the next big wave, not slapping on latex gloves and peering into women's vaginas. "Let's check to see how you guys're doing."

"Wh-who are you?" Stacey stammered, looking up at him, her eyes full of tears while sweat trickled down her brow. I blotted her face and gave her a reassuring rub on the back.

"I'm Dr. Smiley. I'm taking over for Dr. Markham. She's in another delivery right now."

"B-but you're a child!" she blurted out. "You're not much older than ... than this thing." She pointed at her belly. Her eyes flashed to me for help.

Dr. Smiley faltered for just a second and then flashed us both a grin that made him worthy of his name. "I get that a lot. I'm actually almost forty and have two kids of my own, if that helps?"

"Fine, b-but you're too handsome. I can't look at you while I look like this," Stacey wailed.

"Would it help if I told you I was also gay?" he asked.

"Are you?" she asked, pausing and looking up him, suddenly curious.

His lips twisted but then he shook his head. "No."

"Arraaaah!" she screamed. "Get this thing out of me!"

"Let's take a look, Mrs. Gordon. Can you make it back to bed?"

"Saunders!" she hollered.

"Pardon me?"

"Stacey Saunders. No way in hell am I keeping that bastard's last name!" She hoisted herself up into the bed with the help of myself, Dr. Way-Too-Handsome and a nurse.

"Hey! Is Connor a big brother yet?" Jake asked when I finally managed to call him later that day.

"He is." I yawned, wandering through the hospital cafeteria in search of caffeine and sustenance. "He has a beautiful baby sister, name yet to be determined."

"How's Stacey?"

"Tired, but she did incredibly well. Only twenty-two minutes of pushing. Apparently, that's good. She said with Connor she pushed for over three hours."

"Oh God," he drawled, his tone mimicking my own sentiments about the whole child-birthing thing.

"I know."

"So, were you like there ... for the whole thing?"

"Yup." I yawned again. "Not going to lie, it's pretty disgusting. But beautiful at the same time. But gross."

"Okay, enough, I'm eating. How are you?" A warm tingle of something ran through my tired and achy body at his caring words. This guy was full of surprises. Not at all the rude fraidy-cat I'd met on the plane only four days ago.

Had it really only been four days? Why did I feel like I'd known him for so much longer?

I closed my eyes for a moment as I stirred my small paper cup of coffee and paid for my apple and cinnamon bun, secretly wishing that they just sold giant hunks of cheese so I could scurry off to a corner and devour the whole thing. "I'm fine. Exhausted, but somehow I don't feel like I have the right to say that, given the fact that I didn't just expel another human being from my body."

He chuckled. I could hear the sound of dishes being washed in the background and some children's show with a really irritatingly upbeat song. "You're allowed to be tired, just not *as* tired as Stacey. Are you going to sleep at the hospital again?"

"No." I bit into my cinnamon bun and nearly had an embolism from the sudden rush of sugar to my severely depleted brain. The smell instantly reminded me of Jake, and I couldn't help but smile. "I'll stick around until Stacey and the baby wake up, make sure they have everything they need for the night, and then I'll come back. I'll be there probably around six or seven. You need me to pick up anything for you guys?"

"Naw, Connor and I walked to the store earlier today and picked up a few things. We just had some mac and cheese with veggies for lunch, and he's asked for pancakes for dinner. I spied some breakfast sausages in the back of her freezer, so I think I'll cook those up too, get some protein into this kid. All he wants to eat is bloody Goldfish crackers."

I marveled at how easily domesticity came to him. I would have been pulling my hair out in a mild state of panic had I been forced to stay home with a three-year-old, whereas Jake seemed cool as a cucumber. "I guess I should probably ask and not assume that you don't, given your age, but do you have kids?"

He started to laugh. "Why? Because I know how to keep them alive for twenty-four hours?"

"Well ... yeah."

"I have nieces and a nephew who I am quite doting on, but a lot of it's just common sense. When they're hungry, you feed them. Plus, he's three. He's old enough to tell me what he wants. It's not like he's a baby and I have to run through the checklist to figure out why the hell he's crying."

I blew on my coffee and then took a sip, wincing when it burned my tongue. "Yeah, I guess you're right. Thank you again for coming. You really helped us."

"No worries. But I've got to go. The little man wants to play Legos, and I never turn down Legos."

"Okay, see you in a bit." I giggled, my heart warming at the idea of Jake sitting on the floor playing Legos with a three-year-old. He was just so full of surprises.

A few hours later, I knocked on the door, feeling weird about it but not knowing if I should just go in either. Fortunately, I didn't have to wait long, and two men, one tall and one small, both wearing aprons, greeted me with giant smiles and what appeared to be pancake batter on their faces.

"Hello." I smiled, dead on my feet but also starving, my mind and stomach at war in my body over whether sleep or food was more important.

"Pancakes!" Connor smiled, running back to the kitchen and then bringing me a plate with one pancake on it. "Here!"

"Oh, ah, thank you, honey. Maybe I'll eat it at the table though, okay? Will you join me?"

He nodded emphatically and followed me into the kitchen, where we all took seats and then proceeded to dig in to the enormous stack of blueberry pancakes that Jake had just "whipped up."

"So, do we have a name yet?" he asked, his mouth full, while a smear of blueberry marred the corner of his mouth. I fought the compulsion to lean over and wipe it off.

"I think Stacey has decided on Thea Jasmine Saunders, and from the way she was talking earlier, this little dude's going to be getting a different last name soon too." I grabbed another two pancakes off the stack and poured far too much maple syrup on top, much to Jake's delight, followed by a heaping helping of whipped cream.

"Really?" he asked. "Why?"

I stilled. "Oh, ah ... no reason. Uh ... Stacey just wants the kids to have her last name, that's all. Seeing as their dad isn't in the picture, and she's going to change her name back legally too."

"But why? Where's their dad?"

"He's dead," I whispered, giving him the stink-eye, so that he knew to be quiet around Connor when mentioning the "D" word.

He made an apologetic face and then mumbled under his breath. "Did he die with your husband?"

I looked down at my plate and cut my pancakes until they were just a mound of tiny little bite-size pieces. "Uh, yeah."

"Oh jeez." He rubbed the back of his neck. "I'm really sorry. To leave a kid and a pregnant wife. Well, it's lucky that you have each other."

"Yeah." I hated lying, not to mention I was terrible at it. I'd been taught from a very young age that lying only got you further into trouble, and it hurt the person you were lying to as well. Said that you didn't trust them enough with the truth, but I just couldn't tell Jake the truth. It was too embarrassing. He'd probably think I was some pathetic, oblivious looser and would want nothing to do with me, and somehow the thought of Jake wanting nothing to do with me made me almost sick to my stomach.

"Well, why don't you go have a shower, and I'll clean up here?" he said, accepting my answer and not pressing for more. He stood up and began clearing the table. "You look exhausted. And before you get all 'female' on me and say 'so what you're saying I look like shit?' that's not what I'm saying. I'm saying you look beautiful but about to fall asleep into your whipped cream. You've been awake for nearly two days. You deserve to rest."

I gaped at him. Who the heck was this guy? But I didn't have enough energy to argue or question him. I simply nodded, finished my pancakes and, without a word, headed to the bathroom. The water was like warm and welcoming angel wings enveloping me into a cocoon of steam and pummeling my sore body into a pliant heap of skin and bones.

I'm not sure how long I stood under the spray, but I was thankful that the hot water was free in the building and I didn't have to worry about jacking up Stacey's water bill. Eventually I felt pruney and shut the tap off, wrapping myself up in a big towel, only to realize that I'd forgotten all my clothes in my bag, which I'd left in the living room. I thought about calling out to Jake to bring me my bag, but when I poked my head around the corner, I heard a soft tune coming from Connor's room and realized that Jake must have put him to bed, so I didn't want to yell.

Shrouding myself in the oversized sheet, I tiptoed out to the living room to grab my bag, only when I got there, it wasn't where I'd left it. Did Jake take it to the bedroom? Backtracking, I opened the door to Stacey's room only to find my bag on the dresser and the bed turned down. Jake busied himself folding what looked to be Connor's laundry.

No, seriously, who the heck was this guy?

"I—I, uh, I forgot my bag," I stammered, suddenly very aware of my nakedness beneath the towel. I quickly snatched up my entire bag and hurried off to the bathroom, only to emerge minutes later in my hastily packed sleepy owl pajama pants and a worn and faded old Spice Girls T-shirt that was more of a crop top than a shirt.

What was I thinking?

When I walked back into the bedroom, he was still busy folding laundry. I wasn't sure what came over me, perhaps it was the fatigue, maybe the weird heady high of being a part of something bigger than myself for once, a bizarro-world makeshift family. Perhaps I was drunk on pancakes, who knows? But I strode right up to him and pecked him on the cheek. "Thank you so much for everything."

The look he gave me made me take a half step back and my pulse hammer inside my veins. I swallowed as that familiar tingle made its way back into my belly. The man's looks were pure animal. "I don't want to upset you, Freya, and it's not why I came, but if you asked anything of me tonight, I wouldn't hesitate."

"Wh-what does that mean?" I swallowed again, knowing exactly what it meant.

He gave me an appraising look. "I think you know *exactly* what it means. But if you're too tired, you can crawl right into bed without saying a word."

I eyed him from head to toe. He watched me with amusement as I checked him out. A small smirk curved on his plump lips as my eyes stayed just a touch too long on his very tight, very appealing abdomen.

God, had I really dreamt about those lips a few nights ago?

He continued to fold laundry. His hands were big and his fingers long, while a few small white scars on the back spoke of labor, working with his hands. I loved a man who could work with his hands: chop wood, repair a fence, build a shed. A man's man. Those were manly hands, capable hands, hands with stories to tell. I bit my lip fighting off a yawn that had been building. "I am tired," I finally admitted.

His face didn't twitch. He just continued to fold the itty-bitty shirts and pants. "Then go to sleep."

"Where are you sleeping?" My gaze fell to the big queen-size bed. He must have slept in here last night. Was he expecting to sleep in here again tonight? A mild rush of panic took over, but it was mixed with something else, something pulse-racing ... interest?

He looked up at me from beneath his lashes with a lopsided smile. "I'll crash on the couch."

"Oh."

He finished what he was doing and scooped up all the clothes, planning to take them out of the room. I wandered around to the side of the bed he'd turned down for me. The electric charge surging around the room between us was enough to fry bacon. I was at a complete loss of what to do. I'd never seduced anyone before. I wasn't even sure I wanted to seduce him. I just didn't want him to go. I crawled into bed just as he turned off the light and reached for the door.

"Jake?" It was more a breath than a whisper.

"Yeah?"

"*A word?*"

I heard his breath snag and the laundry fall to a heap in the hallway. He was back in the room and next to my side of the bed in less than a second.

"Freya? Are you toying with me? Don't toy with me. We called a truce, remember?" Suddenly the jokester was gone, and in his place was an incredibly sexy, menacingly handsome, virile man. There was no *child* or *boy* here. He was ALL man.

I shook my head and swallowed again, looking down at the intricate pattern on the purple and white bedspread. "No. I ... I don't know what I'm doing."

"Do you want something to happen?"

I couldn't look at him, but I gave a small nod. "I think so." I could scarcely believe my own boldness. I'd never done anything like this before in my life.

"Freya," he whispered, the tenor of his voice rough and husky like twelve-year-old whiskey. "I'm crazy about you, but don't tease me."

"I ... I don't know what I'm saying. I've never done this before."

"Do you want me?"

My face felt warm, and my chest rose and fell fast and uneven. "Yes," I whispered. And before I could think any further, his hand cupped my cheek and his lips brushed mine. I closed my eyes and melted into his touch, leaning my face into his hand and opening my mouth to grant him access.

But he pulled away, tilting my chin up in the process, his gaze soulful and penetrating.

"You're a widow and grieving. I don't want to take advantage of you."

I shook my head and smiled softly. "I'm not, and you're not."

"Are you sure?"

I ran my tongue between the seam of my lips, tasting his kiss. "I think so." My nipples pearled against my Spice Girls T-shirt, and my breasts felt heavy and needful. The way he looked at me, with such hunger, the way a starving man might stare at a loaf of bread in a shop window, it saturated my senses and had me drenched with longing. I was no longer thinking with my mind. This was purely primitive, purely physical and all body.

Slowly, like a panther stalking his prey, he stretched out on top of me, pressing my body into the bed. His lips trailed warm, wet kisses along my neck and chin. "You're so beautiful," he purred. "Your skin is like ivory and soft as silk."

Was this guy for real? Ted never waxed poetic like this.

"Jake ... " I panted, not knowing where to put my hands and letting them awkwardly fall to his shoulders, "kiss me."

And kiss me he did.

He lips captured mine, devouring me, savoring me. His tongue thrust inside, stroking and massaging until I was needy and greedy, shamelessly arching into him, desperate for friction.

"Let me taste you," he murmured, his mouth traveling down my neck and chest to my stomach. "It's all I've wanted to do since we met."

"N-no, no, no!" I stammered, attempting to wriggle away. "You don't have to."

But he slid his hands beneath me and cupped my butt. His tongue swirled around my navel, forcing a groan to bubble up at the back of my throat. I couldn't stop myself, and my hips lifted from the mattress, pushing into his attention.

Blowing cool air on my center, he pushed my legs farther apart.

"Relax," he cooed. "Let me. You're so tightly wound, and you won't tell me why. Just ... just let me, please?" I had to hand it to him; he managed to pull off some pretty convincing puppy-dog eyes, and the man was essentially begging me to let him give me pleasure. I was hard-headed, but I wasn't stupid, and if Jake did *other* things as well as he kissed, then I was almost certainly in for an unforgettable night.

One great night.

I deserved it, didn't I? And that's all it was, I had to remind myself, one night. When we returned home, this couldn't and wouldn't happen again. Never again.

"Okay," I sighed, letting my muscles go lax and my body dissolve into the mattress. "But I should warn you ... " He quirked an eyebrow at me as his fingers deftly peeled my bottoms and underwear down my legs. "I'm not like these newfangled women who wax it all off."

He grinned salaciously as he chucked my clothes to the floor and came face to face with my bush. He chuckled. "All natural. I like that."

"You don't mind?"

Shaking his head, he positioned himself on his stomach and wedged his hands beneath me again, pulling himself so he was flush with the juncture of my thighs. "Not at all. I think it's a beautiful little pussy. A firecracker, just like you." And with that, his fingers spread me open and his tongue dipped inside. "Mmm," he hummed. "So sweet."

I closed my eyes and sank farther into the bed, my hands traveling down to rest on his bobbing head, letting the deluge of sensations wash over me. I lifted my head and watched as this insanely beautiful man ate me out with diligent fascination. His one and only focus was bringing me pleasure. A finger slipped inside, and I pushed up into his face.

"You're so tight," he murmured, the hum of his voice reverberating through me like a euphoric wave. "And greedy."

"Jake, I ... oh God." The man was an expert, through and through. Dedicated to his craft. The twists and twirls of his tongue had me close within seconds. "I'm ... I'm close," I sighed, patting his head. "Y-you can stop now."

Looking up at me, but not stopping his efforts, he lifted an eyebrow and murmured, "Why would I stop? I want to hear you come. Come for me, *Freya*."

Even if I wanted to, I wasn't able to stop it. The pleasure took hold of me like a feather in a gust of wind, whipping me up high, higher than I'd ever been before, only to send me sailing back down toward earth in a giant spiral of enraptured sensations.

I bucked and thrust into his face as every nerve ending in my body seemed to stand on end and fire at the same time. I panted as if I'd just run a marathon, and a light misting of perspiration beaded across my chest and forehead

Jake popped up like a prairie dog, a wide and triumphant grin on his face, his lips glistening with my arousal. "You're not a tough nut to crack at all. Here I thought I might have to be down there half the night, you were so tense." He snickered, crawling up toward the headboard and planting a big, noisy kiss on my lips. "How do you feel?"

I squirmed under his intense gaze. Just because we did things didn't mean we then needed to discuss them. "Fine," I whispered, avoiding his face.

"Look at me," he said quietly, gently turning my face with a finger beneath my chin. "You okay?"

I sat up in the bed but then I realized I was naked from the waist down. I quickly pulled the covers up to hide myself. "I'm fine. Thank you very much for that. It was nice."

His laugh made me jump. It was so loud and abrupt that at first I thought he was angry. "You're *fine*? It was *nice*? Did you just thank me? Who the hell are you, woman?"

"I ... I don't know what you mean?"

"I just ate you out and you came in record-breaking time, albeit quietly, but you're behaving as if I just finished painting your garage or installing new grout in your bathroom. 'It was *nice*?'"

I didn't understand what he was getting at. Was I not supposed to orgasm? He'd told me to. Ted only ever went down on me as foreplay, and then once I was turned on, we'd have sex, which is why I had tapped Jake on the head to let him know I was close. So why was he mocking me now?

I shook my head. "If you didn't want me to get off, why did you tell me to?" I finally asked, not understanding anything that was going on and feeling uncomfortable with the entire topic.

Now it was his turn to look confused. "Of course I wanted you to get off. I wouldn't have put my face between your legs if that wasn't my end goal. Besides, you came on to me. You're a really confusing woman, you know that? I can't figure you out."

"I—I don't know what you want from me," I stammered, pulling my legs up to my chest beneath the covers and hugging them. "This conversation is making me really uncomfortable."

Quickly his frustration and confusion dissolved and he reached for my hands. "Freya, have you never been allowed to orgasm from oral sex before?" I looked away and focused on the duvet cover again. Why was he so set on talking about this? "Look at me," he whispered.

I shrugged. "That's just not how Ted and I did things. He would go down on me but it was only to ... to start things. Never finish them."

He nodded solemnly. "And the orgasm, how was it ... *really?* You're an English teacher; use some big English words. If it was actually just *nice,* then next time I'll try harder, but if you're just embarrassed to express your pleasure, then don't be. You're a beautiful, sexy, red-blooded woman who is entitled to enjoy her orgasms and sing it from the rooftops." I rolled my eyes, but he just grinned. "So," he went on, "how was it?"

I couldn't stop the small smile that played at the corner of my mouth. "It was really great. Really, really great. I"—I looked down at the duvet again—"I've never come like that before. That hard, I mean."

"But you hardly made a peep. That's why I'm asking you how it was, because I honestly couldn't tell. Are you normally that quiet? Or is it because there's a kid sleeping in the next room and we don't know how thin these apartment walls are?"

I twisted my lips and shrugged. "I think so."

He shook his head. "Well, we'll have to change that. My new goal is to make you scream." His smile was all wolf. Instinctively I felt my whole body respond and reignite. I didn't have the heart to tell him that this was a one-time thing.

"So." His eyelids sank to half-mast as he rolled over and pushed my legs down so that he was spread out on top of me. The weight of his body on mine made my heart rate pick up and my core clench from the memory of his mouth. "Ready for round two?" And before I could answer, he pulled the covers down, and his lips were on me again.

Okay, THIS is the last time.

8

I hadn't opened my eyes yet, but I felt him move in the bed next to me.

"Wow!" he breathed out.

He had that right. *Wow!*

Jake Leeman had, as the kids say it, "rocked my world." Not that I had much to compare with, considering Ted was the only man I'd ever been with up until a few moments ago, but Jake ... I squeezed my eyes even tighter, hoping to relive the last half hour.

His hands, his mouth, his ...

I'd come twice. Yes, twice! And he'd even waited for me. Ted rarely waited and often went soft before I could finish.

But not Jake.

He had remained like the rock of Gibraltar until the very end. His hip swivels and deep thrusts left me mesmerized. The way his mouth ravished my nipples until they were hard and aching and sensitive to his touch had me whimpering for more. Not a square inch of my body was left unkissed, unappreciated, uncaressed by the time I came down from my last orgasm. He had worshipped me until I was the one calling out to God.

Yeah.

Wow!

He shifted on the bed again and reached for me. I opened my eyes and rolled onto my side to face him.

"Hey, gorgeous."

Hiding a smile, I lowered my lashes. "Hi."

He tucked a strand of hair behind my ear. "You're amazing."

"Thank you. You too." I nibbled on my bottom lip. I wasn't used to the pillow talk.

His thumb trailed down my jaw and tugged my lip from my teeth, rubbing the spot he'd kissed so thoroughly. "You taste so good."

Squirming from all the compliments and attention, I pulled the sheet up to cover my breasts. "We should probably get some sleep."

He nodded with a yawn, before stretching like a lithe and satisfied jungle cat and tucking his hands behind his head. "Go pee."

I shot him a startled look. "What? Why?"

"Don't you know that you're supposed pee after sex?"

"No, since when?" I went on the hunt for my underwear and pants while keeping the sheet wrapped around my body for modesty. "And how do you know?"

He shrugged, looking incredibly sexy all spread out in his naked glory on the bed, not caring at all that he was completely nude. "Sex-ed. But," he snorted a laugh, "but also Justin and Kendra. Those two have no filter and figured it was their place to talk to Jess and I about safe sex.

"Really?"

"Yeah." He nodded. "It was super awkward at first, especially since at that point I was already sexually active and knew the whole 'no glove, no love' spiel, but after a while it actually became quite interesting and educational. My brother and his wife are very open and honest people, not judgmental at all and willing to answer even the dumbest question. I mean, don't get me wrong, it was kind of awkward hearing it all with my little sister right there." He shrugged. "But they were actually pretty knowledgable. That's where I learned that women need to pee after sex."

"Yeah, but why?"

How did I not know this? But he didn't seem to notice my unease and just continued to prattle on. "My sister seemed to really appreciate it, as my parents are such tight-lipped, pious, right-wing nutjobs. They actually had arranged for her to marry the leader of my mom's quote un-quote church, which is really just a cult, when she was fifteen, but Justin and I put a stop to that." I made a face of surprise. He simply nodded with buggy eyes. "Though I for one would be more inclined to ship her off to a nunnery. I can't bear the thought of my sister having some guy do to her what I just did to you." He bared his teeth. "Makes my blood boil."

I chuckled. "She's a woman and a grown-up. She's allowed to have sex. She's probably already *having* sex."

"She's not a *woman!*" he exclaimed, with more vehemence in his voice than I'm sure he intended. "She's my baby sister. And she's too sweet and pure and innocent to be having sex. I just ... I just can't think about it."

I shrugged. "Then don't. But I'm sure one day your sister will have sex, if she isn't already, and that's just something you need accept."

"I know," he sighed. "But I can pretend she doesn't."

I smiled. Things were just so easy with Jake. "You can pretend a lot of things. Doesn't make them true."

"Go pee, woman!" he growled, closing his eyes. "And then come back and sit on my face. But for now, I'm going to *pretend* that you're doing it." And he started to dart and waggle his tongue in and out of his mouth, making all sorts of disgusting and dirty sounds.

"You're sick." I giggled, heading off to the bathroom.

"Lovesick, maybe," I heard him murmur before I closed the door.

Staring at myself in the mirror, I was startled by the woman that looked back at me. She didn't look like me. She looked ... happy. As much as I'd told myself that it was only a one-time and then a two-time thing, I'd asked him if he had a condom and let him show me *all* his skills.

Even if it just was for the night and one night alone, I was going to enjoy myself. I deserved it. He made me feel alive in ways I'd never felt before. He hit places and erogenous zones inside my body I never knew existed, and he worshipped and possessed me in ways I'd never even knew were possible. I peed as I was told to do, found a washcloth and quickly washed myself and then made my way back to the bedroom.

"Come on, woman," he grinned, still in the same position I'd left him in, "this face isn't going to sit on itself."

That night I wound up having one of the best sleeps since Ted died. I never woke up to pee. I'm not even sure I stirred or changed positions. I was down and out for the count, not waking up until I heard faint voices in the hallway. Rolling over, I found Jake's side of the bed vacant and cold. A sharp pang of disappointment stabbed me in the solar plexus.

It was one night. Don't forget that.

Slowly, I pried myself out of bed, reveling in the faint aches throughout my body from long-denied pleasure. The chatter in the living room grew louder, and from the sounds of things, Jake and Connor were engaged in a pretty heated game of go-fish.

"Morning," I croaked, surprising myself with how hoarse my voice was. "Coffee?"

"Fresh pot." He grinned, giving me a small, playful wink before turning back to Connor. "Do you have any puppies?" Clearly this was a simplified version of go-fish, because I couldn't for the life of me remember playing the game where there were any "puppies" on the cards.

"So, are we all going to go and see baby Thea today and bring her and her mommy home?" Jake asked, after I'd poured myself a much-needed cup of coffee and joined them in the living room.

"Actually," I blew on my mug, "Stacey just texted me a few minutes ago to let me know that they're making her stay another night. Apparently, she and the baby are having some breastfeeding issues, so the doctors want to make sure they have a solid latch before sending them home. But I think you should bring Connor today to see his mum. And I called a nanny agency last night on my way home. They're sending a few candidates to the hospital this afternoon so Stacey and I can vet them and see if anyone will be a good fit to help her out for the first little bit."

"That's a good idea." He nodded. "I still can't believe you *both* lost your husbands."

I twisted my mouth and took a sip of my coffee.

Darn, even his coffee was amazing.

"How did it happen?" he asked, scooping up all the cards and putting them away as Connor had decided he was done and had gone off to play with his dump truck.

"How did what happen?"

"Your husbands."

"Oh ... uh ... car accident."

"They were in the car together?"

"Um ... yeah, sure." I looked away and took another sip.

"Freya ... " He stood up and grabbed his empty coffee mug, taking it to the kitchen to pour himself more. His bare back was chiseled and muscular, and I found myself hypnotized by the way the muscles bunched and flexed as he moved. "What aren't you telling me?"

My daydream fizzled. "Nothing!" I snapped. "I'm going to go and get dressed. I think the first nanny is coming around eleven." And before he could say or do anything else, I rose from my seat and headed off to the bedroom.

Why did he have to be so inquisitive? Couldn't he just let sleeping or, in this case, DEAD dogs lie?

I chuckled at that thought. A dog was a loyal and protective member of your family, whereas Ted had been anything but loyal, and although he wasn't a mean man, he certainly hadn't protected my heart. No, dog was too good for him. He was more of a rat, or a toad, or a cockroach.

Jake came into the bedroom just as I was peeling off my T-shirt. My breasts were exposed, and I immediately turned around. "Hey, I'm changing in here!"

He snorted. "It's not anything I haven't seen. I seem to remember you quite liked it when I had my mouth on your—"

But I cut him off. "That was last night. This is now."

"And what's changed?"

"Everything!"

"How?"

I saw his confused face in the mirror. Inside, I was just as confused. What *had* changed?

"I don't know." I bit my lip and turned away so he couldn't see my face in the mirror. "It was a one-time thing. I was thanking you for taking care of Connor and being so helpful and wonderful."

"Do you pay everyone who does you a favor with sex?" he scoffed, his face taking on a fierce and irritated scowl.

Had I hurt him?

Meanwhile tension, a sudden living and breathing beast, had emerged and sullied the atmosphere of the room entirely. Gone was the playful air of last night, with our coquettish banter and easygoing, newfound camaraderie.

I rounded on him, buttoning up my blouse. "No! How dare you say that?"

"You just told me the only reason you had sex with me was because you wanted to thank me. How am I supposed to respond? So, are you not even attracted to me? Do you not even like me? Were your orgasms even real?"

I pulled on my pants, averting my eyes. "I ... I can't do this right now. I have to go. Please bring Connor to the hospital in an hour or so. Stacey's keys are in the bowl at the door. Her car is the red Mazda 3 parked on the street."

"Why don't you just wait ten goddamn minutes, and we'll all go together?"

"Don't get angry with me."

He pointed an accusatory finger at me, and I backed up a step. "And why not? You came on to me last night. You initiated. And now, in the light of a new day, you once again can't stand to be in the same room as me? What the fuck? And don't you dare say it was because the sex wasn't good, because you know it was."

"I can't do this right now." I ground my teeth together. This man could be so infuriating.

He shot me a look that would make most normal people cower in fear, but for some reason, it didn't scare me. "Just wait fifteen minutes, and Connor and I will get dressed and we'll all drive together."

"Fine." I pushed past him to head to the bathroom.

"This isn't over, Freya!" he called after me.

He couldn't have been more wrong.

When I looked at myself in the mirror, the happy face from the night before was gone, but I still didn't recognize the person staring back at me. She was sad. Her face looked much older than her thirty years, and there were dark purple bags hanging under her eyes.

I quickly washed my face and brushed my teeth, cursing my pale skin and endless freckles as I continued to scrutinize every pore on my face. A knock on the bathroom door jarred me out of my self-deprecating reverie.

"Other people need the bathroom, you know?"

"Oh, sorry. Coming." I opened the door and squeezed past the two of them, who were both dressed and ready to go. I avoided Jake's eyes and went to go pour myself more coffee.

He and Connor made their way into the bathroom. "All right, dude, let's brush our teeth."

9

"Hey there," I whispered, gently pushing open the door to Stacey's hospital room. "How're you feeling today?"

She gingerly propped herself up on her pillows and hit the button to make the bed hinge forward. "I'm okay. Tired. This little monkey was up most of the night. I seem to remember that Connor slept a lot when he was first born. I think I'm in for a battle with her."

I peered into the plastic hospital bassinet to find a snoozing little Thea, all swaddled up like a sausage with only her chubby-cheeked face poking out. "Connor, come meet your baby sister."

Jake had Connor by the hand and led him over to stand next to me, the heat from his big body radiating like waves and making me sway on the spot. He lifted the little guy up so that he could peer inside. Connor's eyes went wide with fascination, and his mouth parted in awe.

"Little," Connor squeaked.

Stacey smiled. "Very little. We have to be gentle."

Connor looked up at the sound of his mother's voice and instantly changed, his smile illuminating the room. His arms stretched out for her. Jake took him over to the side of her bed in one long stride, and the little boy slid in next to his mother, hugging her and nuzzling into her chest.

"I missed you, buddy," she cooed, tears forming in her eyes. She quickly wiped them away with her sheet. "Have you been good for Jake?"

Connor nodded. "Pancakes for supper."

"You had pancakes for supper?"

He nodded again. "Yep!"

For the remainder of the day, Stacey and I interviewed potential nannies. Jake and Connor hung out for a bit longer before heading home, promising to come back and get me later that day. After sifting through some real weirdos and duds, we finally managed to find somebody that both Stacey and I liked, agreeing that she seemed to know her stuff when it came to kids but wasn't opposed to going with the flow and following Stacey's lead and decisions on child-rearing. Some of the women we met were so rigid and controlling that Stacey felt if she didn't toe the line herself, she'd be handed demerits, while others were such loopy flower children, you got the feeling that if one day if they didn't show up, it was because they were off chasing a rainbow.

But with Daniella, we finally seemed to find a good fit—a woman in her mid-fifties with years of experience working with various families, both as a nanny and au pair, as well as in preschools and daycares. Unable to have children herself, she'd decided to dedicate her life to children and surround herself with their love and curiosity. She'd even noticed before any of the doctors or nurses had that Thea appeared to have mild jaundice and suggested that Stacey go and sit in the chair next to the window with her, so the baby could get some sunlight.

Stacey seemed relieved to know that after I left, someone was going to be there to help her through the first few daunting weeks of having a new baby. But underneath it all, even beneath the fatigue and euphoria that came from having a baby, she was still seething with rage. And who could blame her? I'd moved past my anger and was now just kind of numb. But he'd left her with two children to care for. I wasn't sure I could ever forgive someone who did that to me.

It was closing in on four o'clock and I was softly rocking the baby next to the window while Stacey slept. A quiet rustling at the door made me turn around. Jake and Connor stood there with a big bouquet of flowers and a balloon that said "BABY GIRL" in big Pepto-Bismol pink letters.

"Shh," Jake whispered. "I think your mummy is sleeping."

"No, I'm not," Stacey murmured, popping one eye open and then sitting up as Connor raced toward her, the big balloon bouncing behind him.

"Here, mummy!" he cried, thrusting the balloon ribbon into her hand. "Flowers!" He pointed at the huge bouquet that Jake was setting on the dresser at the foot of the bed.

"They're lovely," she said with a yawn. "Thank you."

I brought Thea back over and Stacey took her, letting Connor get good and close to his sister. "Baby," he cooed, gently brushing his knuckle over her cheek.

"I'm going to go find a washroom," Jake said.

"Okay, spill," Stacey said, giving me a stern look once Jake had rounded the corner. "What's the deal with you two? Because I may have been in labor, but there was definitely a spark between the two of you when you arrived. And now it's as though you can barely stand to be in the same room as each other. What happened?"

I looked toward the door and then back at her. "It's complicated."

She shook her head. "No, my situation is complicated. In fact, I'm not sure I'll ever get laid again. But you, you have all the freedom in the world. How long have you guys been seeing each other? Because you never mentioned him when you were here."

I bit my lip and looked down at my shoes. "We, uh ... we met on the plane home."

She shot me an infuriated look. "You let a complete stranger hang out with my kid!"

"No, no," I protested, shaking my head emphatically and waving my hands. "Turns out he's super close with my friend Emma and her husband. We didn't actually get along on the plane but then ran into each other when I went to Emma's for dinner. We called a truce. It was his brother's private jet that got us here so fast. He's great with kids. Has nieces and nephews."

Her eyebrows flew up. "Private jet?"

"Yeah." I sighed. "Trust me, I don't think he's a threat. Connor seems to love him."

"So, what's the deal with you two then?" she asked, visibly relaxing and seeming to accept my character reference of Jake. Her eyes were probing and eager, begging me to give her the scoop on my love life.

"Like I said," hoping my shrug was nonchalant, "it's complicated."

"You slept with him!" she exclaimed. I gaped at her. How could she tell? "You've got 'multiple orgasms' written all over your face."

I made a face, hoping that it neither confirmed nor denied anything but instead shifted the subject elsewhere. "He doesn't know about Ted. He just thinks I'm a widow." She nodded, understanding completely. She didn't want to advertise how she'd become a widow either. "But he's started asking questions."

She made a face, and I spun around to see Jake coming back in. "Ready to go?" he asked, his face void of emotion.

I swallowed. "You bet."

I helped Connor, who had climbed up into his mother's bed, back out and pecked the baby on the forehead. "We'll be back tomorrow morning to get you and Thea, okay?"

"Okay." She nodded, but as I went to pull away, she grabbed me by the sleeve. "He might be one of the few guys who understands and doesn't run for the hills. Maybe tell him? He seems pretty great. And gorgeous too."

I rolled my eyes. She didn't know the half of just how *great* Jake really was. "I'll think about it. See you tomorrow."

That night, we had another delicious dinner—this time Jake and Connor had made spaghetti, another one of Connor's requests. He'd also asked for ice cream sundaes for dessert. Once the little guy was tucked into bed, Jake and I sat in awkward silence in the living room. The news blathered on in the background, and he played on his phone. I was nose-deep in my e-reader.

"So, are you ever going to talk to me again?" he finally asked, causing me to jump and toss my e-reader to the floor.

"Of course." I shrugged, lifting one shoulder in an attempt to seem cool and collected and not all hot and bothered, even though inside, my stomach, heart, brain and genitalia were in a full-on battle. My brain knew I shouldn't get involved with him. But my heart ached and wanted love again, wanted to feel the things that Jake made me feel. My stomach was doing flip-flops, and my genitalia, well, let's just say it wanted an encore of last night. "What do you want to talk about?"

"Well, your complete one-eighty this morning, for starters. What the hell happened?"

"It was one night." I sighed. "Nothing more."

He growled something under his breath that I couldn't quite hear. "It was not *one* night. Stop saying that. And don't you dare say that it was a 'thank you' again."

I picked up my e-reader and set it down on the coffee table before pulling my legs under me. "What do you want from me?"

"I want the truth. Is that so hard? Don't you think I deserve that?"

"I've told you the truth."

He shook his head. "I don't think you have. Why are you so evasive when I ask you questions about your husband?"

I looked away from his face. Nobody should be allowed to be that good-looking. That kind of handsome should be illegal. It messes with your mind and makes you want to do all kinds of things you know you shouldn't. I bit my lip, twisting my fingers together in my lap. "There's nothing to tell. He's dead. Our marriage wasn't that great. I'm sorry he's dead, but I don't miss him."

"See, I think there's more too it. Why is Stacey changing her and the kid's last names? Did she hate her husband too? Did you guys off your husbands together or something?"

I gaped at him. "Off as in *murder*? Did you honestly just ask me if I killed my husband?"

He lifted one shoulder. "Did you?"

"Oh my goodness! Seriously? First of all, no, we didn't. Second of all, had we, do you think I would own up to it? If I were you and I'd decided to answer you with a 'yes,' I'd be looking for the nearest exit, because I wouldn't be letting you live with the truth."

A coy smile played on his lips. "Fine, so you didn't *murder* your husband. Then what *did* happen?"

"Ugh, you just won't let this go, will you?"

He shook his head again. "No, I won't."

"Fine, if you really must know," I clenched my teeth, "one man died in the car accident. And he was my husband *and* he was Stacey's husband."

He furrowed his brow trying to decipher my ambiguous response, and then the light came on and eyes went wide. "Are you two like sister-wives or something?"

I snorted. "In a way, I suppose, but it was unbeknownst to the *both* of us. Ted was leading a double life. Had me as a wife in one city and Stacey as a wife in another. We didn't find out about each other until after he'd died."

"Seriously?"

"Yeah ... " and then I decided to let it all out. From beginning to end, I told Jake the story. And I guess in some ways it was cathartic, but it also forced me to relive that horrible moment, the moment where my entire world, my life as I knew it, came to a screeching, *crashing* halt ...

10

It was the night before his service, and I was busy cleaning out a drawer, looking for his father's pocket watch so that I could pass it on to Ted's brother, Bob, when I saw him the next day. He and his wife, Sheila, weren't going to be arriving from Omaha until the following morning. So much for helping me with the funeral arrangements like he'd promised. But for some reason, the pocket watch wasn't in Ted's nightstand drawer like I thought it would be, so I continued to hunt, opening up his sock drawer and pulling out his work phone. It was dead. I'm not sure what compelled me to walk over to the charger on the wall and plug it in, but I did, and then set back to the job of finding the pocket watch. Finally, around midnight, because lord knows I wasn't sleeping a wink, hadn't since he'd died, I uncovered it in an old suit jacket pocket of all the unusual places. I set it aside to give to Bob.

The following day, after Ted's service, a bunch of people, including Emma and James, Bob and Sheila, a few of my co-workers who came to support me but didn't actually know Ted, followed me home after the funeral. They were all huddled in my small living room sipping tea and coffee, dressed head to toe in various shades of black. It was somber and depressing, and I wanted them all to leave. But somehow, I just didn't feel as though I could kick anyone out. I didn't have the strength.

The day had been draining, and I barely had enough energy to communicate with people, let alone stand my ground and ask them to leave.

I was sitting on the edge of my big overstuffed gray suede couch next to Sheila as she nattered on about her son having to make the hard choice about whether to go out for varsity basketball or varsity football, that he was exceptionally great at both, but doing both would be just too hard. He had to think long term. Which one could land him a scholarship, and in which one was he more likely to turn pro, and blah, blah, blah. Meanwhile I was trying to remember the last time I'd eaten something and was having a hard time coming up with anything besides coffee and creamer. I was just about to excuse myself to the restroom when an unfamiliar ringing in my bedroom forced me to abandon my dull sister-in-law as I silently hummed the *Saved by the Bell* theme song.

The call display said "Stacey," so it was obviously a contact of Ted's. I was not looking forward to having to tell yet *another* person that he was dead. But such is the job of the widow.

"Hello?" I finally answered, on about the eighth ring, after I'd taken a few deep breaths and composed myself.

"Uh ... uh, hello? Is Ted there?"

"Who's speaking, please?"

"Um ... this is his wife. Who's this?"

At this point, Emma had wandered into the room and was giving me a curious look. "Uh, I'm afraid you're mistaken, because *I'm* Ted's wife." This was by far the weirdest conversation I'd ever had. Never in a million years did I think I'd ever find myself arguing on the phone with a woman about which one of us was the widow of a dead man.

"What?" she barked. "Who is this?"

"Ted Gordon's wife. I'm Freya Gordon. Who are you?"

"Ted Gordon's wife, Stacey Gordon. Listen, can I please talk to my husband? This is a really sick prank."

"You're the one who's pulling a prank," I snapped back. "Calling a dead man's phone and pretending to be his wife." There was silence. I waited and waited, and then finally curiosity got the better of me. "Are you still there?"

"He's dead?" she croaked, her voice barely a whisper. "How?"

"Car accident," I said matter-of-factly, still not believing a word that this woman was saying.

"I—I'm not pulling a prank I swear," she stammered. "But I'm Theodore Wallace Gordon's wife."

The stutter and shock in her voice was enough. I looked up at Emma, and her face mimicked my own—horror. The phone fell from my hand, and my face met the floor. I welcomed the sweet, sweet darkness.

"Holy shit!" Jake blurted out, staring at me with an open mouth and wide eyes, as if he were a child and I'd just told him the world's greatest fairy tale. To me it was more of a horror story.

"So, now you know." I sniffed, looking away from his still-shocked face, waiting for the next big wave of realization to hit him. "You can go ahead and leave now. I'm sure I can handle Connor in the morning, and I'll book myself a plane ticket home."

He scrunched up his face. "Why would I leave?"

"Come on." I huffed. "I'm obviously an incredibly stupid and naïve woman, ignorant as a baby is innocent, and so oblivious to everything going on around me that I wasn't even aware of my husband cheating on me and having a whole second family."

"Who said that about you?" He sat up and looked as if he were getting ready to punch someone in the face.

I shook my head. "No one. But they don't have to. It's all true."

"No, it's not. You're not stupid or ignorant or oblivious. Maybe a bit naïve, but that's not a bad thing. You're not at fault here." He shook his head. "No one but Ted is. You and Stacey and those kids, you're all victims. Ted was too much of a coward to end it with one woman so he could be with another. He cheated and he hurt, and in my opinion, he's better off where is he now."

"Yeah, well, you're not wrong about that."

"I'm not wrong about any of it. Did you honestly think that when I found out what had happened to you that I'd be so turned off that I'd leave you stranded without a ride home?"

I shrugged, unable to look at him for fear of what I might say or do. Because at that moment, all I wanted to do was leap into his arms and have him hold me, let him say over and over again that it wasn't my fault. Maybe one day I'd actually believe him.

"Do you think that little of me?"

My head shot up. "No, not at all. I think the world of *you*. I—I was just afraid of what you would think of *me*."

He was over on my couch in seconds, his hands cradling mine while his face was less than a foot away. I was forced to look at him, because if I looked down, I'd be staring at his crotch, and then a whole new surge of ideas would flood my mind.

"I don't think any less of you. In fact, I think more of you, for finally working up the courage to tell me the truth. Trusting me enough to tell me." He gave me a wry smile. "So you, uh, you think the *world* of me?"

"I do," I whispered, giving no quarter to hesitation and instead choosing blunt honesty. His response galvanized my boldness. I licked my lips and looked down. A tell-tale bulge was forming in his sweatpants. My heart started to hammer inside my chest, and when I glanced back up into his face, his eyes were smoldering. Black had invaded the blue. "I—"

"Say yes, Freya. Because I want you. So badly."

Biting my bottom lip, I ran my thumb over his palm. Rough calluses and faint scars spoke volumes about just what kind of a man he was, a man who wasn't afraid of hard work, and boy, was I going to be hard work. But I wanted him. I needed him. I needed to keep feeling the way he made me feel. Happy and desired, worshipped and cared for. I needed Jake. Only Jake could make me feel that way. "Yes. Please."

Unlike last night, when our lovemaking was slow and languid, two lovers exploring each other's bodies for endless hours, tonight was fueled by fire and passion. Jake's lips were on me in less than a second, his tongue thrusting into my mouth, moving with an all-consuming energy. The whiskers on his chin and jaw made an erotic scratch against my flesh, awakening even the nerve endings on my face. His hands roamed and peeled away my clothes, desperate for skin on skin. He pushed me back down to the couch and managed to make quick work of my pink blouse, shucking it to the floor, leaving me exposed in my lacy white bra. I scrambled to free him of his pants, pulling at the elastic of his sweatpants, frantic to feel him in my hands.

"You weren't wearing any underwear?" I asked, swallowing at the sight of him. I ached to reach out and stroke his length.

He shrugged with a wily grin, taking himself in his palm and giving his cock a couple of sexy tugs. "Only packed one pair of boxers ... whoops."

"Oh." I glanced up into his eyes, and if reading my mind, he gently gripped the back of my head and brought his length into my mouth. I took him willingly.

"You have such a sweet little mouth." He groaned, helping me to set the pace. "This is what you wanted, right?"

I glanced up at him, my mouth full and salivating from the taste of him as he continued to pump. All I could do was hum my response and nod. I wanted this so badly. Jake hadn't given me the opportunity to take him in my mouth last night. He'd been completely and utterly devoted to my pleasure. So tonight, it was my turn. I ran my fingers from root to tip, reveling in the softness of his skin, the thickness of him.

I tilted my head and followed a throbbing vein with the tip of my tongue, encircling the base and then pulling back. A low and feral groan rumbled through him.

"Freya," he panted as I swirled and twirled my tongue around the tip, only to then draw him back to the rear of my throat and suck. "Freya ... " He pulled himself from my mouth, his cock slapping against his belly with an audible *thwack*. "I need you."

With expert finesse, Jake relieved me of the rest of clothes, pulling off my khaki shorts and flicking the front clasp of my bra with the snap of his fingers. I was laid bare for him, ready and willing. He could have me any way he wanted.

"Condom?" I asked.

He froze. "We used my stash last night. I only brought one. And based on how you were treating me today, I didn't think this was happening again."

I gave him a dumbfounded look. I had an IUD. Ted had made me get it, saying that he was nowhere near ready for children and that he was allergic to latex (all lies!). But I had no idea where Jake had been or what his history was.

"What?" I blurted out, shocking myself with how upset I was. "Are you serious?"

The look he gave me was priceless, and then he burst out laughing. "Wow," he said between chuckles, "you're pretty pissed about this."

"W-well yeah," I stammered, slowly becoming aware of how naked I was. My eyes scurried around, looking for something to cover up with.

"Are you on the pill by chance?" Apprehension colored his tone. "Because I'm clean. I got an STI test right before I moved to Victoria. Last girlfriend was a bit of cheater ... "

"I have an IUD."

He gave me a poignant look. "It's completely and totally up to you. I'm okay if we just do oral tonight. But just so you know, I'm totally clean."

My eyes raked his body. The man was perfection. Constructed by the gods when they were in a seriously good mood. Tall and tanned, fit and chiseled in all the right places, with a head of hair most women would kill for and long lashes to match. Turquoise eyes I'd gotten lost in once or twice and the most come-hither smile I'd ever been on the receiving end of. There wasn't a flaw on him, and he wanted me. Little old me. Broken and plain, boring and naïve, Freya. He wanted me. And I wanted him. I needed him. I reached for his hand and brought him down on top of me. "Make love to me."

"No." He shook his head, his eyes growing darker. His lips curled wickedly. "Tonight, tonight I'm going to fuck you, because that's what I think you need. That's what I think you want." And then without waiting for an answer, he thrust inside, sheathing himself to the hilt, hitting me so deep that my eyes flashed open and my head flew back into the throw pillows. "Is that what you ... want?" he growled, his teeth grazing my collarbone and traveling down my décolletage.

"Y-yes, oh God yes," I purred, arching into him as his mouth continued to make its way down my body, finding a nipple, lapping at it and suckling, forcing me to hiss and squeal in approval.

A low growl vibrated deep in his throat, tingling along my body and setting every nerve ending on high alert. "You like that?"

"Mhmm." He nipped and sucked, twisting his tongue around my achy, red bud. "Jake ... " I sighed. "Oh God, yes. Harder. Faster."

I wasn't sure what had come over me. I'd never given Ted any instructions in bed. I barely uttered a word the entire time, maybe the odd "God" or his name, but I'd certainly never asked him to go harder or faster. I was on fire, a full-on raging inferno of feelings and sensations, dangerously close to hurtling out of control toward a breath-stealing, soul-capturing, forbidden precipice.

"You're so tight!"

"Ah, harder!"

"Come on," he said with a grunt, standing up and slipping out. He pulled me by the hands and helped me to me my feet, bending me at the waist with a gentle hand on my back until I rested my elbows on the arm of the couch, the soft microfiber feeling nice and smooth against my skin. He held on to my hips, angled himself at my entrance and drove home.

"*Oof,*" I coughed, as the force of his impalement sent my stomach into the couch, knocking the wind out of me.

"You okay?"

"Y-yeah." I'd never had sex in this position before. It was wild and primitive and so animalistic. I was intoxicated on the intensity of it all, how it seemed forbidden and wrong, something that should be left to the animals. But my mind and body told me that it was all kinds of right, that we *were* animals and I was entitled to enjoy myself.

I pushed my butt back into him, encouraging him to go deeper and harder, loving the weird slapping feeling of his testicles against my skin, the sound blending in with the din of our heavy breathing and groans of passion. I bowed my back and moaned at the divine change in the angle. Jake was hitting erogenous zones inside my body that I didn't even know existed.

"You're close. I can feel it. Come for me, baby. Come hard." He grunted, continuing to hammer into me. I bit my lip as the pleasure speared through me, my sex tightening and my whole body going rigid. Even my toes curled into the carpet as my entire body, even my soul flared to life and gave in to the euphoria.

"Yes, oh, oh God, yes," I cried, tears stinging my eyes as I continued to spiral up, up into sweet oblivion, my orgasm spurring on Jake's release, causing him to come.

I was covered in a thin mist of sweat, my hair hung down around my face like a curtain of fire, and the only sound filling the quiet room was our heavy breathing and thumping hearts. Jake slowly pulled himself from me, and I waddled off to the washroom, only to return a few minutes later to a thoughtful glass of water and a blanket, which he draped over my shoulders.

"So, how're you feeling?" he asked, his smile coy and boyish.

I grinned at him and took a sip of my water. "I feel pretty darn good. Great in fact."

"Great?" His smile turned from boyish to downright cocky.

"Amazing? Stupendous? Terrific? Pick one. Any one will work."

He raised an eyebrow. "How about mind-blowing?"

I nodded. "That too. POW!" I made an explosion sound and gestured with my hand. "My mind is totally blown."

His warm laugh washed over me. "Well that's a much better response than last time."

"I feel like a big weight had been lifted from my shoulders." I said, resting my head on his shoulder. "Thank you for being such a pushy ... "

"Ass?"

I snickered. "Yeah."

He took my glass from me and put it down on the coffee table, guiding my body back down to the couch, covering me with his big, muscular frame. "Oh *Freya*, you have no idea just how *pushy* I can be." He kneed my legs apart and slid home.

11

The next day we welcomed Stacey and baby Thea home. We picked them up from the hospital and brought them back to their little nest with a waiting and eager Daniella sitting in the lobby of the building. Stacey seemed keen to get home and start a routine, but when I mentioned that our flight was scheduled to leave at five o'clock, she burst into uncontrollable sobs, clinging to me as if I were the keeper of all the answers.

"I'll be back to visit soon," I assured her, rubbing her back as she laid her head on my shoulder. I could feel her warm tears dripping down my back. "And you know, I was thinking, it might not be such a bad idea to consider moving. I think you'd love Victoria. Better weather, lots of parks, and then there's the ocean. Connor would love going to the beach and making sand castles."

She sniffed and lifted her head, her eyes red-rimmed, while deep purple circles hugged the skin beneath. The rosy pregnant-lady glow was gone, and now she just looked as though someone had beaten her up and then proceeded to kick her once she was down. Even after everything he did to me, I would never be able to forgive Ted for what he did to Stacey, to his family. He robbed them of so much.

"Yeah." She ran her wrist under her nose and used the sleeve of her big sweatshirt to mop at her eyes. "Maybe. I don't know how I'm going to be able to afford Daniella for long."

"Don't you worry about that," I said, grabbing her hand. "We'll figure it out. But seriously, give the move some thought. Who knows, maybe Daniella would want to move?"

She took a deep breath. "I hate him."

"I know you do." I nodded. "I do too." I gave her hand a squeeze. "But I've been thinking, was Ted big into puzzles, like brain teasers and riddles, when he was with you? Because he definitely was with me." She nodded. "I think we might be missing something. For all his faults he was a very methodical man, a thinker and a planner. I feel like if we dig deep enough, we might find something."

"Like what?" she scoffed. "A buried pot of gold?"

I shrugged. "Or something like that. I just ... I can't put my finger on it just yet, but there are a few boxes of his stuff, mostly papers, that I haven't gone through yet. If there's anything like that here and you have the time, maybe go through it. You never know what we might find."

"Like the deed to an island in the South Pacific or stocks in Microsoft?" She snorted, rolling her eyes but ultimately agreeing with a nod.

"Wouldn't that be nice?"

"I don't know what I'd do without you, Freya," she choked, more tears threatening to fall down her cheeks. "You've been a life saver."

My lips twisted at the uncomfortable praise. "You'd do the same, if the roles were reversed, I'm sure."

She rapidly blinked and then wiped away a few rogue drops from beneath her eyes. "So, tell me ... did you and Jake make up?"

We were just getting ready to head out on to the tarmac and board the plane when I remembered my trip tradition and turned to go back. "Where are you going?" Jake called after me as I hastily dropped my bag at his feet and took off toward the gift shop.

"Be right back!" I called, not bothering to look behind me. I managed to snag the last overpriced box of maple candy and bought it, cringing as the teller handed me my receipt.

That's half a car payment.

"What was that about?" Jake asked, mild irritation in his tone, curiosity on his face.

"Tradition," I puffed. "Whenever my dad and I go on trips, we always buy each other some kind of treat, usually maple candy or something *Canadian-y* no matter where we are. Weird tradition, I know. But it's what we do."

He shrugged. "Okay. Are you done?"

I nodded and reached for my bag, but he just shook his head and carried it out to the plane for me.

"Shit!" he exclaimed as we got ourselves situated and were preparing for take-off. "I totally forgot to go and buy headphones." He shot me a look of mild panic. "Would you mind holding my hand like you did before?"

I gave him a small smile. "Of course not."

And then the jokester was back. "I mean I guess now I *can* ask you to make out with me, right?"

Rolling my eyes, I laughed. Something I was doing a lot more of in the last few days. "I suppose so, yes."

Then his eyes traveled around and behind me to the back of the plane. "And there *is* a bed on this thing ... "

I gave him a mock look of surprise as my whole body sparked alive and my core tingled and tightened in anticipation.

"Don't give me that look." He laughed, his eyebrows bobbing provocatively. "I saw your eyes dart there when we boarded. You were thinking the exact same thing."

I shook my head. "Was not."

The devil himself smiled back at me. "Liar!" and before I could even blink I was hauled out of my seat and dragged back to the bedroom, Jake's hard body covering mine and his lips roaming across my face. "What better way to distract yourself from turbulence than by making some turbulence of your own!" he murmured against my neck, softly biting that sensitive spot behind my ear.

I was weak, helpless against his devotion and attentiveness. Jake had taken hold of my body, my mind and I'm pretty sure my soul and shown me a new level of pleasure. He'd awakened a beast, he possessed me, and there was nothing I could do but give in to his unwavering attention and let him peel the clothes from my body and ruthlessly worship me.

"So, this might be a weird question," he said, as we lay in bed at the back of the plane, our limbs tangled up in a knot so tight I wasn't sure whose legs were whose, "but ... how old are you?"

I looked at him out of the corner of my eye, breathing a small sigh of relief that he wasn't interested in discussing the incredibly naughty things we'd just done to each other. For some reason, talking about it made me very uncomfortable. He was tracing a finger up and down my thigh, and I was finding it increasingly difficult to concentrate. Grabbing his finger and halting his efforts, I looked him in the eye. "I'm thirty. Why? How old are you?"

He grinned, pulled his hand away and then went back to tickling me. I didn't stop him.

"I'm twenty-five."

"Oh."

"Oh?"

"Yeah ... oh."

An impish grin took over his face. "Does that bother you?"

I pursed my lips together, my cheeks growing warm. His finger slowly and not so inconspicuously began traveling farther down my thigh, venturing between my legs.

"I don't know," I finally said with a swallow, frantically trying to engage in some very poor biofeedback practices and not focus on where his finger currently was or what it was drawing delectable little circles around.

"What do you mean, you don't know?" Another finger joined in the efforts, and instinctively I pushed into him, closing my eyes and biting my lip as pure rapture threatened to engulf me.

"I—I don't know what I mean. I guess not. Does it bother you?"

He chuckled when my body clenched around him. "Not at all. In fact, I've always liked older women."

"How much older?" Why was I asking him this when he was doing what he was doing? Did I really care about the answer?

"None old enough to be my mother, let's just put it that way," he whispered, his voice low and deep, like liquid honey in my ears. And then I realized that I was bucking into his hand, shamelessly riding him as he pumped two fingers inside me and his thumb brushed lightly over my swollen clit. "But let's not talk about that. Let's talk about how sexy you are and how you're currently fucking my fingers with your sweet little pussy."

"Jake ... " I sighed. "Oh God."

"Do you want me to stop?"

I pushed into him again. "No, God no, don't stop."

"You're so beautiful when you come."

"Jake ... " I panted again. I was so close, and then with an expert flick of his thumb and twist of his fingers, I exploded around him, my release building and spreading and swelling with his ceaseless efforts. Sparks flew behind my closed eyes as I relished his attentions, brazenly taking every ounce of pleasure he had to give. Finally, I had to squirm and wriggle away, pushing at his hard chest to get away from him. I was so tender, too tender, and every luscious stroke of his diligent digits sent shivers up my spine and made my legs twitch.

"Not ready for multiples yet?" He chuckled, running his hand up my leg and cupping my breast. "We'll get there."

"I'm sorry you were cheated on," I murmured, snuggling into him and resting my head on his chest as he wrapped an arm around me and dragged me down into the bed with him. I realized that I hadn't addressed the fact that he said his last girlfriend had been a bit of a cheater. I knew firsthand what it was like to be the victim of infidelity and my heart went out to him.

He shrugged and planted a kiss on the crown of my head. "Ah, not a biggie. We weren't together long, a month or two, and we never had the 'exclusivity' conversation. Not that I wandered, but she certainly did."

"Well, I'm sorry."

"I'm sorry you were too. Er ... did you guys find out who Ted was with first? You don't have to talk about it if you don't want to."

"No, no, it's okay." I sighed, my hands wandering up and down his torso, marveling at the hardness. "He was with me first. We'd been together almost seven years, and then three or so years into our relationship, he met Stacey at a bar in Edmonton and he got her pregnant that same night. They were 'married' shortly after."

"Jeez," he muttered. "I'm really sorry."

"Yeah, well, so am I. But I've come to terms with what he did to me. It's what he did to her and the kids that I'll never be able to forgive him for."

"And so you shouldn't." He growled. "If he were alive, I'd definitely have a few choice words for him, along with a long *talk*."

I giggled. "Yeah, a *talk*?"

"Hey folks," the captain came over the loudspeaker, making us both jump and look toward the door, thinking that he was right there and breathing out a quick sigh of relief that he wasn't, "just want to let you know that we're about twenty-five minutes outside of Victoria and will be starting our descent in about ten or so minutes."

"I suppose we should get dressed," Jake said reluctantly, unraveling his arms from me and swinging his long legs over the bed and into his waiting shorts.

A sharp pain of something shot through my gut. Disappointment? "I suppose." I went on the hunt for my clothes.

"So, I guess the big question now is," he said, pulling his T-shirt over his head, "is this a 'what happens in Edmonton stays in Edmonton, and the air'? Or are you going to let me follow you home and make you scream all night long?" His smile was downright wicked, and I couldn't stop the laugh that bubbled up.

"Well, when you put it that way." I smiled back as I clasped my bra and shrugged into my blouse. "I guess we'll just have to leave it all in Edmonton and the air, then won't we?"

He was across the bed and had me back beneath him in seconds. "Oh Freya," he hummed, his grin as mischievous as they come. He cupped my face ever so gently, encouraging me to look into his eyes. "That question was just a formality. Let's not play games. And just FYI, I like my eggs sunny-side up in the morning." And with a wink and flip of his wrist, I was back on my feet, and his hand landed hard and fast on my butt.

12

I'm not quite sure how it happened, but we arrived back in Victoria that night and then Jake wound up spending the entire weekend with me.

On Friday I went to go visit my dad, and Jake followed me. I don't even remember inviting him to come, but when I looked over in my car, there he was with a giant grin sitting in the passenger seat.

"So where does your dad live?" he asked, reading my mind and knowing that I was still trying to piece together the shortcut our relationship had taken, and how in just one week's time we'd gone from strangers to enemies, to frenemies to lovers, to, well … in a relationship of sorts.

I let out a big sigh and turned off the main road. "He's in a home. We moved him out here shortly after we relocated to the island. He has severe Alzheimer's, and most days he doesn't recognize me, or if he does, not for very long."

He made a face. "So he wouldn't have even known if you hadn't brought the candy?"

"No. But I would have."

"And your mum?"

"Died when I was six." I parked the car and reached into the back seat for my purse and the candy.

His cocky smirk faltered, and he grabbed my arm before I could open the door. "I didn't know. I'm sorry."

I shrugged. "No one does. It's not something I really talk about. But thank you."

We made our way into the assisted living home and found my dad. As always, because he was nothing if not a man of routine (I came by it honestly), he was sitting in the overstuffed chair at the window, eating apple slices and sipping tea, watching the ducks splash about in the pond just beyond the window.

"Hi Dad," I whispered, coming up and pecking him on the forehead, his skin cool to the touch but not cold. His color looked better than the last time I saw him.

"Freya?" He looked at me, and recognition flooded his eyes. "When did you get here?"

"Just now, Dad. Sorry I haven't been by in a while. I was out of town again."

"Did you bring any candy?" His eyes drifted to my purse, where a box of the maple candy stuck out like a sweet beacon. He licked his lips and then looked back up at me with hopeful eyes.

"Of course, but let's only have a couple for now. You don't want to overdo it."

He shot me an irritated glare but took the box from me anyway. "I'm your father. Don't you be telling me what to do. If I want to have all the candy, then I will!"

I raised my hands in surrender. "Fine, fine, who am I to deny you the little ounce of joy you get from eating yourself sick? What do I know?"

"Hrmmpf," he grumbled, opening the box. "Indeed."

We sat and chatted with my dad for a while. The conversation was rather one-sided, as often my dad would get distracted by the ducks or just completely ignore me. But once in a while, he'd have a moment of clarity and say something relevant and inspiring or reminiscent of our earlier days and my childhood. Jake remained silent throughout the majority of the trip, and my father barely paid him any mind. It wasn't until my dad got up to go the washroom and then came back that he seemed to even know Jake was sitting in the chair across from him.

He sat back down and took a sip of his tea, watching the ducks play and dive and ruffle their feathers in the little pond. This was one of the reasons I'd chosen this home for my father, because I knew that he'd find a lot of pleasure watching the birds every day. When he put his teacup down, my dad gave me a very odd look, as if seeing me for the first time. His blue-gray eyes went wide, almost with terror, and his bushy salt and pepper brows nearly shot off his head.

"Brenna?" he whispered, staring at me. "Is that you?" There were unshed tears in his eyes as he grabbed my hand and brought the back of it to his lips. "Darling, I thought you were gone."

The odd time when I'd come to visit my dad, especially if I wore my hair up in a bun, he'd briefly mistake me for my mother, but it would last only a few seconds, maybe a minute or two at the most. And since I'd stopped wearing my hair up, he hadn't made the mistake again. So when he did it today, while my hair was down, it sent a frisson of alarm straight up my spine.

"Um, Dad, it's me, Freya." I waved at him and smiled. "It's not Mum. I know I look a lot like her, but Mum's been dead for a while now, remember?"

But it was if he were in a trance and heard nothing and saw nothing but my mother. "I've missed you," he said softly, nothing but longing and love in his voice and eyes. And then suddenly his face took on a serious scowl. "We need to tell Freya the truth."

I shot Jake a look, and he sat forward in his chair. "The truth about what, Mr. Lapierre?"

But my father ignored him. "I think she has a right to know that she has a brother."

Suddenly my tongue felt like a lead weight in my mouth, and my stomach did a cartwheel and failed. "Brother?" I finally squeaked.

My dad's brows were drawn tight. "I don't care that you had a baby at sixteen and gave it up. But I think our daughter has a right to know she has more family out there. Once we go, she has no one. Maybe she can find him."

I thought my head was going to explode, but I needed to know more. Why had my father never told me this before he got Alzheimer's? When I was younger but old enough to understand? If he hadn't mistaken me for my mother, would he have taken this secret to the grave? Would I have lived my entire life not knowing that I had more family out there somewhere? Or was this all a manifestation of the Alzheimer's, one of his many confusions and stories?

I hated deceiving my father, but if he thought I was his wife and I could get him to tell me more about this *brother* I apparently had, then I would do anything I had to.

I hinged forward and cupped my father's cheek. "You're right, Roland, but I can't seem to remember which hospital I had him at, do you remember? Or the baby's father. It was so long ago, things are a little fuzzy."

He gave me an incredulous look but then softened and leaned into my hand and closed his eyes. "It's okay, sweetie, we'll tell her together."

"Where, Roland?" I demanded a little bit more forcefully. "Where did *I* give birth?"

"I think she has a right to know," he started mumbling, looking around for another piece of candy and grinning when he spotted the box on my lap.

"Roland!" I snapped. "Where did *I* have the baby? Who was the father?"

Smiling sweetly, he kissed my palm and took my other hand in his. "I think it's time we told Freya though. She's old enough now. I think she'll understand. We can do it together."

I ground my molars together to keep myself from crying at the stunning truth that I had a sibling, so close, yet still so far away. But I swallowed, knowing that I would not be getting the answers I needed today. So instead, I smiled, closed my eyes and leaned into his hand. "I think so too, Roland. She deserves to know."

He gave a small nod, and then his eyes drifted to Jake. "Who are you?" Then back to me. "Freya? When did you get here?" And just like that, I was me again.

"Dad," I said, reaching into my purse for a water bottle and swallowing the lump that had formed in my throat, "this is Jake. He's my, uh ... he's my boyfriend ... I guess."

"You guess?" Jake snorted. I chose to ignore him. Now was not the time to be getting into a discussion over the status of our very whirlwind and somewhat unorthodox relationship.

"Since when do you have a boyfriend? Aren't you married to Ted?" My dad shook his head in confusion. "I remember walking you down the aisle. You wore your mother's Celtic knot."

I nodded with a smile, wishing that I had the pendant on me at that moment. "You're right, Dad, you did, but Ted's dead. I told you that last time and the time before that. He died in a car accident a few months ago."

My dad made a face that wasn't quite a pout. "Hmm, well, I hate to speak ill of the dead, but I hope you're happy with this young man, because I don't think Ted made you very happy."

I felt Jake's hand rest on my back, sending a small shiver of longing coursing through my body. "He makes me very happy, Dad."

"How're you doing?" Jake asked tentatively as we got back into the car and headed for home. "That was a lot of new news to take in all at once. You have a brother!"

I raised my eyebrows and nodded, letting out a big sigh. My chest felt unusually tight, and a tension headache was starting to build right between my eyebrows.

"Yeah, I don't know what to believe. I mean I don't think this is one of his made-up stories. But how did I not know about this until now?"

He shrugged. "When was your dad diagnosed with Alzheimer's?"

"About six or seven years ago. I can't quite remember. It was early onset but didn't really start to show up as more than just mild confusion and forgetfulness until the last few years. Now it's really sped up."

"Maybe he meant to tell you but honestly just forgot."

"Maybe ... " I hummed, still thinking that I didn't have the whole story and wondering what else my dad had been hiding. My mind began to wander. Had my mother really died from a brain aneurysm in her sleep when I was six, or had she died some other horrible way and he was just covering it up? Was Roland even my real dad? All these new questions popped up, and I felt myself get dizzy. The car swerved, and I struggled to right it before we darted into the opposite lane. I jerked the wheel hard to the right, causing the car next to me to honk.

"Whoa, whoa!" Jake hollered, grabbing the wheel and righting it before I mowed down a pedestrian. "Maybe I should drive. Give you some time to think."

I shook my head. "What? Oh ... yeah, maybe." Without even really thinking about where I was, I pulled over.

"Okay, okay," he said, fear in his voice as he ushered me around to the passenger side and helped me climb in. "Let's get you home before we cause an accident."

I buckled myself in and sat staring blankly ahead as Jake expertly weaved us through traffic. My whole life, my whole world as I knew it, it was turning upside down ... again. I thought finding out my husband had been leading a double life was upside down enough, but now to find out I had a brother ...

We pulled into my parking garage, and Jake got out of the car. I just continued to sit there. He walked around to my side and opened my door. "Come on, let's go upstairs," he whispered, leaning across me to unbuckle my belt and help me out. I let him lead me like a puppy on a leash. My eyes struggled to focus as we walked through the concrete bomb shelter that was my parking garage, took the elevator up and made our way down the hall to my suite.

"What can I do?" he asked, watching me toe off my shoes and leave them in the hall. "Freya?" I haphazardly flung my purse into the coat closet and shut it.

"Jake," I sighed, lying back onto my bed, "I just want to be alone for a bit ... please?"

His face fell into a frown, but he nodded quickly and walked out, closing the door behind him. I felt bad for how I had treated him, but the headache had progressed, and I was now having a hard time seeing straight. At the moment, Jake's feelings were not my top priority. He'd go home and we'd talk later in the week, once I was able to make heads or tails of my situation, but for now, I just needed to close my eyes and be alone.

It was several hours later when I woke up to find a blanket drawn across me and the blinds lowered. I knuckled the sleep out of my eyes, scuffing slowly in my slippers and opening up my bedroom door only to be knocked back a step by a delightful aroma. Someone was cooking. Wandering into the kitchen, I found Jake puttering. A purple and white orchid sat in a beautiful yellow pot, and a bottle of decanted red wine was breathing on the counter.

"Wh— I ... I thought you went home?" I asked, coming up to the counter and accepting the glass of wine he'd just poured.

He gave me a puzzled look. "Why would you think that?" He tossed on oven mitts in response to the beeping timer and opened up the oven to retrieve a mouthwatering loaf of homemade focaccia bread.

What couldn't this guy do?

"I don't know. Because I asked to be alone."

"And I left you alone." He shrugged. "Doesn't mean I was going to *leave* you. You feeling any better?" He stirred a pot on the stove and grabbed two plates from the cupboard.

"A little bit," I said, sliding onto a bar stool at the counter to watch him, completely fascinated with how comfortable he felt in my kitchen, in any kitchen for that matter. The man was certainly full of surprises. "My headache is just a dull tapping now, thankfully. And I think I'll try again with my dad, maybe dress up like my mum, put my hair in a bun. I don't like the idea of tricking him, but I need answers."

He nodded, dishing up what looked to be chicken penne in a rosé sauce with Caesar salad and focaccia bread. My stomach gurgled at the barrage of delectable smells wafting toward me. He pointed at the orchid. "That's for you, by the way."

I fingered a silky petal and studied it. It was beautiful. "Thank you. But why?"

"Do I need a reason?"

"Who are you?" I blurted out as he set dinner in front of me and joined me at the bar.

A playful smirk tugged the corner of his mouth. "What do you mean?"

"Dinner, flowers, taking care of Connor. You're perfect. So who are you? What's your goal here? Because honestly, you seem just too good to be true."

He took a bite of his salad before answering. "I like you, and you've been through so much. I think you deserve to be taken care of for once. You take care of everyone else, but," he sipped his wine and looked at me over the rim, his eyes so intense that I felt my breath catch in my chest, "who takes care of you?"

"So, you want t-to take care of me?"

He shrugged. "At least for now. You just got some pretty crazy news. You're allowed to *feel*, to be emotional and break down. You don't have to remain stoic for everything."

"I—"

"Just enjoy it. Now eat your food." He handed me my fork and motioned for me to dig in.

So I did.

Meanwhile this weird and wonderful feeling was creeping up my neck and throughout my body, a warmth, and like a fist it squeezed my chest and around my heart.

I was being taken care of.

13

"You wear glasses?" Jake asked, coming out of the bathroom later that night to find me sitting quietly on the couch with my e-reader in front of me and *Charity's Wish* ready to be cracked opened. Dinner and wine had done a bang-up job of quelling my nerves and stanching my headache. I was now nursing my third glass of wine, and a light and tingly buzz was making me feel happy and calm.

I gave him a mock look of impatience. "Yeah, I told you that the night we met when you made fun of me for having size one million or whatever font on this thing."

"Oh yeah." He grinned. "I must have been too busy staring at your boobs and trying to get you to suck face with me to remember."

I nodded with a sarcastic eye roll. "Don't remind me. But I'm pretty sure you were more concerned with trying to look cool while not losing your biscuits from the teeny tiny bit of turbulence."

"It was NOT *teeny tiny* turbulence. The plane took a fucking nose-dive. We were seconds away from death at least a dozen times!" he exclaimed, managing to look offended, which in turn just made him look adorable.

"All right, whatever you say," I sang, turning back to my book. But he came up in front of me and took the e-reader from my hands. "Hey! What the heck?"

"You need to start swearing," he said matter-of-factly. "You're much too dirty in the sack to use such clean language in life. Say 'fuck.'"

"No!"

"Come on," he begged. "Say it once, for me. Or even just say 'shit.' That's not such a bad one."

"No! Now give me back my book!"

"I will if you say it."

I ground my teeth and glared at him. "Give me back my *fucking* book, you little *shithead,* before I kick your butt!"

He burst out laughing. "You couldn't even finish it with 'ass'? You had to say 'butt'? Who are you?"

I lunged for him, but he dodged me like a panther and skirted around the couch. "I'm the girl who's going to kick your *butt* if you don't give me back my e-reader, now!"

"Oh, she likes it rough. I can go with this. Mistress Freya, do you plan to punish me for this insubordination?"

I stilled. "Excuse me?"

"No?" he queried, his head quirking to the side like a curious kitten. "Not into the BDSM stuff? Okay. How about you leave your glasses on for the rest of the weekend? I'll go put mine on and we can just be two nerds banging each other until the cows come home. It'll be hot."

"You're so weird," I muttered, shaking my head.

"Come on, I'm playing around. You need to lighten up a bit. I think you're super hot with your glasses. Like a sexy, nerdy librarian, all proper during the day, but at night you turn into this wild and wicked little sexual deviant. Bringing men to their knees and making them stay there with just a crook of your finger and flick of your wrist."

Is he talking about me? He thinks I'm a sexual deviant?

"You think I'm hot in my glasses?" I gave him a sarcastic look, but inside, my stomach was churning as if a million butterflies had all just hatched at the same time.

My mind zipped way, way back to the afternoon after my first day of grade one when I'd gone and been fitted with my new glasses, only to show up the next day and be mocked and teased. Danny Willis, the class troublemaker, had stolen and bent them, trying to fit them on his fat face. It had been weeks before we were able to go and get them fixed. I'd hated wearing glasses ever since, which was why the moment I was allowed contacts I begged my dad for them and only wore my glasses on days my eyes were sore.

Jake put my e-reader on the counter and stalked toward me, his gait powerful but so easy and graceful that if I didn't know any better, I would have said he was floating. Taking my hands in his, he kissed each knuckle. "I think you're drop-dead *fucking* gorgeous in your glasses. You are literally, and I'm not making this up, my ultimate fantasy." I lifted one eyebrow. "No, seriously, I've always had a thing for redheads, older women and chicks with glasses. The green eyes and the fact that you're almost as tall as me are just an added bonus. I like 'em tall, and I like 'em feisty. And you, my sexy little librarian," his eyebrows bobbed, "are all kinds of feisty. Why? Did someone tell you that you weren't?"

I sighed with a shoulder shrug and looked away. "Pretty much every kid in school from the day I got them. But I know that kids are just mean. I wasn't bullied or anything. And I've learned to live with them. I mean, I wear my contacts most of the time now anyway."

"Can you just wear your glasses this weekend? For me?"

I laughed. "If that's all it takes to get your engine running, then sure, why not?"

"Oh, baby, you could have your head shaved and be wearing a burlap sack with no glasses and missing half your teeth and you'd still get my engine running," he purred. His hands encircled my waist, and before I knew it, I was tossed over his shoulder.

"Eek!" I squealed. "Put me down!" I smacked his back with my hands and tried to squirm away.

But a heavy hand came down and landed on my butt with a loud *smack*. "Cut it out, woman. Come on, engine's running now, let's make the most of it." He headed off to the bedroom at a steady lope.

Sunday morning Emma called, and I groaned and moaned as I fumbled on the nightstand in search of my phone. "Hello?" I finally managed to croak, opening one eye to look at the alarm clock and seeing that it was nine o'clock.

Had we really slept in that late?

"Freya? Are you home yet?" Emma chirped, her tone much too chipper for the hour or my wine-soaked brain.

"Yes."

"Is Jake with you?"

I hesitated but then decided not to lie. Jake had probably been texting with James all weekend. "Yes."

"Hi, Emma!" Jake murmured next to me. His hand roamed across the sheets until it snaked around my waist and drew me in close to him so that we were spooning naked beneath the covers. A telltale morning bulge prodded me in the back.

"I said make *friends* with him," she playfully chastised. "But I guess if there are benefits involved, who am I to stop you?" I cringed inside, but Jake just chuckled behind me. "Come over for dinner again, you two. Tonight, if you can? Unless you're having a naked weekend and are unable to put any clothes on. Then in that case, please stay home."

My cheeks grew warm. Jake just continued to laugh. He pressed himself harder into me. I couldn't stop myself; I pushed back into his erection and wiggled my butt. "We'll be there," I finally managed to say, closing my eyes when his hand traveled down between my legs and started to explore.

"Great." She paused for a second. "You're not having sex right now are you?"

"What? No!"

"Hang up, Emma, so we can," Jake called out, nipping my ear and kneeing my legs apart. "We're halfway there. Let Freya go."

"Shut up!" I snapped, uncomfortable with the idea of Emma knowing what was going on.

Emma was laughing. "Okay, well, I'll let you go then. We'll see you guys a bit later. Have fuuuun."

Jake's free hand came up, snatched my phone from my ear and chucked it to the floor. His body gracefully rolled on top of mine.

"No, no," I protested, twisting my head away so that I wouldn't breathe on him. "Morning breath."

He rolled his eyes. "Very well, we'll do it spoon-style then. But no way am I wasting this boner."

As agreed upon, Jake and I both wore our glasses for the rest of the weekend. I have to admit, when he insisted upon doing it in front of the mirror later that afternoon, as much as I had been opposed to it to begin with, watching his sexy, nerdy face, so harsh and angular in concentration as he brought me closer and closer to climax, was a HUGE turn-on. We really were just two nerds going hard and crazy at each other. And from the way he couldn't keep his hands off me and continuously buried his face between my legs, even as I tried to make us sandwiches for lunch, my glasses were doing an exemplary job of keeping his engine running.

We decided to pop in and see my dad again before we headed over to Emma's and James's. But even after I wrestled my hair up into the no-nonsense ballerina bun my mother always wore and donned a pair of old acid-wash pleated jeans and a baby blue blouse, my father still didn't open up any more about this long-lost brother of mine. He did mistake me for my mother again and spent our whole visit reminiscing and talking about how proud he was of me for finishing grad school. However, after nearly an hour of suggestions and questions, hoping to lead him in the right direction, we gave up.

The trip wasn't a complete failure, though. We were able to finally track down the person "in charge," and I addressed my father's bedroom window situation.

"I'm sorry, Miss Lapierre." The stout little woman with short dark hair and amber eyes blinked up at me before taking her round spectacles off to clean them. "But Mr. Lapierre keeps trying to climb out the window, and it's not safe for it to remain open.

"But it's the middle of June, and his room is like a sauna," I insisted, the bun on the top of my head pulling my hair until it hurt. The second we walked out of there, I was ripping that stupid thing out.

"I understand that, and we've turned the air conditioning up in his room, but we can't open the window."

"Is there another room we could move him to? One with higher windows or on the ground floor?" I looked at Jake for support, and his hand fell protectively to the small of my back.

"We could put bars on the window," she suggested.

I scrunched up my face in disgust. My father was not a prisoner. "No. No bars. I want ground floor, a screen or a higher window."

"We can't play musical chairs with the residents simply because one man is unable to stop trying to climb out the window," she said without an ounce of compassion in her tone. "It's just not possible."

I fought the urge to stomp my foot but instead flashed her my biggest smile. "Not even this once?"

"What if, the next room with a better situated window that comes available, Mr. Lapierre gets moved there? Whether it be tomorrow or six months from now. Is that doable?" Jake asked, batting his unbelievable lashes at the woman and flashing a smile that I was sure was turning her knees to jelly that very moment.

The woman swallowed as she looked up at him. *Yep, jelly!* "Uh, yes, yes, that seems like a very doable scenario. We can't make any promises, but the next room that becomes available, if the window is better, your father can have it."

I wondered if Jake had something up his sleeve. But rather than give him any kind of questioning look, I just smiled again at the care aide and thanked her, pulling my hair free and shaking it loose as we crossed the parking lot to the car.

"Quick, put your glasses back on," he ordered, casually climbing into the driver's side. I didn't mind that he drove my car. I liked it when he took charge. He made me feel safe, and as he'd said before, taken care of. "You want to go for a ride on my bike after supper?" he asked, bobbing his eyebrows as we turned back into traffic and headed to Emma's and James's.

"God, no!" I practically shouted, causing him to jump. "That thing is a death trap."

"It is not."

"Well, I won't be getting on it any time soon, that's for sure."

He smiled as his hand traveled across the center console and landed on my thigh. "We'll see about that."

"You're drunk!" Emma exclaimed as she opened the door for us and practically threw a baby into each of our arms.

"I am not!" I glanced down at the baby in my arms, not knowing who I had.

"On orgasms you most certainly are," she sang, wandering back into the kitchen. "The two of you are completely blottoed!"

"Ignore her," Jake muttered, turning the baby he had around and around as if looking for a name tag or something. "She's spent far too much time with my sister-in-law, who *loves* talking about sex but tends to do so at some of the most inconvenient and inappropriate times."

Emma shot him a mock look of indignation but then turned to me and shrugged with a smile. "I can't help it if I see two people I care deeply for happy and in love."

"Uh ... " I looked down at my feet, cradling whichever baby I had and rocking her back and forth until I earned a smile.

Love?

"So, which kid do I have?" Jake asked, saving the day by changing the subject. "I can't tell them apart. Can you tattoo one of them or something? Nothing big. Just a little C or G behind their earlobe so I can tell who's who."

James came in through the patio doors, once again the smell of barbecue following him in like a jet-steam of decadence. "It's easy to tell them apart." He took the baby from Jake. "This one is ... Claire. See, there's a tiny little freckle on her knee."

Emma looked up from the salad she was tossing. "That's Grace, dear. Claire has the slightly darker eyes and the pointier chin. Grace is the one with the freckle on her knee and the birthmark on her butt."

James made a surprised face and held his baby out for inspection. He took the one I had and held them both out, cradling them along his strong forearms so that they lay next to each other, staring with innocent awe at their gorgeous father. "You're right. Damn, now I can't even tell my kids apart."

Jake and I started laughing. "Sleep deprivation a factor by any chance?" he asked.

James just rolled his eyes and made a funny face at his babies until they smiled. "They tag-teamed us last night from twelve until five-thirty. If one wasn't up, the other one was." He made a stern face. "You two are killing your parents, you know? If it's not lack of sleep, it's lack of sex. Adorable little cock-blockers!" Both girls just continued to smile at him and squirm in his arms, kicking and flailing their limbs until he couldn't help but smile back at them and blow raspberries on their bellies.

"So, what'd your friend name her baby?" Emma queried when I joined her in the kitchen to help. Jake and James took the twins outside to go and stand over the barbecue and drink beer.

"Thea Jasmine. She said she named her Thea after her grandmother, and Jasmine because Ted hated the name. One last jab at him, I suppose."

"Well, I like it," she said, handing me a bread knife so I could start slicing up the fresh warm loaf she'd just pulled from the bread maker. It smelled incredible, like yeast and rosemary and comfort. After washing my hands in the sink, I rested them on the warm loaf and closed my eyes. Memories of my mother always baking bread and the smell of it filling our house flitted through my mind like a lost butterfly.

I opened my eyes and began slicing. "Yeah, me too. Stacey's still pretty angry with Ted. And I would be too, if I were in her shoes."

"Does Jake know about Ted?" she asked. "Like, the whole story?"

I nodded. "He weaseled it out of me. The man's very convincing."

She smiled. "Just like his brother. The man could make a nun break her vows."

"I'll keep that in mind," I murmured, placing the bread in a basket and walking it over to the table. Just then Jake and James walked in balancing babies, beer and barbecue between their four capable hands. I fought the need to rush over and relieve them, but the two looked very competent and not about to drop a thing.

"So, is this it for babies?" Jake questioned as we sat around the dinner table moments later. He reached for a shish kebab off the platter.

"Yes," James said flatly, while his wife said a very resolute, "No."

Their eyes locked across the table, and you could practically feel the tension flood the room. Clearly this was a hot-button topic. I tried to catch Jake's gaze and get him to change the subject, but he was oblivious to my stink-eye.

"Uh, did I hit a sore spot?" He chuckled, using his fork to pry the vegetables off his skewer.

Emma flashed us both a big smile. "No, of course not. It's just that I'm not ready to close the door on more children, but my husband is."

"Your pregnancy was a nightmare. For both of us," James blurted out across the table. "Months of bed rest, preeclampsia, high blood pressure, gestational diabetes, and an emergency C-section at thirty-six weeks! Why on earth would I want to put you through that again? You were sick for the entire nine months! I'm ready to go and get snipped tomorrow."

There was more fear in his eyes than there was venom, and my heart went out to him. He didn't want to see his wife in any more pain, and I couldn't blame him; Emma's pregnancy had been a rough one.

Meanwhile she just shrugged, brushing it off as if it was old news. "Yeah, but then look what we got." She pointed to the girls, who were gnawing away on a piece of bread each.

"And I'm happy with what we have," James said softly, trying to subdue his wife. "Two perfect little girls. And a perfect wife. Let's not mess with perfection."

She rolled her eyes. "Well, either way, we wouldn't even begin to start trying until the girls were at least two. Let's put a pin in it, shall we?

And move on to a new topic, like the fact that Jake and Freya are sleeping together."

I choked on my cherry tomato. James reached over and pounded me on the back.

14

I had thought for sure that I would be leaving Jake at his place and we'd connect midweek, but instead he grabbed some clean clothes and followed me home on his motorcycle, parking it in the underground visitor parking and joining me in the elevator.

"So, are you sick of me yet?" he asked with a flirtatious grin, his bright eyes gleaming in the fluorescent light. Even behind his glasses, they managed to convey all sorts of mischief and trouble.

I offered him a small smile. "I was actually just thinking that on the way back. I'm surprised that I'm not."

"You're surprised that you're not sick of me?" His mouth hung open in shock. "Wow, uh ... thanks, I guess?"

Rolling my eyes, I shook my head and reached for his hand, linking our fingers together. "You know what I mean."

"I'm not sure I do," he replied innocently. "Maybe it's best if you show me just how *not sick of me* you are."

A warm flush crept into my cheeks. I quickly looked away. I was terrible, if not completely incapable of initiating things of a sexual nature, and my ability to seduce and allure had never even been tested. Which meant at thirty years old, I was pretty sure it didn't exist and never would.

"Hey," he said softly, "what's wrong?"

I shrugged, bit my lip and continued to look away. "I don't know how to be ... sexy. How to seduce."

"You've never initiated sex before?"

I shook my head as the elevator came to a stop on my floor and we headed down the hall to my unit.

"What about with guys before Ted?"

Fumbling with my keys, I just continued to shake my head.

His hand landed on mine and stilled my frantic movements. "Relax. Here." He took the keys from me and opened the door.

"There were no other guys before Ted," I finally managed to say after neatly tucking my flip-flops away in their rightful spot and hanging up my purse on the back hook of the closet.

"So ... so wait, I was your second?" He spun around from where he was retrieving a bottle of white wine from the fridge.

I nodded, apprehension filling my entire body. A sudden chill seemed to have swept through the room.

Ted?

I grabbed my elbows and shivered.

"Why didn't you tell me?"

I looked up him. "Why? It's not like I was a virgin."

"Yeah, but ... "

"But what? You would have gone gentle on me?" I snorted out a breathy laugh. I wasn't getting sick of Jake, but I was certainly getting tired of being treated like something fragile, as if at the slightest shock I'd shatter into a million pieces.

His lips twisted in thought. "Well, no ... but maybe I would have understood things better."

"Understood what? Why I'm so lame in bed? A limp noodle who just lays there like a starfish? Is that what you're saying?" I wasn't even sure how it happened, but my hackles were suddenly up and my hands were on my hips.

"Whoa, whoa, why are you picking a fight with me? And I never said you were lame in bed. That couldn't be further from the truth."

"Then what are you saying?"

"I'm saying that it would explain why you're *timid* in bed, hesitant to make a move or take control. You follow my lead. But baby," he grabbed my hand and brought my knuckles to his lips, "you're anything but *lame*."

My lips dipped into a pout. "You're sure I'm not boring you?"

He let go of my hand and tossed his head back to laugh. "Freya, we've been sleeping together for less than a week. You're definitely not *boring* me. And if you were, I wouldn't have insinuated myself into your world the way I have. You've got me on a leash. I'm yours, woman."

I glanced up at him from beneath my lashes, taken aback by how candid he was able to be. "You're sure?"

"So sure."

Shaking my head, I studied my feet again. "I still don't know how to seduce though. I'm not even sure where I'd start."

"You initiated things the first night," he offered.

I shook my head. "No, I kissed you on the cheek, and you took it from there. All I did was say okay. I have no idea how to be seductive."

He grabbed two glasses out of the drying rack from the sink and poured us both wines, passing me mine and taking a healthy sip of his own. "Well, now that," he grinned wolfishly, "I can help you with."

I took a sip of my wine, my mouth feeling very dry, while if I was being completely honest, other parts of me were growing wetter and needy. "How?"

"Easy. We'll start slow. Tell me what kinds of things you like in bed. What do you like to do?"

"Jaaaake," I whined, growing increasingly uncomfortable with the idea of the whole thing. "I can't."

"Why not?"

"Because I can't."

"That's not an answer. Why not?" he pressed again, cocking his hip into the counter and looking at me with open curiosity.

"Because it's weird. It makes me feel uncomfortable talking about ... you know?"

"About sex?"

I nodded.

"Why?"

"I don't know, it just does."

"But yet you *have* sex?"

I shrugged. "Yeah. I go the washroom too, but I don't want to talk about it."

Another deep and masculine laugh rumbled through my small apartment. "Touché. But I still think we should talk about it. I need to know what you like and what you don't."

"I—" How could I tell him that I liked everything he did? That in the short time we'd been together, he'd given me more pleasure than Ted had in nearly seven years, and that there hadn't been one thing he'd done that I hadn't enjoyed ... immensely.

But he cut me off. "Let's try this instead. I'll ask you questions, and you just say 'yes' or 'no.' Does that work?"

"I guess ... "

"Okay. Let's start." He wandered into the living room and sat down on the couch as if he belonged there. I followed him and perched on the edge of the love seat, my hands folded in my lap and my toes dug into the sage and wheat area rug I'd bought when we first moved in. "Do you like it when I kiss your neck?"

"Yes." I took a big sip of my wine, my face growing hot.

"Do you like it when I bite your neck?"

"Yes."

"Do you like it when I slowly unbutton your blouse and open your bra, letting your sweet breasts tumble out?"

My chest began to rise and fall in ragged breaths. "Yes."

"Do you like it when I take one of your perfect little nipples in my mouth and suck and flick it with my tongue?"

"Y-yes."

"Take off your shirt." I blinked at him for a second, realizing that he'd given me a command and not a question. But after half a second, I complied, sitting there in just my plain white cotton bra and old acid wash jeans. The warmth continued to spread across my skin and along my arms. "Do you like it when I run my hands down your body? Cupping your breasts, kneading them, tweaking your nipples?"

"Yes." I sighed, biting my lip. Our eyes locked, and I nearly came on the spot. The way he looked at me was as if I were a gazelle and he a starving lion. Jake was preparing for a feast. Getting ready to devour me.

"Do you like it when I rub your clit with my fingers?"

"Yes." I panted, licking my lips and crossing my legs, squeezing them in an attempt to find some friction.

"Take off your pants." Once again, I did as I was told, his eyes glowing lambent like a cat's, watching my every move but not flinching. He was a calculating and patient predator, and as we continued with our game, I felt an urge to be caught that grew and grew until it was darn near painful. "Do you like it when I spread your lips with my fingers and then lick your clit? Pumping two fingers inside you?"

"Y-yes." I nodded. "Yes."

It was incredible—we hadn't even touched, and yet I was so turned on, ready to combust on the spot. All he'd done was order me to undress and ask me questions, yet there I was, breathless and wet, needy and wanton, ready to submit to anything he asked of me so long as I could run my hands over his hard, beautiful body.

"Do you like it when I make you stand up and turn around, stick your sweet little ass in the air so that I can fuck you from behind?"

"Yes."

"Do you like being fucked from behind, you naughty girl?"

"Yes."

"Do you want to try being on top? So I can watch you come?"

I swallowed again, the image of me riding Jake becoming all too clear in my mind. "Yes."

"Do you like having my cock in your mouth? Do you want my cock in your mouth?"

"Oh yes."

He quirked an eyebrow up and smiled. My eyes traveled down to the V of his legs, and a blatant erection stuck up proud and eager, trying to punch a hole in his shorts.

"Oh yes? Hmm, good to know. Do you like it when I tell you to come?"

I let out a heavy sigh and licked my lips. "Yes."

"Take off your bra and underwear."

I hesitated for a second but then obeyed, slowly peeling my white cotton briefs down my legs and folding them neatly, placing them on top of the rest of my folded clothes. My matching bra followed suit.

"You're beautiful."

"Jake ... " I whispered.

"Do you like this?" he asked, draining his wine and staring at me with such ferocious need that I thought my heart was going to explode. His hand fell to his erection, and he stroked it within his shorts.

My gaze dropped to his hand. "Yes."

"Good. Now come here, pretty girl. I have something for you." He unzipped his pants. "Up on the couch, on your knees," he urged, his tone kind but with an edge of authority. I did as I was told. It was slightly uncomfortable, but I remained patient and waited for further instruction. Meanwhile, my whole body hummed. "Now, do you like having my cock in your mouth?"

I nodded. "Oh yes." I was surprised at how much I was enjoying this. Jake certainly was a master at seduction.

"*Oh yes*," he mocked. "Well then, show me how much you like it." With a gentle hand he guided my head down. That hand then trailed down my naked back, drawing gooseflesh up on my skin, caressing my hips and lower back, kneading my butt until I shamelessly pushed back into his palm. "Do you like it when I touch you here?" he asked, continuing to worship my bottom.

"Mhmm," I hummed, my mouth otherwise occupied.

"Hmm. I wonder if you'll like it if I do this." His hand continued to travel behind me, dipping into my center and finding me sopping wet.

Two fingers probed and explored, running up through my folds and around my clit only to plunge inside and pump, making me moan and move into his hand.

"Do you like it when I do this?" he asked, his voice growing ragged.

All I could do was nod and squeak out my response.

"What was that?" he panted, his own concentration starting to slip. "Do you not like this?" He pulled his fingers free.

"No!" I cried, my mouth still full of him. "I love it. Don't stop!"

"Love it?" His fingers plunged back inside and caused me to come on the spot.

The spontaneous orgasm rippled through me, hitting every single neuron, cell and fiber of my being in unrelenting swells.

Then Jake found his release.

I sat up and licked my lips. He grabbed a throw blanket from the back of the couch and wrapped it around me before drawing me into his arms. My head fell to his shoulder.

"So?"

"Wow!"

"Yeah. Wow! See, you know how to seduce."

I blinked a couple of times but then gave up on trying to see straight and closed my eyes. "What?" I finally managed to say. "I'm pretty sure that was all you."

"Naw, you took off your clothes. You sat there all hot and bothered, panting and licking your lips like I was a choice cut of meat. You hardly had to say two words and I was absolute putty ... well, most of me. One very important part of me was rock-hard granite." He chuckled, the sound a reassuring rumble as my ear fell over his heart. "And licking your lips when you came up from sucking me off ... and the fact that you swallowed. All hugely seductive."

"Really?"

"Really. You're a little tiger, babe. We just have to let you out of that cage you've built around yourself slowly, otherwise you'll get scared."

I laughed. "That's actually a pretty good analogy."

"Of course it is. Now come on, let's go have a shower. It's been," he looked at his watch, "like five hours since I licked your clit, and I'm going through some serious withdrawals."

15

On Monday morning, I found myself in a bit of a pickle. I was a creature of habit, committed to my routine and its comforting predictability. And ever since Ted passed away, I'd become so reliant on that predictability and how grounding it was that any major deviation left me feeling anxious and lost. So when Jake woke me up that morning with his tongue between my legs and then wanted to spend the day together, I had to figure out a way to gently let him down and, without hurting his feelings, get it across to him that I needed my routine.

"So, what do you want to do today?" he asked with far too much pep in his voice for a Monday morning. He took a sip of coffee and poured himself some cereal.

"Umm," I hummed. "Ah ... "

"Do you have to go in to work today?"

I gave him a regretful nod before scooping half a cup of granola over my yogurt. "Yeah. Don't you?"

He shrugged. "Yeah, I guess I do." His lips curled into a wolfish grin. "Though I'd much rather play hooky with you."

"I know your boss. Best not to piss him off."

He rolled his eyes. "Yeah, you're probably right. Okay, well, what time are you off?"

"Five."

"I can come pick you up."

"Umm ... "

He lifted an eyebrow. "You don't want me to?"

"Well ... "

"What's wrong?"

"I ... it's just that I have my routine. And I always go for a run on Monday nights."

He shrugged. "Cool, I'll come with you."

"Umm ... "

He snorted. "You don't want me to?"

I avoided his probing stare and busied myself stirring my breakfast. "No ... I ... it's my time, my 'me' time and I need it. I'm not sick of you. That's not it. I'm just ... I miss my me time."

"Okay." He cocked his head to the side like an adorable puppy. "Were you afraid to tell me?"

"I just didn't want you to think that I was getting sick of you. 'Cause I'm not. I just need some time to myself." I made a regretful face. "I'm sorry."

He shook his head. "You don't have to apologize for wanting some space. But ... well, I do like spending time with you." He shrugged. "When can I see you again?"

"Tomorrow night?"

He pouted but then thought about it and nodded. "Okay, tomorrow night. Meet you here after work?"

"Actually ... I usually go to the gym with Emma for kickboxing on Tuesdays. It's where we met. James takes the girls for a couple of hours. So after?"

He nodded. "Sure. I'm sure James could use a hand anyway."

"You're not mad?"

"No, of course not." He abandoned his cereal and came up, his arms encircle my waist. "I mean, of course I'm disappointed, but I'm not a monster. I can bring dinner and we can *Netflix and Chill.*" His brows bobbed up and down.

"*Netflix and Chill*, eh?"

"Yeah, with less Netflix and chilling and a lot more sex."

I threw my head back and laughed. "Okay, Tuesday night. But," I checked the clock on the microwave, "I've gotta run. Can you lock up?" I reluctantly peeled myself out of his arms, grabbed my Tupperware container of my breakfast, pecked him on the cheek and was out the door.

That night, after an outstanding and invigorating thirteen-kilometer run around a budding neighborhood on the side of a small mountain—there were lots of parks and children playing with chalk or on bicycles in their driveways and I wanted to live there—I found myself toying with idea of calling Jake and inviting him over. I'd had a wonderful day at work, interactions with my students and co-workers could not have gone better.

I was just getting out of my car in the parking garage when a lone, dark figure moved in the shadows, making me jump.

I squeaked. "Oh, you startled me."

"You Ted's wife?" the big blob growled.

"Uh ... yes."

"Where is he?"

"Dead." I was tired of telling people this and at that moment was too drained to be nice about it.

There was a startled strangle in the big behemoth's throat, but then he coughed and rolled his shoulders. "Says who?"

That's a weird thing to say.

"Says the coroner and the death certificate I have. Why? Who are you?"

"Yanni's not going to like this," he mumbled to himself, but his big baritone made even a whisper fill the concrete room with foreboding sound.

"Wh-who are you?" I stammered, fear finally taking hold of me as my eyes frantically searched the garage for another human being or a security camera. I knew they were in there, but the big lug remained in the shadows and, I was sure, in a blind spot.

"Your husband is in a heap of trouble, lady."

"He's not my husband anymore," I whispered. "I told you, he's dead."

"Then you're in trouble now."

"How am I in trouble? What did Ted do?"

He sighed, his shoulders slumping ever so slightly but not detracting at all from his sinister shape and size. "Your husband was doing some *work* for my boss. He delivered the goods but never got the cash to my boss. And Yanni isn't happy about it."

"What kind of *delivery?*" My mind reeled with what kind of people Ted could possibly have gotten caught up with.

Oh God, Ted, even from beyond the grave you're causing me all kinds of problems.

"If Yanni doesn't get his money, he's going to be pissed."

"How do I know you're not just some stranger trying to shake me down? Who's this *Yanni?*" The words came out before I could stop them, and I quickly covered my gasp with my hand. How stupid could I get? Arguing with an enforcer the size of a Corolla.

With a low and menacing chuckle, he stepped out of the dark and into the hue of the dim orange light. I struggled with the urge to step back, but his face alone made me look away, pockmarked and scarred with a droopy left eye and half an ear missing. Combined with his size, barrel chest and greasy comb-over, he was what nightmares were made of.

"Imma give you thirty days to come up with the money your husband owed Yanni."

"How much?" My heart beat rapidly, as though it was fighting to get out of my chest. I thought I was going to choke, with no one around but this frightening monster to hear my strangled cries.

"Fifty grand."

It was though an elephant had just sat on my chest. "What? I—I don't have that kind of money."

His shoulder lifted, and he snorted. "Not my problem."

Anger built inside me.

Ted and his schemes.

Ted and his lies.

I'd had enough.

No more.

His problems were not my problems.

Not anymore.

I threw my shoulders back and stared him straight in his cold black eyes. "And I told you he's dead, so it's not my problem either."

"You're making a big mistake, lady."

"And you're trespassing." My entire body shook, but thankfully my voice was still pretty even. He couldn't know how terrified I was, how much I wanted to just flee and bar the doors in my apartment and never leave again.

"You're going to be sorry." He turned around and sank back into the shadows, but not before sending me one last, final, gut-wrenching threat. "Oh, and don't even think about going to the cops. I'd hate to have to hurt that pretty blonde friend of yours. The one with the two little kids."

16

"Freya?" James called out beyond the door as I scrambled to unbolt it. "Everything okay?"

"Just a sec." I opened the door, and there he stood like a sentinel of protection with Jake at his side, curious looks on both their faces. My eyes shifted uneasily back and forth between them. If they were both here, then who was with Emma and the girls? "You both can't be here!" I ushered them quickly inside. "Someone needs to be at home with Emma ... the twins. They're not safe."

James's eyes flared to life. "What do you mean they're not safe?"

"You need to go home. Someone needs to be there with them."

"Whoa, hey, slow down." Jake's hands came to rest on my shoulders, a reassuring and grounding pressure that immediately began to level my raging pulse. "What's going on?"

"A—a man met me in the garage. He threatened Emma and the girls if I don't get him the money Ted owed his boss. He ... he knows where you live."

James snatched up his phone and punched in a number. "Yes ... the house. Now. Lock down ... check the cameras ... alarm ... Armed." He hung up. "Brock is on his way over."

Who was Brock?

"Start from the beginning," Jake said slowly, grabbing my hand and bringing me over to the couch. I was still in my running clothes as I hadn't bothered to change and was instantly worried about how I smelled. Meanwhile, Jake once again smelled amazing. Like man and cinnamon. Was that his own scent? Or did he stick cinnamon sticks in his dresser drawers?

I told them both everything, from start to finish. Jake sat with me and held my hand, and James wore a rut in my hardwood floor with his incessant pacing.

"I called Stacey right after I called you," I finally said, taking a deep breath. "Asked her if anybody had approached her. I thought maybe this guy meant her and the kids. She's on high alert and knows not to open the door for just anybody."

"We need to call the police," Jake said with a nod. "They might know what kind of dealings Ted was involved in."

"But ... but the guy specifically told me *not* to go to the police."

James inhaled and exhaled loudly though his nose, his eyes nearly black with rage. A muscle at the corner of his masculine jaw ticked with bottled fury. "No, no cops yet. Let me sit on this for the night, and then we'll see about getting a cop in civilian clothes with an unmarked car to come to the house and take your statement. For now, I want to see if there is anything we can find here that might give us an idea what Ted was involved in." He looked at me. "Do you have any boxes of paperwork or file folders of Ted's that you haven't gone through yet? Or even ones that you have?"

I nodded. "Yeah, there are a bunch of them in the closet that I just haven't gotten around to. I'll go get them."

"I'll help," Jake said, standing up and following me to the closet. "This is crazy," he murmured. "Like something out of a movie."

"Yeah," was all I could say as I opened up the closet and crouched down to retrieve the boxes.

"Listen, if you want to go shower, you can. We can start looking through everything. You look like you're catching a chill." He was almost too good to be true. Even at the peak of all this chaos, he was still looking out for me. How did I get so lucky as to find Jake Leeman?

I passed him a couple of boxes and stacked two more for myself before leading the way out to the living room. "Yeah, maybe I will. I must stink."

He made a low noise in his throat behind me. "You don't *stink*, trust me."

I quickly ran and had a shower, the warm water doing nothing to cleanse the horrible feelings that were wrapped around my heart. But at least I didn't have to worry about choking the guys out with my sweaty stench. When I emerged from the bedroom in a pair of yoga pants and another old T-shirt, a sandwich sat on the coffee table. James and Jake were both eyebrows-deep in paperwork from the boxes.

"You should eat something," Jake murmured, barely looking up from where he scrutinized what looked to be last year's taxes.

"I'm not hungry." I sat down and reached for an unopened box and began leafing through stray papers, scanning them for anything that might be a red flag while secretly cursing Ted and his complete disorganization of these boxes. All my important papers were filed away alphabetically and chronologically in a file cabinet that also acted as my nightstand. I could find anything I needed in less than thirty seconds.

"Did the guy in the garage say anything else?" James grumbled several hours later, after he'd finished going through one box. He took a sip of his coffee before grabbing the next untouched box from the floor. That was the fourth time he'd asked me that question, and each time I gave him the same answer—no.

I'd told them everything, and since they'd arrived, I'd been quietly racking my brain for anything else he might have said or an unfamiliar sound in the garage that could help us. But I kept drawing a blank. Fear clouded my brain, and slowly, as the hours ticked on, so did fatigue.

"You should sleep," Jake said, his brows furrowed in concentration while his eyes continued to scan two documents side by side.

I shook my head. "I'm fine."

"I think I might have found something," he said, passing the papers to James, whose red-rimmed eyes spoke not only of exhaustion but also terror for his family.

James looked the two papers over. "Yeah, you might be right." He looked up at me. "What bank are you with?"

"Cascadia National Bank. Why?"

"Hmm, no other banks?"

"No. Why do you ask?"

"Because there are two very cryptic and doctored papers here with what look to have safety deposit box numbers on them. Two different numbers. But the bank is unknown. That information has been erased."

"And these papers were in a sealed envelope with the word 'Confidential' on them, where as everything else has been very haphazardly thrown in here," Jake added, looking at the untouched sandwich and then at me. "You need to eat."

I rolled my eyes and scrunched up my face. "Safety deposit boxes? We don't have any safety deposit boxes."

"Well, apparently your husband did, or does," James said, tossing me the papers and stretching. I looked them over, and sure enough, that's what they were, but the identity of the bank or banks had been deliberately erased. *What the heck had Ted been up to?*

Jake picked up the plate with the sandwich and held it out to me. "Eat!"

I rolled my eyes again, grabbed half of it and took a bite, smiling at him sarcastically as I chewed, not realizing until then just how hungry I was. The explosion of flavors made my eyes close as spicy mustard and sharp cheese with pickles and zesty mayo comingled and burst on my tongue. The man could put together a mean sandwich!

"Okay, well, I'm going to go home." James yawned. "Jake, I'd like you to stay here with Freya tonight. I've already got a call in for a bodyguard for her tomorrow. We'll reconvene and discuss this tomorrow night at the house. But I think we might need to involve the police."

"Should I start calling some banks, see if they have boxes that match these numbers?" I asked, reaching for the second half of the sandwich and taking a monster bite, much to Jake's blatant satisfaction.

James shook his head. "No, we'll wait to see what the police suggest. We may need you to move to the house, that way we're all under one roof and we can just put a bunch of security around one place. Turn it into a fortress. But we'll see what the cops say. For now, I think you're safe with Jake."

"She is." He nodded.

"Okay, good." James stood and stretched again, his long limbs popping as he strode toward the door. He slipped into his shoes and turned to face me. "Don't worry. You did the right thing, and we'll figure this out."

I'd followed him to see him out, my mouth still full of food, and suddenly I found my eyes teeming with tears as I struggled to chew and swallow.

"Chew." Jake chuckled. "Swallow. Good girl. It'll be okay."

"I'm so sorry," I said softly, my throat tight as I struggled to keep the tears at bay. "I—I never meant to bring your family into this. This is all my fault."

"It is NOT your fault," Jake said with passion behind me. "It's your husband's fault. And he's lucky he's already dead, otherwise he would be now for all the grief he's caused you."

James's face took on an amused expression as he tilted his head to the side and studied Jake, but then he looked at me and sobered. "He's right. It's not your fault, and I certainly don't blame you. Get some sleep. We'll figure this all out tomorrow."

"Couldn't stay away from me, could you?" Jake chuckled as we closed the door and headed back into the living room. "Had to make up some big, scary monster threatening you in the garage to get me to come back over. Come on, Freya, you know I would have come over if you'd just asked." He was trying to lighten the mood, but for some reason I found it hard to smile. I was sick to my stomach. A pit the size of a bowling ball rattled around inside at the thought of anything happening to Emma or the twins. I gave him a small forced smile, then started putting the papers back into the boxes, leaving the one for the safety deposit boxes out on the counter.

"I'm kidding, you know?" he said with apprehension in his voice, reading the room and my mood. "This isn't your fault."

"I know." I sighed. "But it still feels like it is. Like I should have known that he was so dishonest, seen some signs or something. Gotten out way sooner so that none of this would have happened."

"But ... " he shrugged, "then we wouldn't have met."

My heart melted on the spot, and I looked up from the table. "How are you so sweet?"

He shrugged. "Because you are. You've been dealt a pretty shitty hand, and I couldn't imagine hurting you in any way. I think all you deserve to do, for the rest of your life, is smile."

"And you intend to make that happen?"

"I intend to try."

I wasn't sure if it was the emotions from the day, his words, or the fact that I felt safe and desired when I was around him. I put down the box in my hand, moved around the table to where he stood. His eyes followed my every move. I lifted my shirt, tossing it to the floor. His pupils dilated and his lids fell to half-mast as my pants and underwear followed my shirt seconds later. There I stood, naked in my living room in front of a man I'd known for just over a week but who already meant more to me than I was ready to admit.

He swallowed. "We don't have to. You've been through so much. And I can see you're tired."

I put my finger over his lips in a hush. "Shh." Then I went to work on his belt, sliding his pants and boxers down to his ankles. He kicked out of them but remained standing and silent. I slowly unbuttoned his shirt, sliding the sleeves down his arms, taking my time admiring his biceps. Then there we both stood, completely naked, completely vulnerable and completely ready—he certainly was—to do the thing that had in such a short time become so natural and felt so right. The sheer thought of Jake made my body spark alive and hum with the need for him.

I took his hand and led him over to the couch, making him sit down and spread his legs. I dropped to my knees and took him in my mouth, the immense feeling of power causing me to sway, and I placed my hands on his thighs to steady myself. Even though I was the one on my knees, I had all the power. He was at my mercy, mine to control, mine to please, mine to possess. I couldn't get enough of him, enough of his taste, enough of the man. I wanted all of him, everything he was and everything he had to give me. I needed him, all of him.

"Oh God. Your mouth ... so sweet," he said with a moan, his hand landing gently on my head and petting it as though I were some cutesy little animal who had just crawled into his lap. "You're ... so good at this. I'm ... I'm close," he sighed, "really close."

I rose from my knees and climbed on top of him, straddling his big body and placing my legs on either side of his thighs. I lowered down until our bodies joined, the incredible sensation of instantly being full forcing my eyes to close and a moan to escape my lips. Then I rode him, without shame or quarter. I rode him hard and fast, taking every ounce of pleasure I could and giving it in return. The feeling of my butt cheeks smacking his thighs and his pubic bone rubbing my clit was unlike any kind of sex I'd had before. It was sex that I had initiated. I was in control. I was on top—and loving it.

The orgasm spun in my belly like a cyclone brewing in the sky, ready to unleash havoc on an unsuspecting town. And just like a storm, it tore through me with unexpected and reckless abandon, eviscerating my very soul as it ripped through my body from one end to the other in overwhelming swells of pure and newfound ecstasy. I cried out Jake's name, startling myself with my volume, but I didn't care.

He made me not care.

I continued to pound up and down on him, waiting for his release while prolonging my own. He stilled, growling low as his mouth came down and took one of my nipples. He poured himself inside of me, his chest heaving in ragged breaths. A light dew of sweat made our bodies glide against each other as we slowly calmed our efforts. Spent and satiated, he rested his forehead against mine. Still buried safe inside me, he drew delicate trails up my back.

"You ... you definitely know how to seduce," he whispered. His lips found my forehead. "Wow!"

I grinned, beaming with pride and how successful I felt. I knew that I should feel shy and self-conscious, unsure of myself, but I wasn't. I was so pleased that a giggle escaped me before I could stop it.

Groggy with barely open eyes, Jake looked at me. "What's so funny?" I started to full-on laugh, shaking, my body still shrouding his and causing us both to jiggle as tears started streaming down my cheeks. "What is so funny, woman?" he asked again, this time a look of confusion and maybe even unease on his face.

I took a couple of deep breaths before I was able to speak in complete sentences again. "It's just that ... I'm so proud of myself."

His head jerked, and he stared at me. "Proud?"

"Yeah, that I was able to seduce you so well. And that I feel really good about the whole thing. I know there are all these feelings that I should be having—shyness, fear, awkwardness, apprehension—but I feel none of them. All I feel is satisfaction and pride."

Now it was his turn to start laughing. "Well you should feel *proud*. You did a damn good job."

I nodded, still unable to wipe off the smile. "And what's even more hilarious is that with all the crazy stuff that's going on in my life right now—Stacey, my long-lost brother, now this Yanni guy—I should be so upset and pensive, but right now I'm not. I'm so happy and so ... proud. It's all I can think about. It's all I can feel. And for some reason, that makes me laugh."

He stared at me with open curiosity. Jake made me feel amazing, and I wasn't about to let that feeling disappear, not if I could help it.

"Well," he finally said, after softly shaking his head at me in awe, "we've got to do whatever we can to keep you in this incredible mood. Come on, woman." He gripped my butt, still embedded inside me, and stood up. "Time for round two." Then he whisked us off to the bedroom.

17

"Care to tell me why you have like fifteen different kinds of cheese in your fridge?" Jake chuckled, climbing back into bed with a small plate of cheese, grapes and sliced apple.

"No," I mumbled through a bite of Gala and brie.

"Was Ted the mouse?"

"No."

"So, you're the little squeaker?"

"Maybe ... " I said slowly, giving him the side-eye as I reached for a small bunch of grapes and a piece of edam.

"Hmm," he hummed. "Not a vice I would have expected from you, but I still find it adorable. Would have taken you for a chocolate or wine kind of gal."

I shrugged and grabbed a piece of cambozola and more apple. "I like both those things too, but cheese," I closed my eyes and let the flavors dance and melt on my tongue, "cheese is my one true love. My first two words were, 'cheese please.'"

He started to laugh. "Tell me more."

Scrunching up my nose and grabbing a hunk of extra-old aged white cheddar, but not bothering with any fruit, I gave him a confused look. "About what?"

He popped a grape in his mouth and sank back into the pillows, his tanned and toned body flexing as he casually tucked his arms behind his head, not caring two shakes that he was completely naked. "About you. Your childhood, your life. I want to know it all."

I exhaled loudly. "Well, there's not much to tell. Up until the last few months, my life was pretty boring. Routine, predictable, uneventful —lovely, really. My mom died when I was six, and so my dad raised me. He never remarried. My mother was already his second wife and, as he put it, 'the love of his life,' so he never even dated other women as far as I know. He was an English lit professor, and they met when he went over to England for a semester as a guest professor. She was his student, and they were fifteen years apart."

"Ah, so we're not the only ones doing a little cradle-robbing in your family?" He smiled, leaning up and grabbing more food.

I rolled my eyes. "No, I suppose not. They were married and pregnant with me within a year, and my mother moved back to Canada with my dad. She was a stay-at-home mom who was planning to become a professor like my dad. She put her education on hold until they were finished having children. I don't remember much of her, flashes and the odd memory, but she was an avid photographer, so there are lots of pictures, which helps. My dad did the best he could, raising me on his own. Hiring a nanny part-time and then using friends and some of his family to look after me as well. I'm not trying to be conceited here, but I think he did a great job."

He smiled and kissed the back of my hand. "He did."

"We were best friends. He treated me like an equal very early on, spoke to me like an adult, reasoned with me. I was reading by the time I was three and reading children's novels by the time I was six. I ended up skipping the sixth grade, and thankfully the summer before I moved schools, I also sprouted five inches, because before that I was a short, scrawny little thing."

"Was this all back in Ottawa?" he asked.

I nodded. "Yeah. My dad worked at the university there. He was a tenured professor."

"Cool. Hard to believe we grew up only a few hours from each other, you in Ottawa, me in Montreal. I wonder if we ever crossed paths ... "

Shrugging, I snatched another piece of cheddar off the plate. "Maybe, though they're both big cities, and I never got to Quebec very often."

"Do you speak French?"

Shaking my head, I frowned. "No, my dad grew up in Boston, my mum in Ireland. They were both Anglophones, and for some reason I just wasn't able to grasp anything more than a rudimentary understanding of it from school. I would have liked to learn, and I did as far as grade eleven, but I've forgotten most of it now. You do though, right?"

"Yeah," he nodded. "My sister and I are both fluent."

"That's wonderful. I wish I had a second language."

He bit into a piece of apple, and a trickle of juice started to run down his chin. I toyed with idea of leaning forward and licking it off, but he was too quick and mopped it up himself.

"So, then what happened when you skipped grade six?"

"Oh, right ... uh, school was fine. Not a lot of friends, but enough. I was valedictorian in high school, was awarded a fairly decent scholarship to the University of Ottawa, even though because my dad worked there, I got free education. But that didn't stop me from doing well. I remained on the dean's list for my entire undergrad and graduated with honors. I met Ted while I was doing my master's. We were both standing in line at a bank. He'd asked for my number, and I gave it to him. We started dating pretty much immediately, but we didn't live together for quite some time, not until we were married, as I was still living at home with my dad. I finished my master's and then Ted was offered a job as an auditor in Tanner Ridge, B.C., a tiny, quaint little town just ten miles from the U.S. border with lumberjacks and milkmen, where every friend was a neighbor and every neighbor was a friend, so we moved. It was the hardest thing I'd ever done, leaving my dad, but he was supportive, and we spoke almost every day."

Jake snapped off another piece of apple with his teeth. "So how come you don't use big words like Emma does if you're such an English buff like her?"

I smiled. It was true; Emma had a penchant for big and flowery words. Her love for the English language was almost as deep as my own, which was why I think we'd ended up being such good friends. "Ah, well, I can use them, and sometimes I do, but I learned very early on that kids don't like it when you use words they don't know. It can be ostracizing. Makes people think you think you're better than them. Which I know Emma doesn't think," I quickly added. "But it can happen."

"James has a word-of-the-day calendar at work just to keep ahead of his wife." He grinned.

"I know. Emma told me. I used to read the dictionary as a kid, loved it. Would spend hours memorizing the definition of words and practiced using them in sentences. I even made up a game about it and my dad and I would play. But one day in the third grade, I used the word *dubious* when answering a teacher's question and was immediately chastised by my peers. Earned me the nickname Dooby-booby Lapierre." I snorted. "Kids are dumb. That doesn't even make any sense. I have like *no* chest."

"Kids are mean," he affirmed somberly. "I'm sorry they picked on you."

"Ah, it only lasted for a week. But it taught me to use smaller words, just speak clearly and with conviction but don't *jazz* up your vernacular unless you're at a graduate mixer and are trying to impress someone who will actually *be* impressed."

"Good advice." He nodded. "So, is that why you don't swear?"

I smiled and took another piece of cheese. "My dad said that with my intelligence and grasp of the English language, I shouldn't have to resort to using such 'barbaric and uneducated' colloquialisms in order to describe how I feel about a situation. I just grew up in a household where there were no curse words, and I've sort of lived my life that way. I can swear, and I have, but I just choose not to."

"Emma's mum says that *fuck* should be a word reserved only for the bedroom." He chortled. "James told me that one. I've never met Anita Everly, but apparently she's a pistol."

I giggled. "She is. And I can totally see Emma's mum saying something like that."

"So then, when did you move to Victoria?"

I was surprised by how interested he was in my past. Even when we would get off topic, he'd bring us right back to my story and continue to ask questions. It was both touching but also embarrassing. I'd never talked about myself so much in one sitting before. Come to think of it, I rarely talked about myself at all. I was beginning to worry that he might be getting bored, but he just kept asking. Unless he enjoyed boredom, he must have been getting something out of our conversation.

"We were in Tanner Ridge for a few years. I landed a job as a teacher at a middle school, which I really enjoyed. We moved my dad in to live with us after a couple of years of being there. His Alzheimer's had started to get pretty bad, and he had to retire. All of his friends were either too old or dead, so no one was around in Ottawa to help. Then Ted got a promotion to a company here, and we moved to Victoria around nine or ten months ago. We decided that my dad's condition was too much for us to manage on our own and that we needed him to have 24/7 supervision."

"That must have been hard. Making that decision and seeing your dad decline like that?"

I clenched my teeth to keep the tears away. They always threatened to come out when I spoke about having to make the horrible decision to put my dad in a home. "You have no idea."

"You're a good daughter." He took my hand again. "And I'm sure if your dad understood what was happening, he wouldn't blame you for your choices."

I remembered the day the doctors told me my dad's diagnosis like it was yesterday. Up until the day Ted died, and then the day I found out I was a sister-wife, it had been the worst moment of my life, still might be. Because finding out your parent, your only parent at that, is slowly deteriorating from the inside out, is one of the most heartbreaking and devastating things a person can hear. His brain, the thing that made him who he was—a genius, a scholar and an intellectual—was rebelling against him and slowly collapsing in on itself, rendering my dad to a mere shadow of the man he once was. It had been and was one of the worst things I'd ever had to witness.

"An imprisonment in one's own rapidly shrinking brain," the doctor had said. "Your father has Alzheimer's disease, I'm afraid, which is why he's been so forgetful and confused lately."

I sat in one of those uncomfortable chairs in his sterile chrome and glass office and wept uncontrollably while Ted had muttered soothing words of comfort and stroked my back. It was on the drive back to my dad's house that we decided to move him in with us. We moved him from his home in Ottawa, my childhood home, the one he'd nearly torched to the ground when he forgot to take a cake out of the oven for five hours, to our house in Tanner Ridge.

"I'm afraid as your father's brain slowly starts to fail, or die, you will begin to notice significant changes in him, physically and mentally. Eventually, unfortunately, he might not be the father you once knew, and he might not know you." The doctor's words echoed back to me as I tearfully packed up all the books that my father had written, the books he'd co-written and the books he'd read but wished he'd written. "He may become bedridden and unable to move, eat or drink. At some point your father may require round-the-clock care."

My dad had fought us every step of the way, unpacking all the boxes I packed each night after we'd gone to bed. He'd run away to the university and interrupted a class he used to teach, standing at the front in his bathrobe and slippers and calling the current professor an imposter and scoundrel who had usurped his job. Security ended up having to be called, but not before my dad attempted to punch the new professor—a former colleague and friend of his—in the face. We wound up, against my better judgment, sedating him in order to finish packing and get him on the plane. In that one week I had lost nearly ten pounds from the stress of it all.

I swallowed the lump in my throat, the taste of betrayal bitter on my tongue, because that's what it had felt like. I felt as if I had betrayed my father, turned him into a child or a caged animal, with everyone around me saying, "It's for his own good." But each night before bed, I couldn't keep myself from wondering, was it for *his* own good or *mine*?

Joining Jake back in reality, I picked at a piece of loose thread on the sheet hem. "Yeah, well, the guilt is still there. And now I have this long-lost brother to try to find and some kind of enforcer guy demanding I pay him thousands or else he'll hurt me and my friends."

He shook his head and exhaled. "You need to let go of that. You did the best you could. We'll find your brother. Everything will work out."

I let out my own exasperated sigh. "Why are you so positive? I'm bad luck, a jinx. You probably shouldn't fly with me anymore. Just run for the hills. Save yourself before a black cat decides to make this apartment its new home and I walk under a ladder or something."

"Now you're just being silly," he drawled, taking the plate of food and setting it on the night stand. "You're not bad luck. Haven't you ever heard the saying bad things happen to good people? Well, you're a good person who has just hit a bit of a rough patch. It'll get better."

"Can we ... can we just not talk about it anymore?" I pulled the covers up to my chin and slid down into the bed, wanting to drift off into dreamland and forget the entire day ever happened. My proud and euphoric mood from earlier was just a distant memory.

"We can not talk at all," he purred, sliding under the covers and turning me on my side so that his body cupped mine, a familiar hardness poking and prodding at the small of my back.

"You're insatiable, you know that?" I groaned, parting my legs so he could slide home and letting out an involuntary sigh when he hit me deep inside.

Cupping my breast in his strong and capable hand, he brought his teeth down along my neck and shoulder blade. "It's all you," he whispered. "You drive me absolutely crazy. I can't get enough of you. You're like air, Freya. I need you to breathe."

My belly fluttered at his words. My heart swelled and my mind raced.

He needed me to breathe.

18

The next day Jake and I woke to the ringing of my phone. "Hello?" I answered.

"Miss Lapierre? My name is Heath. I was sent here by Mr. Shaw to protect you. Can I come up, please? I'm to escort you to work."

I looked at Jake, who was busy checking his phone. "Just got a text from James about a bodyguard named Heath. Let him up."

"Okay, sure," I mumbled.

"Thank you." Then the man was gone.

I still couldn't believe that I needed a bodyguard to escort me to work. What had my life turned into? Some daytime soap opera that all the women at my father's nursing home watched? Because it was certainly starting to feel like it. Throw in a paternity scandal and a kidnapping, and we'd see you at the Daytime Emmys!

A heavy fist pounded against my solid wood door a minute or so later. I tossed on a terry cloth bathrobe and opened the door to find another big man, only this one looked less like a nightmare and more like The Hulk's big, lesser green-hued cousin, with gun barrels for arms, a chest the size of a small sedan and a beautiful head of blond hair like some California surfer dude. He looked more like another threat than a protector.

"Uh, hi," I whispered, my eyes traveling up and down his enormous frame.

But it was the smile and the eyes that did it. Transformed this gorilla in combat boots into a huggable, squeezable teddy bear ... in combat boots. "Hi, Miss Lapierre, I'm Heath!" He grinned, showing big, straight, white teeth, the corners of his twilight-blue eyes crinkling with delight. "I'm here to keep you safe. Would you prefer if I came inside or stood out in front of your door?"

"Um." I looked back into my apartment and heard the shower running. Jake must have jumped in. Shaking my head free of the confusing cobwebs, I stood aside. "Come in, come in. It'd be weird for me to know you were just standing in the hall. Coffee?"

He ducked under the doorframe and bent down to begin to unlace his boots. "Please."

"Leave your boots on. I need to wash my floors anyway. Have a seat."

"Thanks," he said, his big smile never leaving his face as he walked past me, bringing the scent of what I could only describe as fresh mint and summer ... maybe fresh-cut grass? Either way it was inviting, and somehow he managed to make it masculine.

It was a very strange feeling having this man big enough to be two average-size people sitting on my couch, but at the same time I liked it, immensely. I felt safe when I was with Jake, but now that Heath was here, I also felt that Jake was safe. Knowing he was safe made the fist around my heart unclench. I didn't want Jake getting hurt because he was trying to protect me. If something happened to him, I'd never forgive myself, so now that Heath was here, I felt better about the whole thing.

Jake walked out a few minutes later with a towel slung low on his hips, his sculpted body glistening with water from the shower. His pecs twitched and flexed as he dried his hair. "Hey, dude." He nodded casually at Heath, who was busy reading something on his phone. The two men shook hands and quietly sized each other up. You could practically smell the testosterone in the room, it was so thick.

"Don't mind me, just go about your morning," Heath said with a rumble, sitting back down.

Jake shot me a wicked grin and bobbed his eyebrows. I just rolled my eyes. "I'm going to have a shower. Maybe you should go put some clothes on."

"Spoilsport." He snickered, following me into the bedroom. "He said go about our morning, and we usually have wild and crazy wake-up sex. You not ready to do it in front of a voyeur yet?"

"I'll *never* be ready for THAT," I confirmed, giving him a stern look. "Now play nice and get dressed." I sniffed the air. "Does your body wash have cinnamon in it?"

He gave me a confused look as he pulled a plain black T-shirt over his head. "No, why?"

"Because you always smell like cinnamon."

"I do not."

"Yes, you do. It's faint, but it's there. Cinnamon and fresh linen."

"And man, too, right? I still smell like a man!"

I chuckled as I headed into the bathroom. "Yes, you still smell like a man. A man with cinnamon buns!" I shut the door.

Tuesday at work was uneventful and easy. Heath proved to be a valuable asset in my classes. As it turned out, he'd spent some time working in Central and South America and had learned how to speak Spanish. Which wound up being very useful for a new Mexican student whose English was practically nonexistent. She clung to him like a flagpole in a tornado, and if I'm not mistaken, the incredible sexy and somewhat shy Quetzalia had developed a bit of a crush on the gargantuan teddy bear. I'd bet dollars to doughnuts Heath was not as immune to her beauty or puppy-dog eyes as he would like to think, either. I caught him a couple of times staring at her with uninhibited infatuation, or he'd whisper something to her while the rest of the class was busy, causing her to burst out into uncontrollable little girly giggles.

After work, Heath and I drove to James's house, where I picked up Emma, and the two of us went to our kickboxing class. James had tried to forbid her from going, but when I picked her up, she was dressed for exercise and fuming mad.

"You okay?" I asked as she climbed into the front passenger seat. Heath, who had managed to fold himself in half, took up the back.

"Ha!" she barked in fury. "My stupid husband thought he could *forbid* me from going out. Said I was being selfish and immature wanting to leave the house at a time like this."

"Oh," was all I said, knowing full well that James's and Emma's fights were usually heated and rip-roaring. The two were very hot-blooded and passionate people, and after witnessing the intensity of their affection for each other at dinner a couple of weeks ago, I could only imagine that that passion transferred just as hot to the bedroom.

Heath snorted. "He knows I'm in going in with you guys, right?"

"Yeah, he does," she said, turning around to look at him. "He's just being an overprotective ass."

"We don't have to go," I said with hesitation, not wanting to piss off my friend or her enraged husband, especially since he was footing the bill for Heath.

"Drive!" she ordered, pointing down the driveway. "I spend all day cooped up in that house letting two gluttonous beasts bite my nipples. I need to get out. I need to kick something, and if it's not a punching bag, it's going to be my husband. He can deal with his children for an hour. Besides, Jake and Brock are with him. They've got the girls outnumbered three to two."

"Okay, okay." I put the car in drive and headed down their gravel driveway.

"James has a cop coming by the house when we get back from the gym." She gave me a look that read my mind. "I'm sorry, but it might be a while before you get to shower."

I gave her a small smile. "I kind of assumed as much and packed a bag. James said he might sequester me in your fortress for a while, and honestly, as much as I like my house, I'll do whatever your husband and the cops tell me to do. I'm so sorry you got caught up in this mess, Em." I frowned and looked at her as we came to a stop at the end of the driveway. "The last thing I want is for you or the girls to get hurt."

She patted me on the shoulder. "It's not your fault. And you can just go stay with Jake in the garage apartment."

I nodded. "Yeah, I suppose I can."

Our kickboxing class had been a much-needed bout of catharsis, for the both of us. Emma and I kicked, punched and pummeled the bejesus out of the punching bag and one another's palms until we were saturated with sweat and panting like dogs in the summer. The class was quite busy, but we sparred together most of the time, as our intensity and focus seemed to scare away the rest of the class. I had to admit there were times when even I was a tad afraid of Emma. When she bared her teeth and scowled at me as though she was getting ready to rip out my jugular, it was enough to make anyone retreat a couple of steps.

But we were both channeling our anger and frustration, her toward James, punching the bag instead of his face, while I was envisioning that the punch pads were Ted, kicking his lying, cheating face until it was just a bruised and bloody heap of skin and bones. Meanwhile, Heath stood sentry just outside the studio doors like an intimidating pillar of muscle, earning glances of approval from the women who walked past and envy from the men. By the time we met him out front, he'd given his phone number to at least three women.

When we got back to the house, there was still heated tension passing back and forth between my friend and her husband, so I steered clear and sidled up next to Jake. He was sitting out on the patio drinking beer with another mountain of muscle in a leather jacket and crew cut.

"How was the gym?" Jake asked, groping my butt as I came to stand next to him. I was warily eyeing the enormous man sitting across from him. He looked even more threatening than Heath, if that was even possible.

"Really good. I'm gross." I batted his hand off my butt.

He rolled his eyes and chuckled before taking a sip of his beer. "I don't care. Brock, this is Freya. Freya, Brock."

He lifted himself up from his chair and extended a hand the size of a Christmas ham, engulfing my own and giving it a firm but not bone-crushing shake. "Nice to meet you," he murmured. "I see you met my baby brother."

Just then Heath joined us on the patio with a beer and a fluffy prancing Dave on his heels. "Smile, goddamn it!" He grinned, taking a seat next to Brock and lifting the dog up on to his lap. "You got the happy bodyguard, Freya, consider yourself lucky," Heath said, smacking his brother on the back.

Jake smirked. "Well, the irritability might have something to do with the fact that you insist upon wearing leather in the middle of the summer."

"I'm not irritable, and the heat doesn't bother me." Brock snorted, turning to me with a small but genuine smile. "You just say the word and I can have this ass replaced. There are four of us, and we all do the same job."

I raised my eyebrows. "Four of you? Wow!"

"Yeah, groceries were nearly five hundred dollars a week in our house as kids," Heath added, taking a swig of his beer. "Our poor mother. A jug of milk lasted half a day."

Suddenly the banter and chuckles were interrupted by the silence-slashing chime of the doorbell. All three men cringed while Heath leapt to his feet to go answer it, sending Dave bounding to the ground, none too pleased.

"Shit! Someone forgot to put the 'Do not ring bell' sign back up. Emma will be seriously pissed if the twins wake up," Jake said through gritted teeth. We all stilled, waiting for the ear-piercing wail from upstairs of one or both babies.

Seconds later, we were joined on the deck by Heath and a very plain-looking man in chinos and a white-collared polo shirt under a light jacket. He was plain in that he didn't look like the cop I knew him to be. James had said he was going to call and ask a police officer in plain clothes and an unmarked car to come out and take my statement, just in case I was being watched by any of Yanni's thugs. And as much as I hated to say it, this man was very forgettable. Short, ash-blond hair, light gray eyes and a round and friendly face, but there were no distinguishing features. Nothing stood out about him. No scars or dimples, nothing. It kind of gave me the willies.

A few moments later, James and Emma, both red-faced, joined us on the patio. James pulled out more chairs and propped the baby monitor on the big glass table we all sat around.

"Freya, this is Detective Cosgrove." Heath angled his head toward the cop, who took a seat across from me.

"Hello," I said shyly, being sandwiched between Jake and James while Emma sat across from her husband and inched her chair closer to Brock.

"Hello, Miss Lapierre." He flashed me a small smile, but it was the accent that made my head snap up. He was Irish! Definitely memorable now.

I filled him in and everyone else on what had gone down the night before in the parking garage, and the whole time Detective Cosgrove nodded and scribbled, only asking the odd question about the enforcer's appearance but otherwise letting me tell my story uninterrupted.

"And now here I am," I finished, leaning forward and taking a sip of Jake's beer, then puckering my face in disgust, "with a bodyguard and my only friend and her children in danger. I'm also worried about Ted's other wife, Stacey, and her children in Edmonton. What if Yanni goes after them?"

"Aye." He nodded, flipping his notebook closed. "You've done the right thing. For now, I think it's best if you stay here as Mr. Shaw has suggested. Keep everyone under one roof with security guards."

"You're welcome to stay in the house or the garage apartment," James said with a single nod.

"Thanks," I murmured, realizing suddenly that if I moved in to the garage apartment with Jake, we'd be pretty much living together, but that there was absolutely no way I would be able to stay in the main house without hurting his feelings.

"We'll start looking into what kind of *delivery* service your husband was involved in," the detective went on, "but I'm quite familiar with the Petralia family. Your husband may have been a drug mule."

"Or money laundering or human trafficking," Brock added. "We're familiar with Yanni as well."

I gasped, thankful that my stomach was empty, because at that moment I felt incredibly ill. "No," I shook my head emphatically, "Ted wouldn't get into drugs ... or ... or any of that."

The detective shrugged. "Well, we don't know for sure yet. But we'll let you know."

"S-so what about the money?" I asked, still trying to figure out how to get my hands on fifty grand. "Was it stupid of me to refuse? Should I just find a way to get the money and pay him?"

He stood up and pushed back his seat. We all rose with him. "Hopefully we figure this all out before then. But yes, we'll see if they do anything to retaliate to your refusal."

James growled. "I don't like that we're waiting for them to retaliate. He threatened my family."

Cosgrove nodded. "I understand, Mr. Shaw. You were smart getting security. But until they pose a serious threat or do something besides demand money, we're not going to set up a sting or a drop. Just keep a security guard with your family at all times and you should be fine."

"I know Yanni Petralia and his brother Spiros," Brock said. "They don't usually hurt women or children. It's not their style. Spiros just said that shit to scare you."

"Well it did," I replied. A chill swept over me, causing the hair on my arms to stand on end. Despite the heat of the evening, I found myself shivering. Although I normally caught myself being lulled into almost a dreamy state when hearing the same accent as my mother and her parents, my whole body was on high alert, and at that moment, I wasn't sure I'd ever sleep again. Following the train of people to the doorway, I caught Jake out of the corner of my eye. He ducked into the living room and came back with a blanket, which he then draped over my shoulders.

We were just saying goodbye to the detective, listening to his instructions and heeding his warnings, when my phone on the kitchen counter started ringing. I ran inside to answer it.

"Miss Lapierre?" came a frantic female voice.

"This is."

"It's Nurse Jablonski. Your father is missing."

19

"What the *fuck* are you talking about?" I screamed, causing everyone, including the detective, to spin around and stare at me. "What do you mean he's *missing*? How do you *lose* a person?"

"I ... um ... he was sitting in his chair by the window, and then when they went back to give him his medication, he ... he was gone." She sounded as terrified as I was furious. "We've got him on the security camera leaving the facility and walking toward the bus stop."

"The bus! I'm on my way."

"Your dad?" Jake asked, running with me as I headed to my car.

"Yeah, he's missing."

"Here, let's go in my car," Detective Cosgrove said, ushering me toward his black Chevy Tahoe. "No need for you to be driving in such a state."

I nodded obediently, not really thinking about anything but the fact that my father was alone and confused in a town he was completely unfamiliar with. He could literally be anywhere. At least back in Ottawa, we could check his usual haunts, but here, here he wouldn't know how to find his way back if he tried.

My mind began to race.

What if Yanni got to him before we did?

What if now that Emma was safe, and the detective said he was going to have the Edmonton PD put a car outside Stacey's house, what if Yanni decided to get to me through my dad?

"Any idea where your father might have decided to wander?" the detective asked as we backed down the driveway and headed on to the road.

I shook my head in the front seat. "No, we're not from here. We just moved here less than a year ago. I take my dad out occasionally, but he doesn't know Victoria."

"Maybe the university?" Jake said from the back. "You said he was a professor. Maybe he hopped on a bus that was headed to the university, not putting two and two together that it's a different town." Immediately my mind drifted back to that day he'd run away and interrupted a lecture. Maybe Jake was right.

"Let's go to the care home first, and then we'll follow the trail from there," the detective said, driving the big SUV with such grace and ease you would think he was flying a plane. At first, I wondered how he knew where to go, but then I remembered telling him in my long-winded story that my father was in Shady Ridge Long Term Care Home.

We pulled into the parking lot a few minutes later, and I bailed out of the passenger side before he'd even put the car in park, running full tilt to the lobby and up to the front desk.

"Is he back? Have you found him?" I hollered at the mousy little care aide in peach and pink scrubs.

"Wh-who?" she stammered, her eyes darting around the area looking for help. "Who is missing?"

"Roland Lapierre!"

Another older aide, one with RN on her name badge, came around the corner and paled when she saw me. "Miss Lapierre, we still have no word of your father."

Just then Jake and the detective walked in through the front doors. "Detective Cosgrove," he said, flashing his badge. "Can I have a look at the security footage?"

"Y-yes, of course," Nurse Jablonski stuttered, her eyes flitting between me and the cop and then back to her trembling little protégé, who was still cowering in the corner and watching everything happen, wringing her hands in the front of her shirt.

"I've put out an APB on your dad and we've alerted transit, so if any bus drivers picked him up, we should hear about it," Cosgrove said.

Everything started to blur. The nurse in front of me and her salt and pepper no-nonsense ponytail, the shaking mouse in pink scrubs behind her, and Jake beside me, they all swirled as my feet felt as though they were about to drift out from under me.

"Whoa, whoa, hey, Freya?" Jake said, all panicky and grabbing me under the arms. "Come sit down for a sec."

"No, I can't. We have to figure out where my dad is," I growled, shaking him off but then faltering again and nearly toppling into an elderly lady who was shuffling by with her walker.

"Come sit down," he ordered, practically dragging me over to a row of chairs along the wall. "We need to wait for the detective anyway. Have you eaten?"

"What?" I shook my head and reluctantly sat down. "No, I—"

"We just got a call about your father. A bus driver recognized his description, said he got off in the university bus turnaround," the detective said, coming out and punching something into his phone. "Let's go."

"Go with him," Jake said, standing up and heading toward the dining room. "I'll catch up."

I followed Detective Cosgrove back out into the parking lot, and we climbed into his car. He continued to natter away into his cell phone. A couple of seconds later, Jake came loping out of the building and jumped into the vehicle. "Here, this is all I could grab without getting serious stink-eye. Eat!" He dropped an apple, pudding cup and a giant oatmeal raisin cookie in my lap.

But I couldn't eat, not until I knew that my dad was safe. I thanked him half-heartedly and stared out the window as we raced across town and up to the university. I didn't wait for the vehicle to stop before I opened the door and jumped out.

"She really has to stop doing that," I heard the detective mumble.

But I was too busy to care. I started calling my dad's name, not realizing until that moment that he might have hopped on another bus already and be God knows where. Or be in any one of the hundreds of buildings on campus or wandered into the woods. I saw the detective and Jake speaking to a couple of security guards, and then everyone fanned out and we went on the hunt. I ran around like a fool, getting weird stares, and startling aimlessly wandering co-eds who were making their way back to their dorm after indulging at the cafeteria, but I didn't care. I needed to find my dad before it got dark, before he got scared.

I was just coming out of the student union building when my phone rang. It was Jake.

"I found him. He's at the fountain. We're just sitting and chatting. Do you know where that is?"

"No." My heart beat wildly, and my stomach did flip-flops. "Where?"

"Where are you?"

I spun around. "I'm in front of the student union building." Just then I spotted Detective Cosgrove and a security guard coming out of a big tall building with lots of windows. I waved them down and ran, the phone to my ear. "Jake found him. They're at the fountain. Where is that?"

"Just over here," the security guard said, ushering us around the tall building and past a weird red metal sculpture and a bunch of bike racks. I followed him, wishing that he'd run so I could run too. I did as soon as we rounded the corner in front of the library and Jake came into view; I left them in my wake and sprinted toward my dad.

"Dad," I sighed, slightly out of breath but more from the fear than from the run, "why are you here?"

He blinked up at me, quietly munching on the cookie that Jake had brought for me. "Freya? They've done a lot of changes to the school. I couldn't find my class. They're going to be wondering where I am."

I exhaled loudly, my stomach finally grumbling as hunger took over the fear. Jake grabbed me by the hand and stood up, letting me take his spot next to my dad. Detective Cosgrove and the security guard joined us. "It's okay, Dad. I think your class was canceled anyway. Let's just head home, okay?"

Looking up at me with panic, he struggled to stand, his hands shaking so wildly that the cookie fell to the ground. "Canceled? Why was it canceled? I don't cancel my classes."

"Uh, fire," Jake blurted out. I shot him a dubious look and mouthed the word "what?" but he just shrugged.

"Fire!" my father exclaimed, trying to stand up again, but we helped him sit back down. "In my classroom? In my building? But all my books!"

"Uh, it wasn't a big fire. Everything's safe. But they had to evacuate the building," Jake continued, building on his ridiculous lie. Somehow, against all odds, it actually seemed to satisfy my father, and he sat back down.

"Oh, well, I hope no one was hurt. Will class be moved to another building tomorrow? I'll check my email when I get home to see where they've relocated us." He picked up his cookie from the ground and took a bite.

"No, no, Dad," I said, taking it from his hand. "We don't eat food off the ground. Come on, let's go home and we can get you another cookie, a clean cookie." He batted my hand away like a petulant toddler and reached for it again. "No, Dad, it's dirty."

"Come on, Mr. Lapierre, there's a café in the library, and it looks like it's still open. Shall we go buy you a cookie for the road?" Jake asked, offering my dad his hand, which he took willingly and then linked his arm through Jake's before turning to look back at me and smiling like a child at Christmas.

The detective was busy on his phone, and the security guard had wandered away. I followed Jake and my dad into the library, where we all bought monster-size white chocolate macadamia nut cookies and then slowly shuffled our way across campus to the waiting SUV, where Detective Cosgrove was once again glued to his phone. The sugar rush from the cookie was a much-needed savior to my blood-sugar, and I managed to find it in me to climb into the back with my dad and not keel over across the seats.

"So how are we going to make sure this doesn't happen again?" I asked the detective as we drove back to the care home. "Do we get a tracking device or something?"

He nodded in the front seat, running his hand over his chin, the stubble making a raspy sound. "We might have to. We'll talk to the nurse when we get back, see what they suggest."

I laced my fingers through my dad's and squeezed his hand tight. The liver spots and arthritic knuckles represented grains of sand in the hourglass of his life, and the longer I looked at him, the more grains I saw fall. I realized that every day I saw my father very well might be my last. I choked on a sob and squeezed his hand tighter, not as tight as I would like, because I didn't want to hurt him, but enough that I could feel the pulse in his wrist against mine. His life blood, still pumping, still fighting. He looked at me and smiled, his mouth full of cookie.

20

"We can put a medical alert necklace on him, which acts as both a device he can press if he falls, but also has a tracker in it," Nurse Jablonski said, once we got my dad back to the care home and tucked away in his bed.

Detective Cosgrove nodded. "Yes, and we'd like added security put on the premises as well, please. We have reason to believe Mr. Lapierre might be in some danger."

"Danger?" Her eyes bugged out. "What kind of danger?"

He shook his head. "I'll send out an officer in the morning to discuss things with your supervisor. But in the meantime, please keep the doors locked. I see you have an intercom system to allow people entry. Use it."

I signed the waiver that allowed for my father to have the alert necklace on, once again the taste of betrayal foul on my tongue as I scratched my name on the paper. If my dad knew what I was doing, he'd be so disappointed in me. Not trusting him, putting a tracker on him like some wild animal we could now watch bebop across a screen as a little red dot, like some kind of sea turtle.

I wandered into my dad's room after signing the papers and just watched him sleep, peaceful and probably dreaming of my mother or teaching, completely unaware of the turmoil and panic he'd just caused. I leaned forward and kissed his forehead, letting out a contented sigh and smiling as his nose twitched and he lifted his hand up to rub it.

"See you tomorrow, Dad," I whispered, looking up to find Jake waiting in the doorway for me.

"Ready to go?" he asked, his hand finding its way to the small of my back and leading me out the door to the SUV.

"I need to see him every day," I said, climbing back in to the big, fully decked out, unmarked cop car, but this time sitting in the back seat. "I have to. I don't know how much longer he has."

"Okay," he replied. "We can make that happen." He scooted in beside me, taking up the middle seat and wrapping a protective arm around my shoulder. I leaned into him and closed my eyes, the homey smell of cinnamon and fresh linen along with his warmth and presence a boon of comfort on such a horribly frightful night.

Detective Cosgrove dropped us back off at James's and Emma's with more instructions and the assurance that he'd be in touch. He gave me his cell phone number and told me to call, no matter what the time, if I heard from Yanni or his lackey again. We wandered inside and quickly debriefed James and Emma, even though all I wanted to do was have a shower and crawl into bed. The realization that it wouldn't even be my own bed hit me like a ton of bricks, and before I knew it, I was a crying mess in front of my friends.

"Shh," Emma cooed, coming up and wrapping her arms around me. "Let's get you cleaned up. You brought clothes?" I nodded. "Okay, let's go run you a bath." She placed a protective arm around my shoulder and led me through the garage and out and around the back of the house to a wooden staircase that led up to a big white door.

Inside it looked like anything but an "apartment." It was fully furnished with top-of-the-line everything, state-of-the-art appliances, a big flat-screen television on the wall, leather La-Z-Boy furniture and two giant bedrooms, one with its own bathroom. I could sense Emma's hand at decorating immediately. There were homey touches here and there, and the soft sky-blue walls and camel-hued accents made the place feel big and airy.

"You and James seem better." I sniffed as I wandered into what appeared to be Jake's room and started stripping off my clothes. Emma went to work running me a bath in the big soaker tub. I needed a distraction, and making sure that my friend and her husband were no longer at each other's throats seemed like a good one.

I wrapped a big towel around my body and joined her in the bathroom. She shrugged. "Yeah, we made up. We always do. Our problem seemed quite small considering ... "

Rolling my eyes, I gave her a reluctant smile. "I'm sorry I brought all this into your family."

She rested a hand on my shoulder and squared herself to me, her hazel eyes smiling along with the rest of her. "It's not your fault. It's going to be okay. Now hop in. I'll send Jake in with some food." Then she spun around and closed the door.

Hanging my towel on the hook, I slid into the warm bubbles, letting the heat and steam embrace me, soothing my aches and pains and washing away the debacle and absolute nightmare of the last twenty-four hours. I pulled out my ponytail and sank into the water further so only my face was visible, allowing the water to seep into my ears and drown out the din of the day.

I closed my eyes and lay there, I'm not sure for how long. But when I finally did work up the strength to pop open my eyes, I found Jake sitting on the edge of the tub looking at me.

"Hi," he said quietly. "You okay?"

I sat up and wiped the bubbles from my face. "I'll be okay. It's just been a trying twenty-four hours. I'm exhausted."

"I bet." He grimaced. "Here." He handed me a glass of wine. I took it willingly and drained half the glass in one sip. "Easy. You need to eat something if you're going to drink like that."

"I'm not hungry," I grumbled, studying the glass and then shrugging before I tipped it up and finished it.

He chuckled low and then reached for something on the floor.

"Well, now, you definitely need to eat, you little lush. Here." He picked up a strawberry by the stem and held it to my lips. "Eat!"

I rolled my eyes. "You don't have to feed me."

"I don't have to do anything I don't want to do," he affirmed with a small and satisfied smirk. "I'm a grown-up. Now eat."

Snorting and giving him one last eye roll, I opened my mouth and accepted the strawberry. The sweet and tangy juice dribbled down my chin and into the water. It was an amuse-bouche of summer, fresh and earthy. You could practically taste the sun.

"And we can't forget this," he purred, grabbing what could only have been the biggest hunk of gouda off the plate. "Cheese for my little mouse."

"Is that smoked gouda?" I licked my lips, inhaling the smoky aroma.

"Yeah, one of your faves?"

"Mhmm," I hummed, biting off a big piece and chewing it happily. "Thank you."

"You're welcome." His lips twisted as if he wanted to say something but wasn't sure he should.

"What?" I probed.

He shook his head. "It's nothing."

"Jake ..."

"Fine. I think you should get your blood sugars checked. Your highs and lows are quite severe. I kept thinking you were going to pass out somewhere on campus as we searched for your dad. And then we'd have two people to look for."

I swallowed the rest of my cheese. "Yeah, maybe."

"I'm worried about you. You don't eat enough and your stress level is through the roof." His turquoise eyes were pleading and as much as I wanted to dismiss his idea, I didn't have the heart. Nobody had cared this much for me in a long time, and it felt really good.

"I'll try to get to the doctor."

He nodded. "Good. Thank you." His eyes traveled the length of my submerged body and back again.

I hesitated for a second. "Y-you want to join me?" Realizing that the thing I wanted, the thing I needed the most at that moment, more than food or wine or warm water, was Jake.

He shook his head and held the cheese to my lips. "I'm not expecting anything tonight. You've been through a lot."

I pulled away. "I have, but right now I want to forget it. And you do a really great job of helping me live in the now. Feel in the moment and forget my problems." I reached for the hem of his shirt, exposing my breasts, which were slick and soapy. "Please?" I turned my head and took another big bite of the cheese with a sassy grin.

A low growl escaped him before he stood up and shucked his clothes, his erection hard and eager, slapping against his belly as he peeled off his boxers. He slid in behind me, cradling me against his hardness. "Is this what you wanted?"

"This is exactly what I wanted." I sighed, melting into him. "Exactly."

Grabbing the plate, he continued to feed me, dangling grapes and berries, cheese and more cheese into my mouth until my belly, along with my heart, were both full and satisfied.

"More wine?"

"There's more?" I asked, craning my neck around to try to find my empty glass.

He motioned for me to sit up a bit, and he leaned over the side and brought up the bottle. "We'll have to drink it like—" But I was way ahead of him. I grabbed the bottle and chugged it from the neck. "Hill-billies," he finished. "Which apparently is something you're totally cool with."

"After a day like today ... " I giggled, handing him the bottle. "I'd be drinking scotch from the bottle if you'd brought any."

"I can go raid James's stash if you'd like. The man is a big scotch guy. Got some primo stuff."

I took the bottle back. "Thanks, but I think this'll be enough." I rested my back against his chest and closed my eyes. "Thank you for everything. You've been ... " I swallowed. "You've been a better man to me in these few short weeks than Ted was in nearly seven years. So, thank you."

He wrapped his arms around me and pulled me tighter against him, his still very noticeable erection lying like an iron rod against my lower back. "I'm crazy about you, if you haven't already figured that out."

"I'm starting to." I sighed. "Um ... "

"Um?"

"You um ... you wanna?" I opened my eyes and tilted my head up to look at him. His eyes were big and dark and full of promise.

"Always," he said softly, with zero humor in his tone. "But only if you want to."

"I do."

Taking the bottle from my hand, he emptied the last sip before resting it on the floor, then he helped me spin around and straddle him. His arms came up and encircled my waist, positioning me over his waiting hardness. "You're sure?"

I nodded. "I am. I need this. I need you." I sank down low, sheathing him to the hilt and throwing my head back from the impact. "Oh God."

"Take what you need," he groaned, his fingers digging into my hips. He bucked up to meet me. "Use me." His mouth found one of my nipples and clamped down, biting and flicking with his tongue, making me cry out and push into his relentless efforts, eager for more. Reaching up, I shamelessly pulled and pinched on the neglected other nipple myself. I'd never been so brazen before, heightening my own pleasure. But Jake made me do it. He made me feel free to take and not feel bad or ashamed about it.

"Jake," I whimpered as water sloshed all around us, spilling out onto the floor.

I rose up so that only the tip of him remained inside, churning my hips to tease and torment us both. I loved the feeling of once again having him at my mercy, toying with his pleasure, being in control. He snarled and tried to shove me back down, but I resisted, smiling as I bent my head low and nipped at his ear. "Just wait."

I swirled my hips again.

"Doesn't this feel good?" I asked.

"It ... does," he ground out. "But being deep inside you feels even better."

"Yeah?"

"Baby ... you're playing with fire."

I traced my tongue around the shell of his ear. "Maybe I feel like getting burned."

Then I slammed home.

"Wicked woman." He chuckled low. "Two can play." A curious hand traveled down my body and between my legs. His fingers found my clit, and I sighed, loving the extra attention, but instead of delightful little circles, he pinched.

"Ow!"

"Good ow? Or bad ow?" he asked, stopping his play and looking up at me.

I had to think about it for a second. "Do it again." He did. I closed my eyes and pushed into him involuntarily. "Good ow."

I was so close as I continued to ride him, taking, taking all the pleasure Jake could give me. Taking it all as he had told me to and loving every second of it. I felt wanton and sexy, powerful and confident, a budding seductress, an emerging tigress. It was only a matter of seconds before the climax that had been building and brewing in my belly erupted like a volcano of pure pleasure. It took hold of my body and my being, ripples and surges of blissful sensations cascading through me. I'd never had sex in the bathtub before, and there was something very appealing about it. We were doing dirty things while getting clean. A beautiful paradox if ever there was one.

Jake stilled and moaned, digging his fingers into my hips while his others continued to pinch and rub my clit, prolonging and heightening my orgasm. I felt him pulse and release inside of me, clinging to my body and burying his head in the crook of my neck.

"Oh, Freya," he hummed, our bodies still connected as we sat there in the cooling water. He dropped warm and wet kisses along my neck and shoulder. "You've got me. Completely. I'm yours."

21

The next morning, I wandered into Emma's and James's kitchen to find two new giants sitting at the kitchen bar drinking coffee and eating bagels with cream cheese. Their enormous frames took up the space that would normally accommodate four average-size people, with big muscles bulging out of tight black T-shirts and matching shaved heads that bobbed and twitched as they chewed.

These must be the other brothers that Brock had mentioned. Was I not getting Heath today? Quetzalia would be disappointed.

"Good morning," Emma chimed as she bounced down the stairs with a baby on her hip. James was hot on her trail, blowing raspberries on the belly of the other one. "Freya, have you met Rex and Chase? Brock and Heath's brothers."

Both bald heads popped up from their bagels and spun around to study me. From the back they could have been twins, but from the front they couldn't have been more different. Though both men were equally attractive and intimidating, owning their baldness and appearing comfortable in their own skin.

The green-eyed Vin Diesel-looking one was the first to get up from his seat and shake my hand, his matching dimples looking as though someone had taken a nail-gun to his face. "Hi, I'm Rex." He smiled, reminding me a lot of Heath at that moment, their big grins softening their otherwise alarming first impression. "I'll be accompanying you to work today."

"Like hell you will," Heath growled, coming in from the garage. "I'm going to work with Freya today. She's got a student who doesn't speak any English, and I'm helping her translate stuff into Spanish."

"What he's saying is, he's got a giant crush on Freya's student and wants to go and put the moves on her again," the older and more austere bald brother, who I was left to understand was Chase, pointed out. He took another bite of his bagel before coming over to shake my hand. More big hands the size of Christmas hams.

"No," Heath protested, shooting Chase an irritated look as he wandered into the kitchen and opened the cupboard to grab a mug and pour himself some coffee, acting as if he belonged and did this every day. "I'm the only one of us who speaks decent Spanish, and Freya's student needs help."

Chase chuckled low in his throat, but it was so deep and raspy it sounded more like a Harley-Davidson coming to life. "Whatever you say, little brother." Chase reminded me more of Brock, hard to ruffle and not overly generous with his smiles. He had a scruff along on his chin and a thin white scar that ran the length of his jaw all the way to his ear on the left side. His eyes were a deep midnight blue, like Heath's, and his eyebrows were blond. Unlike Rex and Brock, who had dark brown brows that bobbed along their foreheads.

"I'm not tired. I'm going with Freya," Heath stated again, reaching for the quarter of bagel that Rex hadn't gotten to on his plate and popping it into his mouth with a cocky smirk.

Just then the front door slammed, and we all turned around to see Brock enter the house and come around the corner. The telltale leather jacket was still on, despite how hot the thermometer outside said it was already this morning. "Heath, why are you here? You're off the clock," he barked, nodding at his other brothers and James, who was busying himself with steeping Earl Grey tea for his wife and balancing a baby in his arms.

"So? I'm not tired. I'm going with Freya." Heath lifted his chin at his big brother in challenge. "You're off the clock too. Why are you here?"

Brock snorted, ignoring his youngest brother and accepting the coffee Emma handed him while taking the baby from her arms so she could start preparing breakfast for her little family. I'd already eaten and left Jake in the garage apartment, as he was busy checking emails and looking over something James had emailed him about a new project. But even without him, the big open-space kitchen felt incredibly small with so many people. The four bodyguard brothers were big not only in size but also presence, commanding and dominating with an aura of confidence and testosterone encircling each of them like a giant ball of energy, with each man having a slightly different color. Right now, Brock's was definitely red.

James passed Heath the other baby so he could peel his wife a couple of hardboiled eggs and cut up her grapefruit.

Emma busied herself with James's peanut butter toast.

They were so in sync.

I quietly noticed I wasn't the only person in the room watching them in companionable action, in awe of how seamlessly they worked together and around one another. Then, as if in some cutesy movie, they both stood in the middle of the kitchen with plates in their hands and passed them to each other. James took his toast from his wife, and Emma took her breakfast from James. It was weird and wonderful, and I wanted it for myself more than anything.

"Hey!" Jake said, coming in through the door off the kitchen that led to the laundry room and garage. His eyes went wide as he took in all the bodies in the room. "Whoa, full house."

He did a round of meet and greet with the other two brothers with firm and slightly challenging handshakes before falling in beside me and draping a casual but claim-staking arm around my shoulder.

"Ready to go?" Heath asked, glancing at me before turning his attention back to the baby in his arms and making googly faces.

"Yep!" I nodded. "Just need to run and grab my purse." I took off back up to the apartment, my mind wandering to lunch and thinking that a fish taco might hit the spot. Jake was right, I wasn't eating properly. I was skipping meals and it was wreaking havoc on my body. I couldn't let the stress get to me. I needed to start taking better care of myself. I couldn't leave that job solely to him.

Seconds later, purse in hand, I was on my way out the door when Jake caught me by the elbows and turned me around, pinning me against the wall. His mouth silenced my gasp as his tongue forced its way into my mouth. He tasted like mint and cinnamon, and I felt my knees turn to jelly as I melted into his hard frame. A whimper of need escaped me. I wrapped my arms around his neck, pressing my pelvis audaciously into his growing bulge.

"I ... I have to go to work," I panted, continuing to push into him as his lips traveled down my neck and over my collarbone. His hands deftly began to undo the buttons on my cream sleeveless blouse. "We can't."

"We can," he breathed against my ear. "And you want to. I can tell. You're wearing a skirt. Tell me you didn't think it might be a possibility." My eyes shut as his hand snaked its way down my body and into the front of my panties. "You're already wet. Oh, Freya, I think you want this more than I do."

I swallowed, nodding as I let my purse fall to the floor and dropped my hands to the front of his khaki shorts and made swift work of the zipper. "I think so too." Without much more thought, I leapt up and wrapped my legs around his waist. Jake pulled my underwear to the side and pushed in, sinking deep and forcing a moan to spill from my parted lips.

"So wet ... so tight." He growled, hammering me against the wall, his hands kneading my butt cheeks. His mouth continued to roam across my neck and jaw.

"Oh God," I mewled, my head banging loudly against the wall. "Yes! Harder ... h-harder." He snarled as he bent his knees and adjusted the angle, hitting that sweet spot inside me.

I shattered into a million pieces.

Bright spirals of color twinkled and flashed behind my eyes as the pleasure tore through me. Every muscle in my body clenched and then relaxed, squeezing Jake, never wanting to let him go. I felt him still and let out a deep and guttural growl as he pinned me against the wall and, like a vampire or some feral beast, claimed me as his own, sinking his teeth into my shoulder just as he found his release.

"Uh, sorry," he said, a few moments later with no true remorse in his tone as he ran a finger delicately over the big red bite mark on my shoulder. "At least I didn't break the skin."

I gave him a sardonic look and adjusted my blouse before doing up the buttons. "You're lucky my shirt covers it, you vampire, otherwise ... "

"Otherwise what?" He bobbed his eyebrows up and down and encircled my waist with his hands, pushing me back up against the wall. "You might ask me to do it again?"

I playfully pushed him away. "Yeah ... something like that. Now I really have to go."

A few minutes later, I joined Heath and the others back downstairs, hoping that my clothes weren't too disheveled and my skin not too flushed that they'd be able to garner what I'd been up to. All the guys remained oblivious, thankfully, but it was Emma who shot me a knowing look and a sassy wink as Heath and I headed out the door. I simply shook my head, but the grin on my face gave it away, and she burst out laughing.

"What's so funny?" James asked, trying to spoon-feed one of the twins in her high chair.

"I'll tell you later," I heard her say just as I closed the door.

22

A fter work, Jake and I visited my dad. Heath was off the clock because I was no longer at work or around Quetzalia, so Rex joined us. His bald head shone in the light of the low-hanging sun as we walked across the parking lot and back to my car, grateful that my father was sitting in his chair and watching the ducks and not off catching buses all over town. I'd brought him some more chocolate chip mint ice cream, and the four of us sat there eating ice cream and watching ducks.

Yet, despite how full of thanks I was about having my father safe and in one piece, I feared for his safety even at the care home. What if Yanni found him there? What if he wandered away again and got hurt? Then there was still the bomb he dropped last week that we hadn't even come close figuring out—who or where was my apparent long-lost brother? I continued to ask him questions and try to get him to open up. But his moments of lucidity were becoming fewer and fewer. He barely even recognized me anymore.

As much as I had been worried about "living" with Jake, things were going pretty smoothly. We'd seen each other every day since we'd arrived back from Edmonton, and I found myself missing him even when he just took out the trash.

When we arrived home, Jake poured us both some wine and we took up position on the couch, cuddling like two people who had known each other for far longer than two weeks. I was busy reading my "porno" novel, as he called it, my feet in his lap while Jake watched some action-packed shoot 'em up movie and massaged my aching tootsies. A gesture he'd offered and insisted on, despite how much I'd protested.

The following morning, Jake and I were getting ready for work and he came out of the shower all sexy as sin, dripping wet with his towel slung low on his hips and a cocky smirk on his face. "What?" I asked, my mouth dry and my voice sounding more like a prepubescent boy's than my own.

"I saw that face." He snickered, shamelessly letting the towel fall to the floor and turning around to expose his taut butt while he dug around in a dresser drawer for some boxers.

"What face? I didn't make a face."

"You made a face. A 'holy crap, I could ride his face all friggin' day' face."

"That is *not* what my face said."

He rolled his eyes and nodded. "Yes. It was, and I'm totally cool with it. You can so ride my face all day. Do you only wear blouses?"

My cheeks were burning up, but his change in topic made me falter, and I tripped while sliding into my yellow kitten-heeled pumps. "I like blouses."

"Yeah," he drawled, pulling up his boxers and then grabbing a baby blue T-shirt off the top of the pile. "I like blouses as much as the next person. It's hot ripping them open and sending buttons flying." My eyes went wide at the idea of one of my blouses being desecrated. "But I think that's all I've seen you in. Besides ratty old nineties band T-shirts, which, by the way, are super hot."

I felt very uncomfortable and looked down at the pale pink and white polka-dot three-quarter-length-sleeved blouse I had paired with navy pleated capris. I thought that my outfit was smart and sophisticated, yet young and fun. The perfect combination of business casual.

"I ... I like blouses," I repeated, not sure what else to say. "What's wrong with blouses?"

"Can we stop saying *blouses* for a second?" he asked, pulling on some brown and tan plaid shorts and coming around to my side of the bed. "I just wonder what you'd look like in a tank top or a dress. You always wear blou—those tops, and I just don't think they allow you to relax."

"They're my work clothes. I don't relax at work." I put my hands on my hips and glared at him.

"You wear them on the weekend too." His eyes glittered with mischief.

"So what do you want me to wear?" I snapped, my anger building. What the heck did he want from me?

"Can I buy you something? Would you wear it?"

"I make no promises."

He rolled his eyes. "I'm not going to put you in nipple tassels and assless chaps. Relax."

Clenching my teeth, I glared at him. "I'm going to work." I pushed past him, grabbed my purse off the chair and headed down to meet Heath.

I let Heath drive us, as I was too irritated with Jake and his attack on my wardrobe to focus on the road.

Later that afternoon, Heath and I sat in the sun on a park bench and ate our wraps from the new Fusion food truck and I wondered if perhaps my anger and frustration toward Jake was a bit rash or even misguided. Quickly, Heath and I had developed a very friendly relationship, and I felt as though I could ask him anything and get a straight and honest answer.

"If Jake wants to buy me clothes, should I let him?" I asked, wiping a dollop of sauce from the corner of my mouth.

He shrugged and continued to chew. "Like regular clothes or sexy clothes?"

"I think regular clothes." My face suddenly felt a heck of a lot warmer than the sun from the mention of "sexy clothes."

He shrugged again. "Why not?"

"Well, doesn't that mean he doesn't like my fashion sense or sense of style? That he wants to change me?"

"If you were shopping and saw a shirt you'd really like him in, would you buy it?" he asked, crumpling up his wrapper and tossing it into the nearby trash.

I cocked my head in thought. "I suppose."

"So would that mean you wanted to change his style? That you thought his fashion sense was poor? That you wanted to change him?" He opened up his second wrap and dove in.

"No, I guess not."

"Then why not? If he sees a dress that he thinks would look nice on you, what's the harm? Doesn't it mean he's thinking of you?"

"Yeah, I guess."

He sobered and chewed his food in contemplative thought. "Would you be upset if I asked Quetzalia out?"

My head shot up and I looked at him, somehow more surprised at his question than I ought to be. I knew the two had feelings for each other, the entire class knew it, but for some reason, I didn't think that Heath would make a move, or maybe I thought that he wouldn't consider my opinion on the situation.

I crumpled up my own wrapper and blithely tossed it in the bin, giving a little mental victory dance when I actually managed to get it in on the first shot. "No, of course not. As long as your brother says it's okay."

"Why would I ask my brother if I could date a girl?" he asked, adorably scrunching up his face. "He's not my keeper."

"Oh ... uh, I don't know. I just thought because he was your boss."

Twisting his mouth in thought again, he nodded. "Yeah, I guess. I'll run it past him."

I looked behind me. The sudden feeling of being watched and having eyes on me sent a shiver down my spine as if I'd just stepped beneath a dripping icicle. Heath followed my gaze and stood up, shielding me from the sun and any other harm with his enormous frame.

"What did you see?" he growled, morphing into the big protector he was being paid to be.

"I don't know. I didn't *see* anything. It was just a feeling. Like I was being watched."

"Go back inside the school," he ordered, getting out his phone and grumbling things into it. "Now."

Frantically, I grabbed my purse and slid my feet back into my heels, then scrambled across the cobblestones toward the front door of the building. My eyes darted around the area, trying to get a glimpse of Yanni's thug or someone similar. But all I saw was tourists and regular people going about their day. Quetzalia walked past me with a couple of classmates. They were all sipping what looked to be smoothies from the new juice bar that had opened up across the street. She waved playfully at Heath, but for once, he seemed too preoccupied with his job to notice her affections.

"I don't think anyone's here," I said quietly, pulling on Heath's sleeve as he followed me to the door, covering me as if snipers were sitting on the rooftops. "And if they were, they're gone. I don't have the feeling anymore."

"Doesn't matter. Go back inside. I'm going to go have a quick look around." He made sure I was in the elevator and on my way up before he headed out into the hot afternoon in search of a pock-faced thug with a droopy left eye.

As I had assumed, Heath didn't find anyone or anything suspicious. He returned about thirty minutes later, much to the delight of Quetzalia, who was back in the classroom. His shirt was sweat-stained, and he had the makings of a sunburn on his cheeks.

We spent the remainder of the day inside, and every so often Heath's phone would buzz and he'd duck out into the hallway to chat with one of his brothers. Apparently, they were taking my "feeling" very seriously, and either Chase or Rex was positioned outside the school to make sure there wasn't any more ominous activity or a person lurking around waiting for me.

As we were packing up to leave, a call came through on my phone. Heath was engaged in some serious flirting with the viva- cious Quetzalia, whose siren-red sundress was leaving very little to the imagination. The rest of my class was either packing up and heading out or casually chatting in various corners. I didn't recognize the number but thought maybe it was Stacey calling from a new phone, or her nanny Daniella, so I decided to answer it.

"Hello?"

"I told you not to tell anyone," came a gruff and familiar voice. "Now you have a bodyguard. Who else have you told?"

I stiffened, knowing exactly who was on the other line. My eyes flew up to the happily chatting Heath, and I tried to get his attention. Fortu- nately, the man must have had ninja training. He picked up on my terror and was across the room in seconds, grabbing the phone, listening in.

"Who else have you told?" the enforcer asked again, this time with much more venom in his tone.

Heath shook his head.

"Uh ... no one. I d-don't have a bodyguard. It's just a friend of mine who's in town v-visiting and tagging along with me to work," I stammered.

Heath nodded and then reached for a cord from his pocket and seamlessly plugged it into my phone and then his, connecting the two so that he could listen in and possibly trace the call.

"Don't lie!" Spiros barked. "I know a Hart when I see one. Did you tell the cops too?"

"N-no. You told me not to."

"Good, because if I find out you did, no amount of brainless Hart brother will be able to protect you or your friends and their kids." Then the line went dead. I'd seen enough good-guy bad-guy movies to know that I hadn't been on the phone with him long enough to trace the call, if that was even what Heath had been up to.

Heath let out a big sigh and disconnected our cords. "We need to get back and show this to Brock," he said matter-of-factly. "He'll know how to proceed." He rested a big, meaty hand on my shoulder and gave it a gentle squeeze. "You did great."

I was shaking uncontrollably and wished like heck that I had a sweater or something to wrap around me. Heath sensed my need and quickly unbuttoned his long-sleeved dress shirt and draped it around me, leaving him in nothing but a tight white tank top that showed off his enormous arms and well-defined chest. I heard Quetzalia gasp in the corner, and Heath quickly shot her a come-hither grin.

"I'll be right back." He smiled, sauntering over to his little admirer and punching his number into her phone.

A couple of minutes later, we were outside and shuffled into the back of a waiting black SUV. "We'll drive you to your car," Rex said bluntly from the front seat. "Now that this guy knows you've got a body-guard, we need to be extra careful. He might have been working alone, but now he could bring in reinforcements."

I blanched at the idea of Yanni's thug calling in the cavalry and there being a whole army of those shadow-skulking creeps following me and my friends around.

"He said my *friends* and their *kids*." I turned to Heath, who had climbed in the back with me. "Do you think he meant Stacey and her kids in Edmonton? Or just Emma, James and the girls?"

"I don't know," he said with a stressful tone. "We'll talk to Brock and see what he thinks. Might not be a bad idea to get Stacey and her kiddos down here and under our protection."

Rex pulled up into the parking garage, and Heath and I jumped out. He hit the fob and we climbed in. Only to be followed the entire way home by a very attentive and efficient Rex.

We drove the rest of the way to James's and Emma's house in silence, Heath stewing over my phone call while I was getting increasingly giddy with the idea of having another friend in town, even if the circumstances were not exactly favorable. It would be wonderful to have Stacey and the kids here.

When the gravel crunched under the wheels, it sounded the alarm to the garage apartment, and I wasn't even out of the car before Jake met me in driveway.

"How was your day?" he asked, his face wary given my mood from the morning, but his eyes were bright and eager to hear about me and my day.

I let out a weighted exhale as I slung my purse over my shoulder and followed him around the back and up the stairs. I wasn't quite ready to face everyone inside the main house just yet. "Well, the thug from the parking garage called me."

"Seriously?" He gaped as he held the door open for me, and I slumped inside.

I filled him in, gratefully accepting the glass of wine he poured me and biting into a hunk of watermelon that he'd cut up and placed on the counter.

Did he ever work?

"I think that Stacey and the kids should come here. We can find them a safe house. Or everyone can stay here," he said.

I shook my head. "No, we can't do that to James and Emma. Their life is already so crazy, and now I've gone and added this mess on top of it all. I couldn't bring two more children and Stacey into this house. We'd have to figure something else out."

"They could live in here and we could move back to your place," he suggested, leading me into the bedroom and making me sit down on the bed. He gently removed my shoes and started massaging my feet. His hands felt like heaven.

"But then where would the bodyguards sleep?"

He shrugged. "Not our problem. On the couch, in the hall. As long as you're with me, you're safe." He pulled on my big toe, kneaded the pad, and I nearly had an orgasm on the spot. This man was a miracle worker, making me get all hot and bothered without taking off anything but my shoes.

"Yes, but with Heath around, then I know that *you're* safe too," I said.

With a smile, he put my feet on the floor and slowly pushed me down to the bed, covering my body with his. I melted beneath him, a rush of scalding heat flooding my limbs. I wrapped my legs around his hips and arched into his pelvis, shamelessly grinding myself against him.

"I'll be fine. I promise. Now, I hope you don't mind, but I bought you a couple of things. I saw them, I liked them, and the colors made me think of you ... well, your eyes." He looked at me with hope. "But if you don't like them, I can return them." Then he lurched off the bed and grabbed a bag from the corner of the room.

"Seriously, do you ever work? How did you have time to go shopping?"

His grin was wide and wily. "James hired me freelance. No contract. But I said from the get-go I only wanted a thirty-hour work week. My last job nearly killed me, so I'm taking it easy for a bit. I followed him to the job site this morning, made my recommendations, put in my two-cents, then headed to the mall. Then I came home, did some more work, made dinner, cut up some watermelon, and then daydreamed about you naked in a field of wild flowers."

I rolled my eyes.

"Wearing nothing but those sexy glasses of yours and a smile."

"And sunscreen though, right? I burn so easily."

"Ah, no need for sunscreen, love. I'd be covering your body quickly, shielding you from the harsh glare and dangerous UV rays."

"How gallant of you."

He handed me the bag, his eyes glimmering with naughty intent. "Always the gentleman. Now, open the bag and let's see if I know my shit."

I slanted him a sideways look before taking the bag, opening it and slowly dragging out a series of beautiful summer dresses, skirts and lacy tank tops. "Jaaaake. What? Why?"

"Why not?" He shrugged. "Come on, change into something comfortable for the evening. Here." He picked up a beautiful, white, knee-length flowing skirt and a dark green, lacy tank top. Which to me looked more like a camisole or something that should be *under* a shirt, not the shirt itself.

I wasn't sure if I'd be able to go see my dad wearing this top. I'd probably have to scrounge up a cardigan or something for fear of giving him a heart attack.

"If you don't like how they look on you, then don't wear them. I just wish you'd relax once in a while, and I don't know how you're able to do that in blouses and trousers." He shook his head. "Seriously, the moment I'm done work each day I change into shorts and a T-shirt, or sweats or something. I can't stand the starched and formal look."

"Are you saying you can't stand what I wear?" I asked, cocking one hip and crossing my arms over my chest.

The look he gave me was playfully impatient. "You know I'm not. I'd be crazy about you no matter what you wore. And it's ultimately your choice. I'm not trying to control you; I'm trying to help you loosen up and relax. You're too stressed out. Too tightly wound, and a breeze between your legs might chill you out."

I scoffed, but he took it as an invitation and came over to stand in front of me. He bent his legs until we were eye to eye and put his hands on my waist. "Though, if you'd prefer something *else* between your legs first ... " He bobbed his eyebrows. "I can help you out with that too."

I swatted his chest and laughed. "Thank you for the clothes. I'm sure I'll love all of them." I pushed him away and picked up the white skirt and camisole.

Of course, they fit like a glove. I stood in front of the mirror and spun around, swaying from side to side and loving the way the skirt swished against my legs and how the tank top played up my eyes. I had to hand it to him, the man had good taste.

"Mmm, sexy," he hummed, coming up behind me and wrapping his arms around my waist again, resting his chin on my shoulder. "You still mad at me for this morning?"

I closed my eyes and dissolved against him. "No, I'm sorry I got so frustrated. My life is so discombobulated right now. I just feel really displaced. First the thing with Ted, and now this guy demanding money. A long-lost brother I can't find anything out about, then my dad going missing, the weird safety deposit box numbers. I just feel like I'm barely keeping it together, hanging on by a thread." My voice began to tremble with the force of keeping my emotions in check.

He spun me around until we were face to face, pressing my head to his hard chest. I drew immediate comfort from the steady beat of his heart against my ear. My own pulse beat in rapid response to his nearness. "It'll be okay," he whispered, brushing my hair off my forehead and planting a reassuring peck. "We'll figure it all out."

I let out a heavy sigh and closed my eyes, hoping to God Jake was right, but somehow knowing that not everything was going to turn out *peachy*. Maybe most things would work out, but I couldn't escape that ominous, plaguing feeling that there was a bigger crap storm brewing, and battening down the hatches and hiding inside wasn't going to do us any amount of good.

"Come on," he said, patting my butt. "Let's go see what they have to say downstairs. Then we can eat a quick dinner. I made chicken with salad. Then we'll go see your dad." He linked our hands together and pulled me out the door.

"We've determined that, yes, those numbers are to a safety deposit box, but, no, they're not to any bank here in Victoria. That's as far as we were able to get. You might be able to get further, because you're the deceased's wife," Brock stated as we all sat around the big dining room table at James's and Emma's. Detective Cosgrove had just arrived and was quietly nodding away.

"Aye, we've determined as much as well," he said. "What we do know is that the boxes belong to the same bank. But because they're only four numbers each, and your husband covered his tracks in hiding the name of the bank, we've reached a bit of a dead end. They could be anywhere."

I massaged my forehead with my thumb and forefinger. A headache threatened to incapacitate me unless I heard some good news.

"But we do have some good news," the detective piped up. "We now know that your husband was indeed working with the Petralia family. Yanni is the leader of the family, and his brother, Spiros, is the man you met in the parking garage and most likely the one who called you today."

Brock grunted. "We're familiar with the Petralia family. Yanni was bribing a cop in Krista's detachment a few years ago."

I gave the cop and Brock a confused look as my mind took off in a million different directions. "And how is this *good* news?"

I saw the tired pull to his mouth and eyes, but he gave me an understanding smile nonetheless. "That's a fair question. I guess it's more good news to me. That now I know who we're dealing with. From the sounds of things your husband was transporting drugs from here in Victoria to Edmonton and using his auditor job as a cover, or a reason for all the travel."

I stopped breathing. Everyone else in the room stopped moving. I almost felt myself rise up out of my body and look down on the table scattered with papers and surrounded by people. This was my life now. I felt as though I was in the middle of someone else's dream or adventure. An out-of-body experience of sorts, because my life had gone from boring and dull, predictable and routine, to overwhelmingly insane in what seemed like the blink of an eye.

"Freya!" Jake called out, shaking me from my reverie, only when I blinked my eyes, I found myself on the floor, and a half-dozen concerned faces were staring down at me. "Are you okay?"

He helped me sit up, and Emma passed me a glass of water. "Yeah, I … I guess. I … what happened?"

"Your eyes glazed over, you stopped breathing, and then you fell out of your chair," Heath said, his face just as vexed as Jake's and Emma's.

"Should we take her to the hospital, get her checked out?" Jake asked, helping me stand and find my way over to the couch.

"No, no, I'm fine. I just haven't had enough water today, that's all."

Detective Cosgrove wandered into the living room and sat down on the chair opposite me. "Well I guess that answers my next question as to whether or not you were aware of your husband involved in any illicit activities."

I shot him a sarcastic glare. "Uh, yeah."

"We've got a team together who are continuing to investigate further into your husband's involvement with the Petralia family, so for now what I'd like you to do is try and locate the safety deposit boxes. Call any bank you can think of and mention your husband, that he's deceased and you're just trying to close out some of his accounts. They'll require proof of your I.D., possibly your marriage certificate and definitely his death certificate."

I nodded slowly. "Am I going to have to do a drop of the money that Ted owed Yanni?"

He shook his head. "That's what we're trying to avoid at all costs. We're reluctant to put up any money unless it's a hostage situation. Right now, it's just threats."

Jake wandered over and draped a protective, possibly possessive arm around my shoulder. Did he think the cop had a thing for me? "And what about Stacey and the kids?" he asked. "Should they stay in Edmonton or come here?"

The detective furrowed his eyebrows and made duck lips in thought. "I'll talk to the unit we're working with in Edmonton, but it might not be a bad idea if everyone was here. We don't know who your husband was working with in Edmonton or how much they defer to Yanni Petralia, or whether they'll take things into their own hands."

"We can fly them here tomorrow," James interrupted. "That's not a problem. Just let us know."

Cosgrove nodded and stood up, the same white collared shirt and chinos from the day before making him look like a person that could easily get lost in the crowd. But then when I thought more about it, maybe that's exactly what he wanted. The less he stood out, the easier he could go undercover and not get noticed. Blend in and disappear. He rested a comforting hand on my shoulder. "We'll figure this out, Miss Lapierre, I promise."

His accent held a timber that sent a dagger of longing straight to my heart. I gave him a smile, though it was a struggle to lift the corners of my mouth, and muttered a small thanks.

"I'll go grab your dinner and you can eat it here, and then we'll go see your dad," Jake said, jumping up from his seat, only for his spot to be immediately filled by one very hairy, very eager to have his belly rubbed, Dave. He sprawled out on his back, exposing his belly, and I dutifully ran my nails along his suede soft skin, earning the much-appreciated leg twitch.

"Oh, Dave," I murmured, "I'd switch lives with you in a heartbeat."

"I don't know," James joked, handing me a glass of wine while balancing one of the twins on his hip, "he's losing his junk next week, so that pep in his step might not be so peppy as of next Monday."

I thanked James for my wine and continued to rub the dog's stomach.

Castration and a lifetime of love and table scraps didn't sound like a bad deal at the moment. The only thing I'd have a hard time adjusting to would be having to go the bathroom outside.

I ate my dinner, though I wasn't overly hungry. Jake forced me to finish my salad, watching me like a mother bird until I darn near had to lick the plate. He said I wasn't eating enough or drinking enough water, which was probably why I'd blacked out. So against my protestations and declarations of feeling fine, he sat there and watched me eat every scrap of lettuce and piece of chicken until my plate was empty. And just like the man could pick out clothes, he could also whip up a mean salad. I was starting to worry that he didn't have any flaws, especially when his list of pros continued to grow.

We made a quick visit to see my dad, and although I didn't bother putting on a cardigan over top of my camisole, he didn't seem to notice nor care. He was completely content talking about the ducks in the pond, his "recent" trip to England—even though he hadn't been to England in nearly fifteen years—and about how much he disliked the way the woman who came to clear his plate smelled like cigarette smoke.

Once again, I tried to pull more information from my him about the child my mother gave up when she was a teenager, but instead of him diverting the topic, he grew angry with me this time and raised his voice, telling me that it wasn't his secret and he had to wait for my mother. He called me an "impetuous young woman" and said that I had no right to be asking such questions. It was around that time that a care assistant came by and suggested that we help my father to his room because he was upsetting some of the other residents.

He fought both Jake and I as we shuffled him down the hallway, using articulate and educated verbal abuse as well as trying to bat us off him with the swat of a hand or a misplaced hip-check. It took Rex interfering with our efforts to get him into his room without the fear of him falling and taking us all down with him. I couldn't remember a time when my father had been so agitated. When we left him tucked away in his bed, I stopped by the front desk, my voice trembling nearly as much as my hands with the emotion of seeing my father in such a distraught state.

"Is everything all right with Mr. Lapierre in room 309?" I asked. "My father seems much more irritable than he ever has before. Has the doctor changed his medication without talking to me?"

The nurse at the desk shook her head, her eyes locking on Jake's for just a second and then flitting back to me. "No, his medication is the same. But he's had other visitors besides you and your friends here." She grabbed the sign-in clipboard and handed it to me, her long pink and white French tips traveling down the paper and then stopping on the name *Spiros Petralia.* My breath hitched.

"Why was *this* man allowed to see my father? I thought after what had happened earlier in the week and after what the detective said, you were going to up the security around this place?"

The nurse paled. "I ... I just got back from a two-week vacation. Today is my first day back. W-what happened?"

"That place is a *fucking* joke!" I snarled as we piled back into the black SUV, Rex behind the wheel and Jake and I in the back. Both men spun around and stared at me. "What?" I barked. "I'm allowed to *fucking* swear, I just normally *fucking* don't."

"Well, now's as good a time as any," Jake said, he and Rex exchanging amused glances in the rearview mirror.

My response fell somewhere between a low growl and a "hmm."

"I'll have Brock go and talk to them at the care home. We might need to either move your father or have someone on him at all times," Rex said as he pulled out onto the road and drove us back to the house.

"It'll be okay," Jake whispered, patting my leg and giving me a reassuring smile, but I wasn't interested. I rolled my eyes at him and stared out the window, willing myself to wake up from this godforsaken horrible nightmare.

Back at the house, I couldn't bring myself to be around a bunch of people again, so I made my way up to the apartment. Jake and Rex went and filled the rest of the house in on the new developments.

I was just towel-drying my hair when Jake walked back in, a somber expression on his face. "Brock's going to put a guard on your dad, and Chase is flying up in Justin's jet on Friday to get Stacey, Daniella and the kids and bring them back on Sunday, after they do some packing and organizing. We're not sure where they'll stay just yet, but Detective Cosgrove called and said it's probably best."

I clenched my teeth and let out the breath I'd been holding. "Well, I guess that's good then."

"You're not happy?" He came into the bedroom and peeled off his shirt. "I thought you'd be happy that they're coming here."

I watched him send his shorts to the floor. "I am." I shrugged, pulling back the covers and climbing into bed, not caring at all that it was still light out and the hum of a lawnmower off in the distance along with songbirds chirping out the window sang the song of long summer nights. "I'm just so tired of bad things happening."

His face fell. "It'll get better."

"Please stop saying that," I mumbled, turning off the light and rolling away from him. "Because right now I'm not sure it can."

23

Normally I looked forward to Fridays. My weekends, although not overly exciting, were full of fun and predictable things. I always went grocery shopping, which for some strange reason was the highlight of my week. Cleaned my house, made myself a delicious dinner and then sat in front of the television and binge-watched Netflix while eating popcorn and drinking wine. But Fridays I usually treated myself to a pizza. I'd order a large, just for myself, always trying a new pizzeria, despite the fact that a very good wood-fire place was located right across the street from my house. For some reason I felt the need to branch out and try other places. The pizza was my lunch all weekend and my guilty pleasure. Gooey cheese and crusty dough, with lots of veggies and meat. It was one of the few things I allowed myself to indulge in. But it was also a nostalgic throwback to my childhood when my father and I would order pizza on Fridays and play cribbage.

But not this Friday. This Friday I couldn't go home. I had to once again be escorted by armed men to an unmarked car and then whisked away like a celebrity or a convict. I still wasn't sure which one I felt like more at my secluded hideaway where I was barely allowed to leave the premises, and if I did, I had to be accompanied by a bodyguard. It was no life I had ever dreamt or wished for, and I was now, more than ever, grateful for how low-key my life had been when Ted was away. At this point, I found myself craving boredom.

I schlepped up the stairs of the garage apartment, craving pizza and my dull old routine, not so much dreading seeing Jake as I was dreading the unfamiliarity of it all. No matter how much I faked it, I just wasn't able to relax in the apartment the way I was able to in my own home. Jake was busy on the computer in the spare room and barely paid me any mind, so I quietly changed out of my blouse and trousers and into another new outfit. This time I chose to go with a light and airy jersey-knit, aqua-blue summer dress that felt like butter against my skin. The day had been a scorcher, so I quickly fastened my hair up into a ponytail, relishing the immediate relief and the breeze that blew over my neck and back.

"I ordered us a couple of pizzas for dinner," Jake said, coming into the bedroom and sitting on the corner of the bed, watching me dress and undress. "I figured we'd pop in and see your dad and then pick them up on our way home." He waited for me to respond, but all I could do was freeze.

Had he read my mind?

"And I'm not sure how your day is tomorrow, but I'm ordering pizza because we have like no food left. Can we hit the grocery store at some point? I don't mind going alone, but I figured I'd ask, in case you wanted to come too. And then I thought—" by this point I'd spun around and was gaping at him. "What? What'd I say wrong?"

"Nothing," I said slowly. "Finish what you were going to say."

He gave me a perplexed brow lift but then continued, "I was going to say, I thought since life has been kind of never-ending chaos for the last couple of weeks, it might be nice to just make a nice dinner and hunker down in front of Netflix and drink too much wine while eating popcorn. What do you think?" I just continued to stare at him. "Freya, say something." Finally, all I could do was sit down on the bed, put my head in my hands and cry. "What did I do wrong?" He was at my side in less than a second, pulling me into his lap.

"Nothing," I blubbered, finding his shoulder and resting my cheek on it, the tears quickly soaking that spot on his shirt until the moss green was more of a dark spinach color. "You've done everything right, more than you'll ever know. I ... I just ... I don't even know why I'm crying."

"It's okay." He rubbed rhythmic and reassuring circles on my back. "You don't need a reason."

"What is your flaw?" I blurted out, sitting up gawking at him. "You're perfect. Seriously, what is your flaw? Do you have an evil twin or a psycho baby mama out there?"

His mouth twisted into a reluctant smile, and his eyes twinkled with an amusement he was unable to hide. "I have flaws. Everyone does."

"No." I shook my head. "Not you. Because I wouldn't even consider you being a jerk on the plane a flaw. I'd say that was your fear getting the best of you. Seriously, what is wrong with you? Please tell me, because I'm starting to get freaked out by how perfect you are."

He shook his head. "I'm messy ... um ... I don't like my food touching on my plate. I, uh ... I've given fake names and numbers to women I've slept with but had no intention of seeing again. I tend to let my nose hairs grow a little too long before I trim them ... the trimmer hurts. Does that help?"

Letting out a resolute and grounding breath, I nodded. "It does, thank you. Though I don't consider not wanting your food to touch a flaw so much as a weird quirk."

"Where's this coming from?" He tilted my chin up with a gentle finger, his eyes probing, seeing right through me, past my skin and bone and straight through to my soul.

"Because it's like you know what I need before I do. I was craving pizza and my old routine of groceries and Netflix. Pining for my easy and boring life before all this craziness happened, and then I get home and you have pretty much planned my old weekends down to a T. How did you know?"

A wry smile caught on his lips as he shrugged innocently. "The pizza was Emma's suggestion. I'm not going to lie. She said pizza was your Friday night guilty pleasure. But the rest, well, it's what I like to do too. We're not so different, you and me. I'm a homebody at heart too. I just don't like seeing you so unhappy. You're prettiest when you smile, so I want to keep you smiling at whatever the cost."

"Who are you?" I whispered, shaking my head as our fingers found each other and laced together.

He shrugged again. "I'm Jake. And I *really* like you."

Thankfully, the visit with my dad was uneventful in comparison with the night before. Rex had been posted at the care home with my dad all afternoon and was being pulled off duty once visiting hours were over. He had nothing suspicious or ominous to report, and like every other visit, my dad had no new information regarding my long-lost brother. I was beginning to think I'd never get it out of him or that he'd made it up. We didn't stay too long, as I was tired, especially after my cry-fest, and my dad was eager to get into his room and watch *Jeopardy*. So, Jake, Rex and I stopped and grabbed our pizza, and then we wished Rex a good night and retired to our little sanctuary.

"I don't understand how you can like this crap," Jake said between bites as we lounged on the couch and ate pizza. My newest zombie romance series played on the television. "It's complete garbage. I mean, aren't zombies considered a new species once they become zombified? So then wouldn't that be a form of bestiality or cross-species inter-breeding? That just seems wrong."

I rolled my eyes and reached for my fourth piece of pizza, not caring one iota that I was gorging myself in front of Jake. For the first time in a while I had an appetite, so I was going to take advantage of it. "It's a TV show. They can do whatever they like."

"Yes, but these two, what're their names again?" he pointed at the male and female leads.

"Leon and Odessa."

"Yeah, they just keep going back and forth between wanting to kill each other or fuck each other. Like seriously, pick a goal and stick with it."

"You're ruining my show." I growled, secretly loving the playful banter.

He ignored me and continued to complain, "I just don't understand how he can hunt her down, hold her at gunpoint and then, once he gets close enough, fuck her senseless against that crumbling brick wall. What if she gets pregnant? Will the baby be a zombie? Will she try to eat it if it's not? Will it be half human, half zombie? Is there such a thing?"

"I'm not sure zombies can get pregnant."

"How do you know?"

"I dunno, something about their bodies deteriorating. Seems to me that their reproductive system would be the first thing to go."

He nodded in contemplation. "Yeah, perhaps. I'd like to see some science behind it though."

Wiping my hands on a napkin, I nodded. "I'll get right on that."

The show ended, and we paused the screen before another episode started. We both stood up to clear the coffee table of dinner, and Jake topped up our wine. The fact that the setting sun was peeking in behind the drawn blinds didn't bother either of us one bit. It may have been a beautiful summer night, but I was enjoying myself exponentially spending it indoors and glued to the boob tube.

I was on my third glass of wine and finally feeling a semblance of calm embrace my body and mind. I whipped out my phone and sent an email to Jake, who had ducked into the bathroom after cleaning up dinner.

"Well, these are very pleasant surprises," he said, wandering back into the living room, studying his phone. "Especially your third preference. I never would have thought."

I bit my lip and gave him a coy smile, playing with the hem of my dress and tucking it over my knees. "You told me to email you with five things I'd been interested in using."

"I did." He nodded. "And I must say, I'm quite impressed."

"So, which three are you going to pick?"

"Ah, ah, ah," he scolded, as I careened my neck around to try and get a glimpse of which ones he was going to add to his cart, "you'll have to wait and see until they arrive."

I pouted. "You're no fun!"

"Oh, honey, I'm *tons* of fun! So," he bobbed his eyebrows up and down salaciously and poured the rest of the wine into my glass before joining me back on the couch, "have you googled all the positions I gave you?"

Giving him my best poker face, I blinked. "Yes, I have."

"Annnnd?"

"Annnd, there are definitely a few I'm interested in trying. I also googled a few other ones myself and have added them to the list."

"There's a list!"

I nodded. "Mhmm."

"And what ones are on the list?"

"Wellllll ... " I smiled. Feeling the wine, I brazenly lifted up from my seat on the couch and straddled him. My arms rested on his shoulders, and my breasts were aligned with his eyes. "Sticking with your theme, I'm interested in something called the *Dirty Sanchez*." I watched his eyes bug out. "And if we could get those bodyguards on board, maybe a *Bukkake Circle*. But I'd definitely like to try the *Cleveland Steamer*. Sounds dirty."

"You're kidding, right?" He laughed choppily. His palms grew sweaty against my thighs. "Right? You're not serious?"

I fought off a laugh. "About as serious as you where when you thought it'd be funny to slip in having a bowel movement on my chest, you freak!" I swatted him playfully on the pec. "I seriously hope you were kidding, otherwise I'm outta here."

His hands found their way up my dress, and he cupped my butt, pushing me against his pelvis. I ground against him and closed my eyes.

The other night Jake had casually suggested we push my boundaries a bit in the bedroom. He sent me the link to a website where we could order some sex toys, as well as a list of sex positions I was to research and decide which ones seemed good. I'd been bit reluctant at first, not comfortable with the idea of looking at a website with such suggestive material, but after he brought up the link on my phone and started scrolling through the online store, I was rather intrigued. It didn't take too long for me to make up a list and send it to him, along with the sex positions I thought sounded like fun.

"There were other things on that list of positions too," he said, pinching my butt cheek and making me squeak. "Anything else pique your interest?"

I bit my lip and toyed with the hair at the nape of his neck. "Mhmm. I liked the idea of the waterfall, reverse cowgirl and the wheelbarrow."

"The wheelbarrow?" He looked at me with surprise. "Really? That one's going to take some balance."

It must have been the wine talking, or maybe it was just Jake and how wonderful he was and how comfortable he made me feel in my own skin, but I drew my dress over my head and deftly unclasped my bra, letting my breasts spill out. "Well, I'm certainly up for the challenge," I said. "I guess the question is, are you?"

His eyes raked my body. His gaze was passionate, but almost severely so. It rocked me to my very core. "Absolutely. I'd do anything for you. You drive me crazy. I can't get enough of you. You're like air, Freya. I need you to breathe."

Just like the first time he'd said it, my belly fluttered at his words and my heart swelled.

He needed me to breathe.

"And I need you." I leaned over and grabbed his wineglass, draining it, then reached behind me for my own and did the same thing. I let the euphoria of alcohol sweep me away from my disaster of a life, peel away the layers of confusion and chaos until all that was left was the two of us in our safe cocoon, untouchable by the outside world and its dark scariness. If even for just a moment or two, and if we were lucky enough, the whole night.

"Freya," he finally whispered, "I ... "

"Shh," I cooed, prying myself up off him and grabbing his hand, leading him to the bedroom. Grinning, I turned around and rested my palms on his chest. "You have far too many clothes on for what we have planned."

The wolf was back, and he smirked at me, his eyes daring but also dark with promise. I felt like Little Red Riding Hood, his eyes so big, while his mouth ... *all the better to eat you with, my dear* ... I licked my lips.

"Well, that can easily be rectified," he purred, and in no time he was naked, hard and ready. "But before we try anything like the waterfall or wheelbarrow, we need to get you good and wet." He pushed me to the bed before kneeling on the floor and gently nudged my legs apart, bringing my ankles up to rest on his shoulders.

He had me writhing on the bed, wet and wanton in a matter of minutes, clawing at the duvet cover and shamelessly pushing into his relentless ministrations.

"I—I'm close," I stammered. "I don't want to come like this." Patting his head, I tried to pull away, but he wouldn't let me. His arms were draped across my thighs, and his fingers spread me open. I continued to squirm and wriggle until I was a pleading, begging mess.

Popping up from between my legs with a smile on his face and a very hard, very impressive erection bouncing against his stomach, he pulled me to my feet. "All right, now that you're ready, which would you like to try first?"

I worried my bottom lip between my teeth and thought about it. "Um, reverse cowgirl, then waterfall, then finish off with wheelbarrow."

His eyebrows nearly shot clear off his head. "The whole gamut in one night, eh? You naughty little wench. All right." He climbed onto the bed and tucked his hands behind his head. "Have your way with me, woman!"

And I did!

Despite how much wine I consumed on Friday night, I managed to be up and at 'em with the sun and the birds on Saturday morning. Emma and I headed to the gym for a rebounder class, where we bounced ourselves into hot sweaty messes on our own individual trampolines. Then, after a hot shower and another new summer dress,

Jake and I headed out to go grocery shopping and run errands for the afternoon, accompanied, of course, by Heath.

"So I went out with Quetzalia last night," Heath said as he drove Jake and I around.

I perked up in the back seat and caught his baby blues in the rearview mirror. "Really? How'd it go?"

"Well, his eyes have thick purple bags under them, and he has a giant smile on his face. How do you think it went?" Jake snorted, leaning forward and patting Heath on the shoulder in testosterone-filled congratulations.

Heath's eyes crinkled at the sides, and a satisfied chuckle escaped him. "It went pretty well."

Deciding to feign ignorance, I plastered a curious smile on my face and ignored the innuendos passing back and forth between the boys. "Where'd you guys go?"

"Uh … " Heath's eyes flashed to Jake and then back to me. "We went out for dinner and then back to her place."

"Freya," Jake chastised with a chuckle, resting a hand on my arm, "leave the poor guy alone. He got laid. Let him enjoy his high without the third degree."

"But I wasn't—"

"It's okay." Heath laughed, pulling into the parking lot of the local grocer. "We went out for Italian. I took her to that new pasta and prosecco bar on The Gorge. It was really good. You guys should go." I stuck my tongue out at Jake and snickered while giving Heath a triumphant grin in the mirror. "And then we went back to her place and humped like convicts on a conjugal." Then it was Jake's turn burst out laughing as he took in the look on my face.

24

Saturday night, Jake and I wound up cooking in the kitchen together. He hooked his computer up to the television and played some modern rock while the two of us seamlessly danced around each other in the tiny apartment kitchen.

"Dear lord, it's hot in here," he panted, coming back from the small balcony, where he'd been tending to the fish and vegetables on the barbecue. "I think it's hotter in here than it is outside." He pulled off his shirt, carelessly tossing it onto the couch. I gaped at him, licking my lips as I dried my hands on the tea towel.

He was perfection.

Every lean, sinewy, hardened inch of his raw maleness, couple with the way he stared at my lips, it was what erotic dreams were made of. "Get your mind out of the gutter, young lady." He grinned. "Unless you'd like to put dinner on hold and dive headfirst into the gutter. Then I'm totally game."

I rolled my eyes. "Cool your jets. Let's eat first."

But his engine was revved and his playful side was out, though I'm not sure he ever truly put it away. "Oh baby, I could *eat* right now." He stalked toward me, his lip curled into an entertained smirk, an expression I was coming to know all too well.

My nipples pearled against the shelf bra of my pale pink tank top. The denim cut-offs I was wearing had made me feeling like Daisy Duke all day long. "Jake, dinner," I said, my voice a tremulous whisper as his hands came behind me and cupped my butt, lifting me up onto the counter.

"Dinner can wait," he murmured, coaxing my lips apart until he found my tongue and challenged it into a duel.

My hands wound their way into his hair, and I pulled him down to me, further fueling his passion. He drew the straps of my tank top over my arms and rolled a hard and tender nipple between his thumb and forefinger.

A savant in seduction, he made such quick and deft work of my shorts that I was barely aware of him popping my button and sliding them down my legs. "Now, I believe I said I could *eat*." He grinned, once again hunkering down and sliding his face between my legs.

I ran my fingers through his hair and pushed into his face, not caring at all that I was essentially naked in the kitchen or that an incredibly handsome and talented man was eating his fill of me. The pleasure was inebriating and dissolved my modesty. All I currently cared about was finding my orgasm.

His tongue was pure, unadulterated magic, anticipating my wants and cravings before I even knew what they were. The slip of a finger and then another sent me over the edge, and within a minute, I was crying out his name and teetering precariously on the counter as I rode out my orgasm on his face.

"All right then," he said, standing up to his full height, licking his lips in a consciously sensual way, "back to dinner."

Seconds later, and I mean *seconds* later, there was a knock on the door, and James poked his head around the corner. "Hello?"

"Hi," I squawked, surprising both myself and the men with my bird-like voice. I hastily buttoned my pants and made sure my breasts were firmly tucked away. Could he tell that we'd just done something terribly naughty? Was my face flushed? Did the room smell like sex? I watched James meander in, and even if he had an inkling that all kinds of debauchery had just taken place, he wasn't letting on. "What's up?"

He seemed strangely reluctant to speak, worrying his lip between his teeth and avoiding my eyes. Eventually he lifted his head, and his eyes drifted back and forth between Jake and I, finally zeroing in on me. "Um ... Spiros Petralia tried to go and see your father again this afternoon." He saw me blanch but pressed on. "But thankfully Rex was there. Spiros didn't get anywhere near Roland."

Although I knew terror *should* have been my initial reaction, for some reason it wasn't. The heat of anger, no, fury, rushed up my throat and face and into my hairline. The taste of rage was thick and acrid on my tongue. I was so sick and tired of Ted's mistakes haunting my life and the people in it. Clenching my jaw tightly, I spoke with clipped words, "And then what happened?"

Both men took a step back when they heard my tone. "He left," James said. "But not before he and Rex had a few words. He knows you've got bodyguards, but he doesn't seem to think that that's going to stop him if you don't get Yanni his money."

"He said as much on the phone." I snorted. "Is he just trying to scare me?"

He nodded again. Jake made his way to my side, standing sentry and ready to comfort or protect me, depending on what I needed.

"We can't figure out what Spiros's game is. But we've called Detective Cosgrove, and Chase has confirmed that he, Stacey, the nanny and the kids will be on Justin's plane tomorrow afternoon. I've arranged for one of my vacant townhouses to serve as temporary quarters for them."

My eyes went wide. "James, you don't have to do that. They can stay here, and Jake and I can move back to my apartment. Rent out the townhouse. That's how you make money."

He made a dismissive pout and shook his head emphatically. "Don't be silly. It's got four bedrooms, enough for Stacey, the kids, the nanny and Chase. I've been meaning to get a painting crew in, so it's not rentable at the moment anyway. And I have *plenty* of money, even without the income from that rental."

"Okay," I whispered, my dander slowly dissipating and being replaced by a melee of other confusing emotions. "Thank you."

Rage was exhausting.

He shrugged again. "Don't worry about it. But I just came to let you guys know what the latest is. Spiros isn't the type of guy who makes mistakes, but he also isn't known for harming women or children. So, if anything, he and Yanni might think Ted is still alive and that we're all just hiding him. They might be trying to flush him out."

"That's not a bad thing," Jake finally piped up, "to have them thinking Ted is still alive. Less of a likelihood they'll come after any of the women or kids."

James nodded again. "That's what we're thinking. But for the time being, we're going to remain on high alert and keep you covered."

"Fine." I crossed my arms in front of my chest. "We're going to go and see my dad tonight. I need to see for myself that he's okay."

"Rex didn't let Spiros get close to him," James affirmed, giving me a resolute stare. "He's very good at his job."

"We're still going."

"Understandable."

"Anyway, dude," Jake sighed, draping a casually protective arm around my shoulders, "thanks for the heads-up, but we're going to start dinner, and I'm sure you have gruel to shovel into the mouths of some very cute little babies."

James gave a noncommittal murmur, seemed to ponder something and then flashed us both a big toothy smile. "All right then. You two have a good night." With a small nod, he was back out the door.

"You okay?" Jake asked after James had shut the door.

I nodded and shrugged him off, walking back into the kitchen to resume mixing my cheesecake batter. "I think I'll take my dad a piece of this when it's cooled."

"Freya."

I avoided his gaze. "It's fine," I muttered. "Let it go. I'd rather not discuss it right now."

"Please look at me." Slowly I lifted my head, my eyes giving away my mood. "You're allowed to be mad. You're allowed to scream and cry or punch something. You want to punch a pillow? Do you want to hit my chest?"

I rolled my eyes and snorted. "Leave it alone. Stop flogging things like a dead horse, forcing me to talk about it. I just ... I just want to think about some things ... just ... let me be." The last came out on a faint sigh. I was so tired. Tired of it all.

I showed him my back and grabbed the lemon off the counter, keeping my eyes cast down as I grated zest into the bowl. By the time I looked up again, he had retreated back out to the balcony and shut the screen door. Tendrils of barbecue smoke wafted past through the screen to let me know he was tending to dinner.

I felt bad for how I had spoken to him. He was only trying to be supportive. But no matter how much he said he understood what I was going through, tried to assure me that things would get better or encourage me to talk about it, he just. Didn't. Get it.

He didn't get the feeling of being responsible for so many other people's lives suddenly being turned upside down and threatened. Or that my father, my only living relative, essentially, didn't even know who I was anymore.

He just didn't understand the increasing weight and guilt that continued to stack up on my shoulders and that no amount of reassurance and support could lighten that guilt or guarantee anybody's safety. I felt alone, despite all the support I was getting from these people I hardly knew, alone in my guilt and alone in my responsibility to make sure none of them were harmed.

Pouring the cake batter overtop my cracker crust, I felt more tears threaten and sting my eyes. I quickly banished them away with the back of my hand, silently cursing Ted, and for the first time since he'd been gone, found myself actually glad that he was dead. Even after everything he'd pulled, I had never wished him to be gone. I'd never wished for his life to be over. If anything, I wanted him here so he could answer for his actions, pay for his crimes against the women he'd professed to love and the children he'd brought into this world. But now, now I found myself happy that he was gone. And that feeling made me hate myself.

Tidying up the kitchen and grabbing a couple of plates for dinner, I had my head down and was quietly thinking about how I could go about getting ahold of the money and making the drop on my own. No cops, no Harty boys, just fix the situation myself and save everyone the headache. I was so deeply immersed in my thoughts that I didn't even hear him approach, and the apprehensive clearing of his throat made me jump.

"Sorry," Jake murmured, plunking the plate of fish and vegetables on the counter before maneuvering around me to grab a beer from the fridge.

We ate in silence, cleaned up in silence and went to see my father in silence. Heath's eyes drifted back and forth between Jake and I, asking questions and willing one of us to break the mounting tension in the car and say something.

Neither of us did.

We spoke to my father but not each other, and it was as though my dad could sense something was off. He remained evasive and closed off from me, but he addressed Jake like he was his son or a nephew he hadn't seen in ages.

It was bizarre.

I found myself sitting in the big high-back green velvet chair across from my dad, staring out the window at the ducks, while Jake and my father bantered and gossiped like two old blue-haired biddies with calluses on their crochet fingers.

"So tell me, Roland," Jake said, after they'd discussed everything under the sun, from politics to the weather, Hemingway to Dr. Seuss, "your wife, you mentioned before that she had another child. Do you remember what hospital she delivered him at?"

I spun around and gaped at him while silently willing my father to finally break his streak of tight-lipped stubbornness and let the cat out of the bag once and for all.

My dad chewed on his bottom lip. He reached with a trembling and bony hand for his teacup, the lukewarm camomile sloshing around as he brought it to his lips. "Limerick, maybe?" he finally said, and with enough of an upward inflection that even he was questioning himself.

"Limerick, you say?" Jake said. "And where is that?"

My dad gave Jake an incredulous look, as if he'd just asked him what color the sky was. "Don't be daft. You know where it is. Freya, it's time for *Jeopardy.*" He turned to me and motioned to get out of his chair.

Scrambling out of my own seat, I leapt to my dad's side and helped him out of his chair. Jake was on his other side and wedged an arm around my father's back and eased him up. The three of us shuffled off to my dad's room to get him tucked into bed, with Alex Trebek and the Daily Double humming away on the television. I kissed him on the forehead and told him I loved him before I softly closed the door. I met Heath and Jake, and we headed down the elevator to the front doors.

"Miss Lapierre?" an unfamiliar nurse hailed, waving me down. Her voice was soft and wobbly. "Do you have a minute?" She was cute, shorter than me by at least three inches, with eyes the color of coffee beans and hair to match.

I stopped and nodded. "Yes, of course."

"I was told ... " Her eyes darted to Jake, and she licked her lips. "I was told that your father was to be moved to another room if it should become available."

"Yes, that's correct." I nodded again.

Nerves had her biting her bottom lip, and her eyes continued to travel back and forth between Jake and Heath, almost avoiding me. "Well we have a room available. Mrs. Deo died yesterday."

"I'm very sorry for her passing," I said robotically, not knowing who Mrs. Deo was or whether or not this little nurse had even known her. "Is her room available and suitable for my father?"

She nodded, still focusing on Jake. "Uh huh."

"All right then." I shrugged, not understanding why she was behaving so oddly but writing it off as her young age—I put her at about twenty-two or so—and that both Jake and Heath were very big and very handsome men. "What do you need from me?"

"Huh?" Her eyes were glued on my boyfriend.

"What do you need from me?" I said again, this time a touch sterner. The rush of heat to her cheeks and the way she continued to gaze at Jake triggered a streak of possessiveness in me that rattled me to the core.

Was this what jealousy felt like?

Jake cleared his throat and shot the nurse a big grin. "I think Ms. Lapierre is talking to you."

"Huh?" She shook her head and looked at me. "Oh, uh sorry. We just need your consent to move him to a different room. On the main level."

"Oh." I made a face of understanding. "So his room would be just down the hall?"

She nodded, fighting the urge to look back at a grinning Jake.

Was he flirting with her?

My hackles started to rise, and I clenched my molars. "Do you need me to sign something?" My eyes flew to Heath, and he was barely able to contain his laughter. I glared at him and he quickly sobered, turning around to examine a photo of The Queen as if she were some Victoria's Secret model.

When we finally climbed back into the SUV, Heath was chuckling like a hyena. Jake and I continued to avoid each other's eyes.

"Come on," Heath said, maneuvering the vehicle out of the parking lot, "you have to admit, that was pretty funny. She was eye-fucking the bejesus out of Jake. Couldn't have been more obvious if she'd tried."

I grumbled something rude under my breath but didn't look at either of them. Instead I just glanced out the window until the houses grew familiar and we turned down the driveway to James's and Emma's. Jake and I both bailed out when Heath parked the car, and without saying anything, we trudged up the stairs.

"You need to talk to me," he finally said, grabbing my arm once the door was closed. "I know you said you wanted space, and I've tried to respect that, but now you're treating me as if you're mad at me. Have I done something wrong?"

Letting out an exasperated sigh, I brought down a wineglass from the cupboard and upended half a bottle into it until there was nary a millimeter of the rim free of wine. Jake's eyes danced with amusement, but his mouth remained stern. "I know you're trying to help, and ... " I shot him a pleading look, "and you are. But I'm still in this alone."

"No, you're not. You have me and James and Heath and his brothers. You have Emma and Stacey. We're all in this with you."

I precariously took a sip. "See? That's just it. You're in this *because* of me."

"We're in this because of Ted," he said without an ounce of compassion in his voice.

"Same thing." I shrugged. "You're all tangled up in this ugly mess because of me. Because I foolishly picked Ted to be my husband."

He shook his head with a scoff. "That doesn't make any sense, and you know it. You need to start trusting people again, Freya. We're not mad, and we want to help."

"But you can't!" I snapped. "You can't."

"Then tell me how I can?"

Taking a long and mouth-filling sip of my wine, I glared at him over the rim of the glass. "I don't know ... do you have fifty grand you can spare?" I snapped sarcastically. "Because that's pretty much the only thing that's going to get these guys off my back and out of our lives."

He sobered. "Is that what it will take to make you trust me? To make you believe I'm not one of the bad guys who's going to hurt you? Because I have it. I can go to the bank in the morning, and we can be done with all of this bullshit this time tomorrow."

Shaking my head, I looked down at my feet. "No. Just leave it."

"Oh my God." He growled, running his hands through his hair and spinning on his heel only to pace the room. His face was such a heated tangle of emotion, I wasn't sure if he was going to scream or laugh. "You are so fucking annoying sometimes, you know that?"

My head flew up and my mouth hung open. "I ... ah ... annoying?"

"Yeah." He nodded. "Annoying. You won't let people help you. You won't let people in. You just keep everything bottled up, which just makes your problems grow bigger and harder. You're stubborn, pigheaded, blind and so incredibly annoying, and you drive me absolutely crazy."

"I ... um."

"Like seriously," he went on, "get off your high horse and drop the woe is me act. Your husband died, you have a sister-wife, big fucking deal. You're still alive, and at least *you* weren't saddled with two kids and no husband. Stop making other people's problems and issues *your* problems and issues."

"Jake ... I ..."

He let out an enormous sigh, grabbed my wineglass from the counter and drained it. "There. I've gotten it off my chest." He gave me an apologetic half smile. "Sorry, but it needed to be said. Do you hate me now?"

Something strange happened. I wasn't sure how to explain it, but Jake snapping made everything in my head fall into place, and I felt neither anger toward him or myself. Instead a weird and eerie calm settled over my body. A giggle bubbled up from my chest and escaped my mouth before I was able to stop it.

"Are you laughing at me?" he asked, surprise but also intrigue on his ruddy-cheeked face.

"I ... I've just never seen you like that ... you ... " I continued to snicker. "You were unhinged."

Transforming yet again, he stalked toward me, his smile impish. "That wasn't unhinged, sweetheart, that was barely a simmer. But I must say, I do feel better. I wish you'd start trusting me."

Looking up into his soulful gaze, I softened and moved into him. "I do trust you. I just don't want to see anyone else get hurt because of me."

"We won't." He kissed my forehead. "I'm sorry for some of the things I said." I didn't bother to remark on his use of the word "some," because if I was completely honest with myself, everything he said was true. I was in a bit of a woe-is-me funk and pitying myself as well as hating Ted for what he'd stuck me with. Meanwhile Jake's "simmer," as he'd called it, ignited something inside me, and I felt a familiar stirring in my belly. Had his heated diatribe actually turned me on? I was one sick puppy.

"You were right, though," I whispered, my hands traveling up and resting on his shoulders, "I need to start letting people help me. Letting people in."

He nodded. "Will you let me in?"

"Yes." I led him to the bedroom, where we slowly peeled off each other's clothes. "I want to thank you," I said, my teeth nipping at his jaw as he kicked his shorts off into the corner of the room.

"Yeah?" His voice was whiskey-thick and gravelly. "For what?"

"For letting me see another side of you. I was starting to worry that you might be perfect. But it's nice to know you have a breaking point. That even Mr. Perfect can be annoyed and driven nuts."

He barked out a hearty laugh and tossed me into the pillows. I was in nothing but my underwear. He prowled up the bed and hovered over my body. "Well, you certainly drive me nuts. I'm fucking crazy about you."

I grabbed his ears and brought his mouth down to mine, our lips brushing with just a whisper of a touch. "The feeling is quite mutual." Then he took me, making me forget every single bad thing that was happening in my world, until my body was humming and my brain was mush, hopped up on dopamine and loving life. At one point I wasn't even sure of my own name.

25

S unday, we welcomed Stacey, Daniella and the kids to Victoria. James and Emma had outfitted the townhouse with everything imaginable. From couches to beds, spices to flatware, they'd taken care of it all. Besides clothes and personal effects, there wasn't much Stacey and the kids needed to bring. Chase had flown up to retrieve them from Edmonton and was going to stay in one of the guest bedrooms as an extra bit of protection. We'd all gone over to help move them in, catch up and smell Thea's delicious baby head.

Despite the circumstances, I was excited to have another friend in the city. Emma and I had already discussed it—once Stacey was comfortable leaving Thea for an hour or so, we were all going to kickboxing. Stacey had a lot of pent-up anger she needed to let out ... more so than most.

After leaving Stacey and the kids, with the promise of returning later in the week to see how they were settling in, Jake and I went back and shared a bottle or two of wine with James and Emma out on their patio. So come Monday morning, my head was a bit fuzzy, and I woke up expecting to go to work with a mild hangover only to have Jake laugh in my face as I stood ready in the kitchen wearing my mint and white polka-dot sleeveless blouse and black capris. I inhaled breakfast and chugged my coffee because he'd kept me in bed late, and I was worried I was going to be late for my first class.

"It's Canada Day, silly." He chuckled. "Ditch the getup and put on your swimsuit. Let's go find a lake and go swimming."

"But ... "

"No buts. I'll pack a picnic. You put on the skimpiest bikini you can find. I want to see as much of that sexy body as I can. And I want all the other guys around to be drooling." Then he smacked my butt and sent me stumbling off toward the bedroom.

"I hope you guys don't mind, but I invited Quetzalia to join us at the lake today," Heath said as he pulled up to a swanky-looking condo building not far from the university. "She texted me and wanted to hang out."

I shrugged. I'd never made it a habit of socializing with my students in the past, but Quetzalia seemed like a nice enough girl. And Emma had said before that she'd gone out for dinner or drinks with her students in the past, especially the older ones who were eager to work on their everyday conversation and get tips and pointers from native English speakers on how to pick up or meet people. "Sure, I don't mind."

"Just as long as you two can keep it in your pants while we're all together." Jake snorted.

"It'll be tough," Heath teased, pulling up to the curb where Quetzalia was standing, waiting for us. Her ebony hair was tucked up into a carefree messy bun on the back of her head, while a soft peach sundress hung effortlessly on her curvaceous frame. "I'm like a fine wine, man. Fine Canadian wine. The ladies can't get enough of this rare and delicious vintage."

Quetzalia opened the door. "*Hola.*" She smiled, climbing in. "Hello, Miss L-Lapierre."

"Call me Freya." I grinned. "Hi, Quetzalia. This is Jake."

They shook hands. Meanwhile Jake and Heath were sharing a very inside, very personal joke between them as their eyes continued to shift back and forth in the rearview mirror.

What was going on?

Heath, being Victoria-born and -bred, knew better than the rest of us where the best swimming holes were. So after about thirty or forty minutes of driving through rural farm country, with nothing but fields and cows as far as the eye could see, we turned down a dirt road and into a small parking lot with only a smattering of other vehicles.

"This way." He nodded, leading us in the opposite direction of the marked path. We meandered through the low shrubs along what looked more like a deer trail. Tall evergreens stood sentry and offered much-needed shade. Sporadic gaps in the branches allowed for peeks and snippets of lake to pop through, and the shrill cacophony of beach-goers dissipated the farther away we hiked. The sweet smell of summer filled the air: warm earth and pine. I took a deep and calming breath, inhaling it all. My worries floated away with the summer breeze, even if only temporarily.

We walked for another couple of minutes before he had us take a hard left, and we found ourselves on a small bluff overlooking a perfect little circular lake. The people across the way at the public beach were no more than moving specks on the yellow sand.

"Cool," Jake murmured, and without further ado, he peeled off his shirt and back-flipped off the rock and into the water, sending sparkling droplets up over the rest of us.

"Maybe I should have told him there are sharp rocks at the bottom and it's only like five feet deep," Heath said casually, tearing off his own shirt to reveal a chest and stomach Adonis would be jealous of.

"WHAT?" I screamed, scrambling to the edge only to see a happily swimming Jake making his way around to a small ledge and pulling himself up.

Heath was laughing while also trying to explain in Spanish the joke to Quetzalia. Clearly, she found it about as funny as I did and batted him playfully on the shoulder with a scowl.

I'm not sure why, but I was reluctant to take off my clothes. Quetzalia was busy making herself comfortable on a sprawled-out towel in her sexy-as-sin string bikini, her copper skin glowing against the canary yellow, while her breasts practically heaved out of the cups. She was stunning. I felt almost translucent next to her with my pasty skin.

"Come on, gorgeous," Jake huffed, climbing up the small path from the water's edge. "Strip and come swimming."

I shook my head. "I'm okay for now."

Jake's eyes followed where I was looking. The beautiful Quetzalia was busy basting herself in lotion. He read my mind. The man could be a detective, he was so astute. "Get your sexy ass in the water, woman! NOW!" he ordered, stalking toward me and pulling the halter tie of my dress at the nape of my neck. The dress fell to the ground in a pool of purple at my feet, and before I could even utter a squeak, let alone a protest, Jake scooped me up and ran full tilt off the cliff.

We landed in the lake a mass of tangled limbs, Jake holding me so that my butt hit the water first. As soon as we were weightless, we came apart and I kicked to the surface, pushing my wild mane out of my eyes.

"What the heck!"

"What?" He grinned, swimming toward me and drawing me close. My arms seemed to be drawn by magnets, the way they instinctively floated toward him and rested atop his shoulders. My legs deftly wrapped around his waist. "You loved it." He nipped at my bottom lip, teasing me as his tongue traced my mouth. I gave way and allowed him access.

"Get a room!" Heath hollered from shore, lying down next to Quetzalia and offering to lotion up her back.

"Just close your eyes, children." Jake chuckled. "Things are about to go from PG to PG-13." He fished his hands in the cups of my sky-blue bikini and began playing with my nipples.

"There are people on the beach," I whispered. Though secretly, I was getting a bit of a high from the naughtiness of it all, not to mention how good it felt.

"So? They can't see a thing." He continued to play.

"How good of a swimmer are you?" I asked, spying an island in the middle of the lake and thinking it would only take us about ten minutes to swim to it.

"The best in the world." His megawatt smile made me laugh. "Did a couple of triathlons in college. And then Justin forced me to do the Penticton Ironman with him last year. Why?"

I pushed away from him so I was a few feet closer to the island and then headed off at a pretty good speed. "Race you!" Then we were off.

"Oh, Miss Lapierre, you are playing a dangerous game," he said with glee, speeding ahead of me at a brisk front crawl. "What do I get if I win?"

Knowing that he was going to beat me, but thoroughly enjoying myself, I continued to swim as hard as I could. "Whatever you want!" I called ahead, stopping him in his tracks, so much so that he sank and I managed to pull ahead.

We were neck-and-neck for a while, the water sloshing around us while our breathing became ragged and we were grunting each time our faces popped up. Making good time, we were just meters from the island when it became a sprinting game. Jake and I looked over at each other and laughed as we kicked and fought our way to the rock sticking out from the low-hanging cliff.

With one final ditch effort and the most unladylike snarl, I lunged, propelling myself forward. But even then, my efforts were in vain, and Jake touched it just a second before me.

"Good race," he panted. His eyelashes were spiked with water, and his cheeks held an adorable pink flush. "But," his hands encircled my waist, his own chest heaving with his efforts, "it would appear I won."

I was short of breath, and my hair was in my eyes, but I couldn't mistake his smile. "It would appear so, yes," I said, wiping my face. "So?"

"So ... you said I get whatever I want."

Wrapping my arms around his neck, I pressed my chest against his. "Mhmm."

"Wellllll ... " His teeth grazed my chin before his lips traveled up my jaw until they found that spot just behind my ear, making me groan and push into him. "What I want ... " Now his fingers were back in my cups, my hard nipples being expertly pulled and pinched. I felt him smile against my shoulder right before he bit it. "Is to fuck you sense-less right here, in the water, up against the rocks."

All I could do was nod and whimper, my legs finding their way back around his waist. I ground against him, riding his erection and letting the beautiful friction from the fabric of my bathing suit rile me up. His hands roamed across my skin until they made their way to the bottom of my suit. My fingers made quick work of his drawstring and the Velcro of his board shorts. Pushing my bottoms to the side, he lifted me up until I was just hovering over him. His tip teased and taunted me.

"God, you're so beautiful." He grunted, pulling me down on to him. "So fucking beautiful. So fucking perfect." His teeth raked across my jaw and one hand made its way back up to my breast. "I love your tits. They're fucking perfect." His mouth traveled down my neck and he latched onto a tender peak, flicking his tongue back and forth over the hardened nub. "Fuck, you taste good

"More ..." I arched my back and pushed my nipple deeper into his mouth. "Please ... more."

"Oh, baby, of course." His mouth moved over to the other nipple and he gave it just as much attention as the first.

It was hard to tell who was riding who as we floundered there in the water, connected in the most intimate of ways. Our bodies writhed with the pleasure but also the need to stay afloat and in one place. My back was against the hard rock and it hurt, but my mind was elsewhere. I focused on the eroticism of it all. Having sex in the middle of a lake, in broad daylight, where anyone could happen upon us.

It was hot, so hot.

For a moment I felt as though I was having another out-of-body experience, the sensations lifting me up out of the water so that I was able to just hover above us and watch. Jake's face was set into a deter-mined and need-driven scowl. I bit my lip and let my eyes flutter shut, taking it all in and letting my senses drive me.

Then I heard it ... the distant sound of voices and lapping water.

"Jake ... " I whispered. "I think I hear people."

Before we could pull apart or duck for cover, two kayaks poked their noses around the corner, followed immediately by their paddlers. Two young men who couldn't have been a day over twenty-one, all bare torsos and bronzed skin. Their eyes knew what we were up to even though their mouths struggled not to smile.

"Hello," Jake said, lifting his hand from my breast and giving them a wave, his cock still buried deep inside of me. "Nice day for a kayak."

"It's a nice day for a lot of things," the older-looking of the two said with a smile, his eyebrows bobbing. The two of them continued on past us and back out to the center of the lake and then toward the beach full of people.

I tucked my face against Jake's shoulder and mewled. "Oh my God!"

"I know, hot, right?"

My head shot up, and I just stared at him. "What!"

"That was so hot, getting caught."

"No, it wasn't."

"Well, that's a lie. You're so turned on right now. Maybe a little embarrassed, but mostly turned on." He thrust into me again, and I couldn't stop the groan that burst free at the back of my throat. "I'm beginning to think I know your body better than you do."

With an eye roll and a thrust of my own, I gave in to the need and I let him take me, hammering me into the rock. His hard body glistened in the warm summer sun, and his blue eyes pierced mine, glowing in the reflection off the water. He was a god among men, making my whole being explode into a thousand tiny pieces.

He knew my body. He knew my mind. I was pretty sure he knew my soul, better than I did.

"Welcome back, exhibitionists." Heath laughed as we climbed back up to join him and Quetzalia on the bluff. "Looks like you had some voyeurs."

Jake grinned triumphantly, and I dug around in the cooler for an apple. The swimming and the sex having caused me to work up quite the appetite.

"I'm surprised you didn't take advantage of the privacy yourselves," Jake said, opening a beer. "Or are you afraid you might burn your butt?"

Heath's smile was wide and wolfish. "I'd only burn my ass if I was on top, and who says we didn't? You guys were just too preoccupied to notice."

We spent the remainder of the afternoon lounging and laughing, swimming and sleeping. It was a beautiful, carefree day. I knew all kinds of worries and woes were waiting for me back in reality, but it was nice to escape them, even if just for a few hours. Quetzalia, although quiet, was very sweet, adding to the conversation when she could and appealing to Heath as if he were some all-knowing deity if she found herself confused. And Heath doted on her, almost sickeningly so, but at the same time it was adorable. He made sure she had lots of water, constantly asked her if she was hungry and offered to lotion up her skin for her nearly every thirty minutes.

By the time we got home, I was exhausted, which hardly made any sense given how little I'd actually done. But I was, and after a delicious barbecue dinner downstairs with Emma, James and the twins, we retired to bed early. The sun had sucked the life right out of us until we were nothing but limp noodles half a shade darker than when we'd started.

"You got a bit of a burn on your shoulders," Jake murmured as we lay on the bed, not touching because of how hot it was. "Do you want me to put some aloe on it?"

Not bothering to open my eyes, I grunted a yes and then I felt him leave the bed, only to return a few seconds later and straddle my upturned butt. "Get off me. It's too hot to be skin-to-skin," I moaned, already feeling the sweat getting trapped between us.

"Quit moaning, you big baby. Let the doctor work." His hands were sorcery, even with just the aloe. He massaged and rubbed, thumbs kneading into knots I didn't even know my shoulders had until I was a puddle of human butter, supple and pliant. I must have dozed off or something, because Jake's voice startled me. "Are you close?"

"Close to what?" I murmured.

"Coming."

My eyes popped open, and I craned my neck around to give him an eyeball. "No, why would I be close to coming?"

"The way you were moaning ... kind of thought you might have been having a bit of feminine hysteria." His smile was all playful, and his hands grew more and more brazen as they curved around from my back, cradling my ribcage and cupping my breasts.

"Feminine hysteria?" He helped me roll over until I was on my back and he was straddling my front.

He nodded. "And now, I see that you burned your chest a bit as well." He clucked his tongue while shaking his head. "Silly, silly. Best to take your swimsuit off and let me apply more aloe."

Rolling my eyes, I obliged. "You're incorrigible."

"Shh, crazy lady. Let the doctor do what he needs to do."

He continued with his tireless ministrations until an all-too-noticeable bulge appeared in his shorts. His hands, which had started on the burn on my chest, had somehow made their way down my stomach and were probing beneath my bottoms. "Again, you fiend?" I moaned. "I don't know if I can."

He pulled them down my legs until I was naked on the bed. The fan in the corner hit my aloe-cooled skin, causing a sudden chill to sweep over me. "One more time, and then I'll let you sleep. You don't even have to do anything, you can just lie there and enjoy." Then he ducked his head between my legs and all was right with the world ... at least for that moment.

26

Unlike the previous week, which dragged on like wet sand in an hourglass, the following week just flew by. I'd barely had enough time to run and see my dad after dinner each day, what with all the assignment grading from work during the day and evening and the insatiable man in my bed in the morning and night. I'm not sure what had come over Jake, but that whole week, he poured his feelings and his desires out in bed, bringing me to orgasm so hard there were tears in my eyes, and one time, I was pretty sure I'd blacked out for a second or two.

Finally, though, it was Thursday night, and we were visiting my dad again at the home. Rex was still on duty, so Heath ran out to grab some dinner. Jake was deep in conversation with my father in front of the window looking out onto the duck pond while Rex gave me the lowdown on the day.

"He seems less agitated today," I said, letting my gaze drift to the top of my father's head, the gray wisps standing on end. He'd be mortified to know he didn't look "church ready," as he called it. He was always so put together, and now ... now he preferred to wander around in his pajamas and kept misplacing his comb.

Rex nodded. "Yeah, it's been a good day. Was upset yesterday about the fact that they were serving quiche for dinner when he could have sworn it was prime rib night, but today he's happy."

I smiled. "Was it prime rib night?"

Rex's midnight blue eyes twinkled. "The man went back for seconds. I'm not sure where he's packing it away."

"And nothing mentioned about my mother or brother?" I knew there was probably no sense asking. My dad had been tight-lipped ever since that fated day when he'd mistaken me for my mother.

Rex's brows furrowed, and he glanced up to see Jake watching us. The two seemed to share some unspoken conversation before Rex's big, bald head snapped around and he pinned his gaze back on me. "No, nothing. Sorry."

I shrugged. "I'll keep trying."

"I keep asking too," he said, following me back over to the window where my dad and Jake sat.

"Hey, Dad," I said, coming up behind my father and pecking him on the side of the head. "Rex says it was prime rib night."

My father's eyes lit up. "Your mother makes a mean gravy. If I was a less civilized man, I would have licked the plate."

I chuckled. "That she does." I moved in front of him and perched on the edge of the coffee table, taking his hands in mine. "Listen, Dad, I want to ask you again if you remember anything about Mum's baby. You know, the one she gave up when she was a teenager. Was it an open adoption? What year was it? Any information that can help me find my brother ... " I figured since he'd had a good day and his favorite dinner, he might be in a better frame of mind and willing to talk. Some nights when he'd had a frustrating day, the mention of my mother and the baby she gave up sent him off the rails.

His body stiffened, and his eyes hardened. "Not my story to tell." Anger laced his tone. "Talk to your mother." Another dead end.

I let out defeated sigh. "Okay, Dad. I will."

Jake's hand landed on my back. "We should probably get going. It's getting late."

I nodded, not ready to leave my dad but knowing it was time. I squeezed my dad's hands a little tighter, feeling his pulse beneath my fingertips. Slow and steady. "We'll be back tomorrow, okay? I'll bring you some ice cream. What flavor would you like?"

The frustrated look on his face evaporated, and his milky gray-blue eyes shone with childish glee. "I'm thinking pistachio this time."

"Pistachio? That's a new one. You're always asking for mint chocolate chip or something with butterscotch." I stood up, and Jake's hand slipped to the small of my back.

"Well, I want pistachio. It was your mother's favorite."

My heart melted like an ice cream cone in the middle of July. Even if he didn't remember where he was or who I was very often, he was holding on to every shred of my mother he possibly could. A love like that seemed to even transcend his illness. He'd remember her for always.

"Pistachio it is." I blinked back the tears.

"Would you like help to your room, Roland?" Jake asked.

My father shook his head. "No, thanks. I'm going to stay and watch the ducks a bit longer. Good to see you again, Jake."

He remembered Jake?

I crouched down next to the side of my father's chair. "Bye, Dad." I pecked him again on the head. "I love you."

He smiled but didn't look at me, and no recognition of who I was or my voice shone in his eyes. "Nice to meet you," he said blandly, his gaze locked on the ducks.

I had to bite the inside of my cheek to stop from crying.

Rex took a seat adjacent to my father's. "Mind if I watch the ducks with you?"

My dad shrugged. "They're not my ducks."

Jake pulled me up and linked his fingers through mine. "Let's go. If we come a bit earlier tomorrow, he might remember you."

My chin and lower lip trembled as I let him lead me to the front door. "Yeah, maybe."

Later that night, we were snuggled up on the couch watching the only movie we could agree on—some action flick where the CGI was out of this world, but the acting was subpar—when Jake's phone buzzed on the coffee table.

"Hello?" he answered, standing up and walking into the kitchen. He showed me his back and brought his voice down low.

Who was he talking to that he didn't want me to overhear?

This was new.

Normally he wouldn't have even moved an inch and just answered the phone right in front of me, possibly even put it on speaker.

Against my polite upbringing, I brought the volume of the television down a touch lower and strained to hear what he was saying, but all I could get was a series of "mhmms" and "yeahs."

Fear ratcheted up my spine.

Who was he talking to?

What were they talking about?

Why was he being so secretive?

Jake spun around but didn't bother looking at me. Instead he grabbed a piece of paper off the end table. "Okay, I've got a pen and paper." He scribbled something down, but my spot on the couch was a terrible vantage point, and I couldn't see a darn thing.

He finished writing and clutched the paper in his hand. "Thanks, Rob. Email the rest of the information. Thanks again, I really appreciate it." He hung up from "Rob" and joined me back on the couch.

"Everything okay?" I asked, unsure if I should pry. I didn't want him thinking I was a nosy girlfriend and *had* to know who he was talking to. I did trust him. Didn't I?

Without bothering to answer me, he took the remote from my hand and turned off the television. Then, carefully placing the remote back on the coffee table, he faced me, took my hand in his and finally lifted his eyes to mine.

"Well." He swallowed. "I found your brother."

I stilled, staring at him. Not even able to blink. My pulse quickened, and my throat dried up. "Y-you found him?" I croaked. "Where is he? What's his name?"

His smile was small. "His name is Liam Kennedy, and he lives in Thailand with his wife and children."

"Thailand?" I shook my head. "Was he adopted by Thai people?"

"No. He and his wife moved there, opened up a hostel and work as English teachers at an ESL school. He was adopted by an English couple and raised just outside of Brighton."

"Okay." I pulled my glasses off and rubbed the bridge of my nose, shaking my head in disbelief."

"He has two daughters," Jake went on, "and he's open to getting in touch with you."

He is? How do you know?"

A sheepish expression fell over his face. "The PI I hired to find him has been in touch with Liam."

"He has?" My heart beat wildly in my chest, and my palms were sweaty. I could hardly think straight as the realization that my long-lost brother wasn't so long-lost anymore sunk in.

Jake nodded. "Apparently, he's been very curious to know if he has any other siblings out there. But seeing as your mother has passed away, and Seamus Allen, Liam's father, is also deceased, he's had a really difficult time tracking down any leads."

"How? How did you do all this?"

He shrugged. "James has me doing a lot of desk and computer stuff right now, so I've been working from home. Most days on my lunch break I go and visit your dad. I've been slowly drawing more information from him. And then Justin gave me the number of a PI he's used before. Took me nearly two weeks to get your dad to tell me the name of your mother's high school and her boyfriend. And even then, he only told me the guy's first name. Do you know how many Seamuses there are in Ireland? It's like Michael here. Talk about a needle in a freakin' haystack."

I swallowed. My mind was still a blur and my pulse still raced, but my heart, my heart was expanding. Ready and willing to let in new people.

Family.

And not just a brother; I had nieces and a sister in-law.

I still couldn't quite believe it. "I have a brother?"

"You have a brother." Jake smiled, closing the gap between us and pressing the small piece of paper into my hand. "This is his email address and phone number. He's really looking forward to hearing from you. He said he'd like to Skype with you some time if you're willing."

I nodded again, feeling like my head was going to fall off my neck, I was doing it so emphatically. "Yes ...yes, I'd love to Skype with him."

"Okay." He smiled. "Well, the ball is in your court now. He knows you exist; you know he exists; the rest is up to you."

There were tears in my eyes when I threw my arms around his neck, pulling him down to me until our eyes locked. "Thank you."

His gaze softened. "I'll do anything to make you happy, Freya. I know that life is a shitstorm right now, but we'll make it right, I promise. I just wanted to bring a smile to your face, help you find the family and connection you crave."

My chest felt ready to explode with the sudden rush of feelings and emotions flooding in.

That's when I knew, at that moment, that this incredible man had stolen my heart. It was wholly and entirely his. I'd loved Ted, but he hadn't owned my soul the way Jake did.

He was all-consuming.

I needed *him* to breathe.

I swallowed and cupped his cheek. "Jake?"

His eyes sparkled down at me, and he leaned into my palm. "Yes?"

"I love you."

I didn't even have time to blink, let alone breathe or think, and Jake was on me. Covering my body with his and capturing my mouth in a passionate and devouring kiss. When our lips parted, I was on my back and we were face to face, his arousal digging painfully into my hip.

I blinked up at him and looped my arms around his neck. "You don't have to say it back. I just wanted to tell you how I feel. You've changed my life. You've changed me. You've awakened this part of me I didn't even know existed, awakened my sexuality and my zest for life. I like who I've become since having met you, and it's all thanks to you. I ... I love you."

He studied me for a second, his eyes wandering over my face. A myriad of emotions seemed to wash over him. "Freya ... "

"Shh," I cooed, grinding against his shorts and locking my ankles around his back. "Let me thank you properly. Ditch the shorts."

A short while later, after I'd thanked Jake—more than once—and we'd called it a night, we were huddled up in bed, a tangle of limbs, despite the summer heat outside. It was amazing that in such a short span of time, I slept better when he was next to me.

I felt safer. More at peace.

I was just drifting off to sleep when a buzz on his nightstand caused us to break our spoon so he could grab his phone.

"Fuck," he murmured.

"Hmm?" I asked, the drugging effect of good sex and a long day pulling me off into dreamland. "What's wrong?" Lazily, I rolled over to face him. He looked like he'd just been punched in the gut.

I pushed myself up to sitting and leaned back against the headboard. The evening breeze ruffled the gauzy drapes over the window and swept across my heated skin, cooling it like a balm.

"Hmm?" I probed again, knuckling sleep out of my eyes. "What's wrong?"

He was still staring at his phone, his jaw slack and his eyes wide. The bedroom was dark, but I could see the outline of his face, and I knew he wasn't happy.

"Jake?" I shook him by the shoulder.

"Huh?" He shook his head a couple of times and finally lifted his head to look at me. "What?"

"You're freaking me out. What's wrong? Who messaged you?"

"Justin," he said on a defeated exhale, his shoulders slumping until he was practically hunched over.

"Is everything okay?"

"No."

Oh, no. His brother. His nieces and nephew. My mind began to reel with the possibilities. I knew firsthand what it was like to lose a loved one.

I scooted closer to him and wrapped my arm around his waist. "It'll be okay. We'll get through this. What happened?"

"My parents and sister are coming to visit."

I had to resist the urge to haul off and whack him. Here I thought someone had died or been diagnosed with cancer or something. In fact, I was no longer able to resist the urge and *did* haul off and whack him on the chest.

"Jake!"

His startled, almost hurt expression made me falter.

"I thought someone had died."

He shook his head. "No, nobody died. Sorry, didn't mean to scare you." Appearing to almost be in a trance, he put his phone back on the nightstand.

"Your family is coming to visit. That's a good thing, no?"

He didn't say anything.

What the heck was going on? I'd never seen him like this.

"When are they coming?"

"Saturday."

"Like *this* Saturday?"

He nodded.

"Oh. A spur of the moment flight deal?"

"No. I knew they were coming, but I thought it was next month. Justin just texted me and asked me what ferry I was catching tomorrow. He wants me to go over a day early to ... *prepare*."

Prepare for what?

Almost fast enough to give himself whiplash, he faced me, his eyes pleading with me. Even in the dark, they were so full of emotion, so full of need. "Come with me. Please." He grabbed both my hands and cupped them, holding on tight and pulling me toward him so that we were sitting across from each other on the bed, knees to knees. "I need you there."

I nodded. "Okay. I'll see if Ruby can cover my classes. I'd like to stop and see my dad in the morning though."

Releasing my hands, he scooped me into his arms he kissed me hard on the mouth. "Thank you."

He didn't release me as we slid down beneath the sheet and let our heads fall back onto our pillows. I spun in his arms until my head rested on his chest and my leg draped over his. He seemed to want, to need the connection, and despite the heat, I was going to give him what he needed. He always knew what I needed, often before I did, so I was determined to be that for him too.

Before I knew it, he was asleep. Whatever demon had haunted him at the news from his brother had disappeared, and he finally seemed at peace. His breathing was deep and even, and his chest rose and fell rhythmically while a strong and beautiful heart beat beneath my ear.

Thankfully, Ruby had no problem covering my classes, so after a quick visit with my father, we were on our way. Rex had offered to bring his tablet to the care home so I could Skype with my dad while I was gone. I wasn't sure if he'd go for it, but I was a little uneasy leaving him knowing it'd be several days before I saw him again. His condition seemed to be getting worse and worse and his moments of lucidity few and far between.

"I love this dress on you," Jake said as we made our way down the outside deck along the starboard side of the ferry. He reached for my hand and twirled me out, then twirled me back in.

"Jake ... " I giggled, worried that people would be watching us.

"What?" he asked with a smile, bringing me back beside him and planting a kiss on my temple. "It's not like I unzipped your dress and took you animal-style right here." He twirled me out again. "You're gorgeous."

I raked my teeth over my bottom lip, hiding the smile of glee I got when Jake, the eternal romantic, made me feel like the most beautiful woman in the world. The *only* woman in the world he could see.

The boat had just left the terminal, and people were flocking outside to enjoy the beautiful summer day. The wind was a welcome reprieve from the scorcher, and whipped my hair around my head like an orange tornado.

"Well, I know I was against it at first," I started, wrapping my arm around his waist and leaning into him as we continued our stroll, "but thank you for knowing what I needed before I did and buying me some new clothes. You were right, I needed to step out of the blouse box and get adventurous."

His eyes took on a wicked gleam. "Oh, baby, we can get *adventurous*." Sex grated through his voice. "How *adventurous* would you like to get? Shall we run down to the vehicle and have ourselves a forbidden quickie? No one's allowed down on the car decks en route. We'd be *breaking* the rules." His hand fell to my butt cheek, and he cupped it. "Don't you want to be a dirty little rule breaker?" He pinched and I yelped.

Chuckling, I rolled my eyes. "Maybe on the way back. It's too nice a day to not enjoy this view." We were at the bow now, and although we couldn't stand *Titanic*-style right at the front, it was still a pretty amazing site to behold. The gulf islands surrounded us while the water sparkled with a million diamonds and silky wisps of white clouds looked like someone had taken a paintbrush to the sky.

Standing in companionable silence, we took in the view, arms around each other. My mind drifted back to last night when I'd told him I loved him. He hadn't said it back, and even though I knew he cared about me deeply, I couldn't deny the pain I felt in my chest because he hadn't responded in kind.

Blinking back the tears, I plastered on a big smile and let the wind dry my eyes. I was with a man who was crazy about me. Those three little words didn't mean everything. His actions spoke louder than his words. He cared.

But as hard as I tried to convince myself that it didn't matter, the longer we stood there in silence, the more I realized that it did matter.

Had I said it too soon?

Was I more invested in this relationship than he was?

I mean, up until that moment, I hadn't really felt the age gap, but now—he was only twenty-five. Maybe he wasn't ready for a girlfriend, wasn't ready to be tied down to one woman.

Was this just a summer fling? Only to fizzle when the season changed and Jake realized he wasn't interested my baggage and the chaos that seemed to follow me around like a balloon tied to my wrist. He had his whole life ahead of him, a budding engineering career and a new city to date in.

"Freya?" He reached for my hand and pulled me around so we were face to face.

I swallowed the hard lump in my throat. "Yes?"

"Thank you again for coming with me. It means a lot."

I smiled sweetly. "Of course."

"I mean, I want you to meet my family. You're my family, and I want you to meet them."

What?

I shook my head. "Jake ... I ... about last night ... I ... " I trailed off. Words failed me. Possibly for the first time in my life, words had failed me.

"Freya," he started, "I—"

But I cut him off. "I don't expect anything from you. Calling me *family* is sweet, but it's okay if you don't mean it. This relationship is what it is. I shouldn't have said what I said last night and put that kind of pressure on you. I'm sorry."

He made a deep and feral growl in his throat. "Would. You. Let. Me. Finish. Woman?"

"I—" He put his finger over my mouth to stop me.

"I love you too, and you *are* family. If you'd let me get a word in edgewise once in a while and stop cutting me off or downplaying the whole thing, you would have known by now that I'm fucking in love with you, you hard-headed, exasperating woman."

"Sorry," I muttered, looking down at my feet. But inside, my heart was swelling and dancing and flying from his beautiful words.

"Look at me," he commanded.

I did as he asked. This man had my heart. I'd do anything for him. When I looked up, I saw something I'd never seen in another man's eyes before—obsession. Lust and love, need and desire. Ted had never looked at me as if he couldn't breathe without me, but Jake, Jake looked at me as though he would give me his last breath on earth.

"I love you, Freya. I've fallen hard, I've fallen fast, and I've fallen madly in love with you."

I swallowed and took a deep and grounding breath. "I love you, too."

He cupped the back of my head and threaded his fingers through my hair, pulling me close, so close that all I could see were those impossible blue eyes. Endless pools of azure that saw right through me and into my very soul. "We're in all this shit together, you and me. You got that?"

I nodded, blinking back the tears.

"My family shit. Your family shit. The Petralia shit. We're in this together. We'll figure out what to do when we get back, meet your brother and start our life together."

My lips parted. "Our life together ... "

His intense gaze softened, and his mouth curved up into a wolfish grin. "You didn't think I was going to let you get away, did you? This is the real deal, baby." My skin heated and tingled deliciously as he gripped my hair tightly in his fist. "We've said the 'L' word, you're about to meet my family, and if you don't run for the hills, I'm keeping you."

I licked my lips. "I'm keeping you too."

IF YOU ENJOYED THIS BOOK

If you've enjoyed this book, please consider leaving a review. It really does make a difference.

Thank you again.
Xoxo
Whitley Cox

ACKNOWLEDGMENTS

There are so many people to thank who help along the way. Publishing a book is definitely not a solo mission, that's for sure. First and foremost, my friend and editor Chris Kridler, you lady are a blessing, a gem and an all-around amazing human being. Thank you for your honesty and hard work.

Author Jeanne St. James for doing a thorough beta-read for me, your notes, brutal honesty, insight and ideas were so helpful. You really are my sister from another mister.

Thank you, Justine and Krista for your beta-reads as well. I love that I can hand you the rough, unedited stuff and you'll read it and give me your feedback.

Tara at Fantasia Frog Designs, your patience with my indecisions when it comes to covers is appreciated. You never disappoint.

My Naughty Room Readers Crew, authors, Jeanne, Erica and Cailin, I love being part of such a tremendous set of inspiring, talented and supportive women. Thank you for letting me learn, lean on and join the team.

My street team, Whitley Cox's Curiously Kinky Reviewers, you are all awesome and I feel so blessed to have found such wonderful fans.

The ladies in Vancouver Island Romance Authors, your support and insight have been incredibly helpful, and I'm so honored to be a part of a group of such talented writers.

And lastly, of course, the husband. You are my forever. I love you.

SNEAK PEEK - HARD, FAST AND MADLY

PART 2

Does unconventional breed more unconventional? Because not that I'd been neck deep in the dating pool—ever, but I thought that it was a touch early for me to be meeting Jakes family. Especially all of them at once.

Was that sweat between my boobs?

I shifted in my seat. Yep, that was sweat.

Great.

Nervous boob sweat.

I grabbed some tissues from the glove compartment of my Volvo SUV and blotted down the V of my dress. Jake grinned at me from the driver's seat as we sat waiting for the ferry to unload.

I was meeting his family.

There was no turning back now.

Deep breaths.

Oh man this was early.

But nothing about our relationship had been conventional or followed the normal progression of how people date. We'd been what I would have called enemies first, then friends, then lovers faster than I ever thought possible, and now he was my boyfriend.

I needed him like I needed to breathe.

He was my air.

From our first meeting on that jet flying over The Rockies, to our trip to Edmonton to help Stacey, our relationship, for being still so fresh and new, was already full of ups and downs and the *L* word.

Yes, that little four-letter word that means so much when said by the right person. I'd said it, then regretted saying it, only to be filled with a joy I never knew existed when Jake said it back. So of course, even though I was shaking in my flip flops about meeting his parents and siblings, I was in love and would do anything for him.

He was my light.

I'd fallen into the darkness after Ted had died. Willingly let the bleak absorb me. Sure, I still put on a happy face when I was around people, and went about my routine at home. But the hole inside me was vast. I was missing something. Light. Love.

And Jake had restored both.

He flipped on the switch and illuminated the entire world again. He showed me that not all men were two-timing, untrustworthy cads, and that I was worthy of not only love, but pleasure.

He introduced me to a new, sexy side of myself. Showing me that I am a sensual being, entitled to pleasure and that contrary to what I thought, I can seduce. And apparently, I can do it well.

So yes, I was nervous about meeting Jake's family, so much so that when we drove off the ferry and the car nearly flew up and off the ramp I thought I tasted vomit and quickly scanned the interior of the vehicle for a bag to throw up in.

But I was also excited.

He had done so much for me in the short span of our relationship, that I wanted to reciprocate. He practically begged me to come with him the night before, so I knew this was important to him. And the way he reached for my hand as we drove off the ferry, told me he was happy I was with him.

I was happy as long as I was with Jake.

"You okay?" he asked, following the heavy flow of traffic only to have to abruptly stop because the car in front of him tossed on the brakes.

"*Oof,*" I exhaled as my chest slammed against the seat belt. "No."

"What's wrong? You sick?" He had a mild look of panic on his face. I melted at the sweet sight of how much he cared. So, rolling my shoulders back, I plastered on the biggest, fakest smile I could muster.

I could do this for him.

I *would* do this for him.

I shook my heady dully, feigning nonchalance. "Just had a bit of a headache, but it's gone."

He studied me out of the corner of his eye. "You're nervous about meeting my family, aren't you?"

My chest rose and fell with a weighty sigh. He already knew me too well. "Yeah, maybe a little. I just wish I wasn't meeting them all at once. Couldn't you ease me in? One person at a time?"

He grinned. I'd quickly come to find out that a smile on Jake's face was about as intrinsic as his nose or his chin. It was always there. He was always happy. How was that possible? "That's why we're going over today and not tomorrow, so you can just meet Justin and Kendra and the kids. My parents and sister don't get in until tomorrow night."

The anvil on my chest suddenly felt a hundred pounds lighter. "Really?"

With a nod, his hand fell to my bare thigh and he gave it a reassuring squeeze. Meanwhile, the beast inside of me wanted to tell him to move that hand further up my leg. "Justin and I kind of figured it might be a little overwhelming to meet them all at once."

"Thank you." I licked my lips as my eyes fell to his hand.

"Damn girl, do I have to pull over and fuck you on the side of the highway?" he asked, watching my physiological response to his touch. "Or can you take care of yourself?"

"What!"

"Yeah." He made a satisfied sneer and nodded. "That'd be hot. Touch yourself, baby."

"NO!" With much reluctance I pushed his hand away.

"What! Why not?"

"Because I don't do that."

His eyes nearly popped out of his head. "Ever?"

I gave him an indignant look. "Of course not."

"Why the hell not?"

"B-because. Can we please not talk about this?"

"Have you truthfully never masturbated?" he pressed on, ignoring my request, but instead putting his hand back on my thigh, only higher up this time.

I shot him an irritated scowl, my dander slowly rising. "Of course not." Then my curiosity betrayed my upbringing. "Have you?"

"All the damn time, woman!" He howled. "Since my first stiffy at like eleven or twelve I've been spanking the monkey non-stop."

I stared at him, startled by his candor. The emotions inside me debated on whether I should be repulsed, intrigued or turned-on, and darn it if it wasn't leaning towards the latter. The idea of Jake sitting with the heavy weight of his cock in his hand made me salivate.

"I uh...I think chronic masturbation is a serious problem," I finally said, not sure what else *to say*.

He rolled his eyes. "It's not chronic. It's not like I had to leave in the middle of class or duck out on a date to go beat off in the public wash-room. You know, a couple of times a week, when I felt the urge."

As much as the image of Jake touching himself was turning me on, the desire to change the subject was greater. "I don't want to talk about this anymore, please."

"Why not? Seriously, Freya, you need to touch yourself. How'd you survive all those weeks when Ted was away for work. Or the months after he died?"

"I...I don't know. I just did." Truth be told, at night, when Ted was gone, it had been hard. We weren't sexually charged the way that Jake and I were, but Ted and I had a marital bed and when he was gone I missed his touch. But, the idea of taking care of myself had never really come to mind.

My father had never had the sex talk with me. He'd left that to an older female friend, who was in her seventies by the time I was ready to learn about the birds and bees. And to "Aunt Ellie," which is what I called her, sex was a duty. I was never to deny my husband and my pleasure was not the priority. She never brought up masturbation or female enjoyment, oral sex or foreplay. She hadn't even talked about contraception. That I had to learn in school, with a cucumber. To Aunt Ellie, sex was just another facet to a marriage, and was just something the women had to lie there and endure. She even told me to compile my grocery or to-do list for the next day in my head while he "went about his business." I'm ashamed to admit, the first few times Ted and I had sex I'd actually done just that. It was so awkward and uncomfortable that I thought it would be like that forever so I'd mentally pour over the grocery store flyers or plan my meals for the week.

"Well," Jake piped up, making me jump in my seat, "we've got to change that. I'd love to watch you play with yourself."

My bottom lip dropped open and I gaped at him across the car.

He wanted to watch me touch myself...

A roguish smile took over his face as he raised one dark brown slanted eyebrow. "Interested?"

How could I lie to this man and tell him that I wasn't, when deep down I was? From the moment we'd met he'd seen right through me, to the marrow of my bones. I bit my lip. "Maybe. Though not this weekend. Someone could hear us."

He gave me an impatient look. "It's called locking a door and stifling your cries of euphoria with a pillow." He shook his head and clucked his tongue. "Tsk tsk, Freya. So much to learn when it comes to being dirty."

I let out my own impatient sigh. "Whatever, Jake. New topic please."

He nodded. "We'll put a pin in it and come back to it later." His eyebrows bobbed. "Like tonight."

"We'll see."

"How do you think Stacey and the kids are settling in?" he asked, slowing down as the traffic slowed down. We were getting ready to go under a big tunnel.

"I think okay. It's nice that Daniella and Chase are there to help her." I blew out a frustrated breath. "I hate that they're tangled up in this Petralia nightmare."

We emerged on the other side of the tunnel and continued on the highway. Thankfully, it was a beautiful day and the mountains to the

East and North provided a weird ominous comfort the closer we got to Jake's brother's home in North Vancouver.

"Just remember," he said, "none of this is *your* fault. Ted was the one who decided to become a fucking drug mule or whatever for some Greek crime family, only to take the money and run."

"He didn't run."

"Well he didn't walk it directly to them and keep you safe. He died before they got their money and nobody knows where the hell it is."

I shook my head. That was true. Ted, boring, predictable, old-fashion values Ted had traded in his job as an auditor to become a drug mule for a Greek crime family. Then he'd two-timed me with Stacey, marrying her *as well* as me, and having two children with her. Only neither Stacey nor I had found this out until after Ted had died in a car accident.

So now, Stacey and I were unlikely friends, she'd moved to Victoria to be closer to protection from the Hart brothers security firm, and Yanni Petralia was hounding us for the fifty thousand dollars that Ted apparently owed him.

You know, *normal* everyday problems.

We stopped at a red light and Jake shifted in his seat, leaning over and cupping the back of my head. "We will get through this, Freya. I promise."

I swallowed. He couldn't make such a promise.

The light turned green and he repositioned himself back facing the road.

"This time next year, baby, we'll be laughing. We'll be worry free and living in our own house with maybe a dog and a bun in the oven. Just you wait. All this Petralia shit will be a distant memory very soon."

My eyes went wide.

A house.

A dog.

A bun in the oven!

"Uh ... let's not get ahead of ourselves," I said with a slight shake to my voice. "Let's get through the weekend with your family first."

"That's probably best." He nodded. "Because we're here." He

pulled down a long driveway lined with oak trees, their branches connecting overhead to create a luminescent green tunnel. The trunks stood like centuries old sentinels, guarding the house and leading the way.

I gaped out the window at the mansion before us, opulent didn't even begin to describe its magnitude or prestige. With a circular driveway, five car garage, pillars outside the main entrance like it was the white house, and a giant fountain in the middle of it all. I looked down at the blue and cream floral dress Jake had bought me and suddenly felt very drab and underdressed, inadequate and wishing that I'd packed a couple of more blouses or a blazer or something. What were these people going to think of me?

I was so plain.

Jake laid on the horn and a couple of seconds later the front door flew open and two little pixies with fairy wings sprinted out. One was darker skinned and taller with a sweet round face and jet-black hair braided into numerous small plaits that trailed behind her like ebony tentacles. The other was the spitting image of Jake. Big beautiful blue eyes, unruly chestnut hair trying desperately to escape her pigtail braids and a smile so full of mischief you'd think she'd been born with tricks up her sleeve.

"Uncle Jake!" they both cried, running around to the driver side and opening up the door before he could even get out.

"*Bonjour!*" the taller one said. "*Comment ça va?*"

He caressed her head while hoisting the younger one up on to his hip and giving her a swift peck on the cheek. "*Ça va très bien, merci. Et toi?*"

"*Ça va très bien, merci,*" she replied. Her eyes drifted to me as I sat stock still and terrified in the passenger seat. "*Qui est-ce?*"

"You can get out, you know?" Jake chuckled, turning to look at me. Then he looked back down to answer her. "*Elle est ma petite amie. Auntie Freya.*"

Both of the little girls' eyes went wide with surprise and then delight as Jake walked them over to my side of the car and opened my door for me.

"I want Auntie Freya to hold me," the little one in Jake's arms whined, struggling to get free.

Jake rolled his eyes and passed her to me where she instantly started fingering my curls and petting my face. "That spit-fire there, is Chloe. And this...this is my little Maggie." To the little girl's elation, despite her size and height, he lifted her up like he had her sister. She giggled shyly and then wrapped her arms around his neck while her long legs hung down nearly to his knees.

"Auntie Jessica is here, too," Chloe said to me, running her curious little fingers over my eyebrows. "And grandma and grandpa."

Jake stiffened next to me, his whole demeanor morphing in the blink of an eye. "I'm sorry, I thought they weren't coming until tomor-row." But as much as my nerves were making me ill, it was the change in Jake that had me worried. Within a matter of seconds his smile faded, his shoulders slumped and it was as though he collapsed in on himself. His larger-than-life, happy-go-lucky personality was gone. And the remorse and reluctance lacing his tone told me that he very well may have been just as sorry for himself as he was for me.

As we made our way up to the front of the house a series of voices and shadows spilled from the doorway. Then there they were—Jake's entire family. It was easy enough to tell who was who. He looked so much like his siblings and his mother that they all could have been in a Gap commercial. Meanwhile, Kendra was a petite and slender beauty with dark red, wavy hair that fell over her breasts, and eyes the color of hanging moss. She had a little boy on her hip, with hair the same colour as his mother's, who was vehemently gnawing on an entire apple which he clutched greedily in both hands.

The sore thumb in the crowd must have been Jake's dad. It was a process of elimination, and sore and thumb-like he was. Where the rest of the family was long and lean, Mr. Leeman was short and stout. His eyes were near black, and they squinted repetitively like a serpent's. He was bald, or almost bald, with a dusting of hair encircling the base of his scalp, giving his head almost a crop circle look. But it was his colour that caught me off guard the most. His skin held a yellow-ish hue, very sickly so. The shade most people associated with jaundice or cirrhosis of the liver. I thanked the stars above that Jake had inherited his looks from his mother.

I followed Jake up the steps and stopped when he stopped, deciding to take my cues from him and do as I was told. "Hello," he said solemnly, looking at his mother and father as though they were relatives he'd only met once or twice and wasn't overly familiar or fond of.

"Hello, Son," his mother said, sweeping past Kendra and wrapping her shapely arms around him. Her steely gray eyes traveled up and down my body in blatant appraisal. Jake passed Maggie off to her father and gingerly hugged her back.

"Hello, Mum."

"It's good to see you, dear."

He released her and looked down at his feet. "Yes, you too."

"Hello, m'boy," Mr. Leeman croaked waddling the few steps over and sucking spit in through his teeth before looping a meaty arm around Jake's shoulders.

"Hi, Dad."

My eyes darted back and forth between everyone. It was such a cold and formal greeting that I wasn't sure what was going on. Was I not supposed to be here? Was this a family only thing?

And then the vision stepped forward and Jake's eyes reignited with the spark I'd come to love so much. This had to be Jessica, and she was just that—a vision. Poker straight chestnut hair that she'd pulled back into a simple ponytail which showcased her long and elegant neck, the same big gray eyes as her mother and flawless porcelain skin. She was what modeling scouts would deem "the jackpot." She threw herself at her big brother, forcing him to take a step back and they both shared a moment of murmurs and whispers in one another's ears that no one else could hear but had her smiling—at me.

Jake and Jessica pulled apart and he stepped back, looping his arm around my waist. "Uh, this is Freya, everyone. Freya, this is...everyone." He proceeded with the introductions, and I shook everyone's hands, shifting Chloe to my left hip so that I didn't have to awkwardly offer the wrong hand to people.

"Hi," I finally squeaked, feeling Mrs. Leeman eyes scouring me like a hawk, judging me and deciding if I was worthy of her son. By the way her lip curled up into a small sneer, she'd already decided that I wasn't.

"Well come in, come in," Justin boomed. "Chloe, you can walk, sweetheart." He turned to me. "You don't have to carry her, she's almost four, she can walk."

"It's okay," I whispered, moving her back to my right side. "It's a good workout."

"Can Auntie Freya sleep in my room?" Chloe asked, lightly playing with my dangling earring.

"I think that's a wonderful idea," Mrs. Leeman piped up. "Good idea, angel." I shot Jake a look of fear, meanwhile his sister and brother gave him one of sympathy and Kendra just rolled her eyes. "Well, they're not married," Mrs. Leeman went on. I could have sworn I heard her say "thank the Lord." "So it's only right if Jake and Freya sleep in separate rooms. Don't want to give the children the idea that sharing a room or a bed out of wedlock is acceptable," Jake's mother went on, pouring herself a glass of cucumber lemon water from a big glass pitcher on the kitchen counter.

"Do you share a room and a *bed* in Victoria?" Justin asked coming around to stand in front of me. He had the same intense and soul pene-trating stare as his younger brother.

I squirmed under his unwavering scrutiny. "I uh...."

"Of course they do," Kendra interjected, laying a supportive hand on my shoulder.

"Okay then! My house, my rules, you'll share a room," Justin decreed, holding his index finger up as if making a grand announce-ment. "You can have the one at the far end of the hallway upstairs. The one you usually take."

My gaze shifted to Jake and he just stood next to his sister, the two of them studying their feet, quiet and withdrawn as if they were chil-dren who only spoke when spoken to.

"Jake dear, come sit with your father and I. Tell us about your new job," his mother cooed, wandering around into Justin and Kendra's warm and inviting beach cottage inspired living room.

Dutifully, Jake and his sister followed their parents and sat down next to their mother, meanwhile it was suddenly as though I didn't even exist. Jake didn't even look at me. He just abandoned me in the spacious kitchen, next to a tray of chocolate chip cookies that smelled like heaven and looked like decadence.

"You want a cookie?" Maggie asked, coming up next to me and lacing her fingers through mine.

I could have kissed her perfect, sweet little face. I had a friend. "I'm okay," I said, for some reason feeling like I needed an adult permission before I was actually allowed to have one.

"Mags, why don't you take Freya upstairs and show her to her room," Kendra said. "I'll be up in a second with some fresh towels."

"Come on," Maggie said, pulling me along until we stood at the base of a wide sweeping staircase with a shiny wooden bannister. "Your room is this way." She hauled me up the stairs and down the hall. "This is your room."

Opening the door, I wandered inside to find an enormous king-sized bed taking up the center of the room with a desk and wardrobe tucked into opposite corners. Maggie leapt on to the bed, followed by a tiny little ball of brown and black fluff. "Who's this?" I asked, perching on the corner and scratching behind the pup's ears.

"Sally Jessie Ruff-ael, but we just call her Sally for short. Are you going to marry my uncle?"

"Maggie," Kendra scolded, coming into the room with an armload of towels. "We don't ask those questions. At least not until we've let our guest breathe and release the tension from of her shoulders." She gave me another sympathetic look.

"That's right," Justin added, coming up and plunking our two duffle bags on the bed. "Though calling her 'Auntie Freya' wouldn't be a bad thing, right?" He gave me a big grin, the same one his brother always made when he was kidding around.

"Um, n-no, of course not. Auntie Freya is fine by me."

"Listen," Kendra said, helping Maggie climb off the bed, "Jake's parents are a little weird, and Jake and Jess turn into shells of their normal selves when their around their mum and dad. It's a coping mechanism they've developed in order to just *deal*. We're still trying to figure out how to bring them out of their shells all the time, but it's a tough process."

Justin nodded. "I was the same way until Kendra smacked some sense into me. My mum..." he scratched the back of his neck as if trying to choose his words wisely, "she's very *set* in her beliefs and her ways. She's a tough woman to win over. So don't beat yourself up if you don't."

"I still haven't." Kendra snorted.

Justin slapped me on the back and smiled. "But we like you, and that's all that really matters. Come on, let's go get some liquor in you, that always makes dealing with my mother easier."

Kendra nodded. "Amen! And it's the only way I can even remotely tolerate *Jeff*!" She ushered Maggie out. Justin and I were tight on their heels.